What the
Irish Goddess
Told Me

What the Irish Goddess Told Me

by
Mary Alice Cullinan

ISBN 0-9721680-0-1

Manufactured by the National Publishing Company
Division of Courier Corporation

Cover photograph by Mary Alice Cullinan © 2002
Editing, layout and book design by Victoria Rose Ochocki
Chapter heading graphic design by Cari Buziak © 2002

I would climb the high hills of the land,
I would swim to the depths of the sea,
For one touch of her lily-white hand,
Ach ar Eirinn ni neosainn ce h-i.
(*Ireland over all*)

The Groves of Blarney
Traditional Irish song

I would like
to dedicate this work
to my mother
who stands behind me,
my sister
who has walked beside me,
and my daughter
who runs before me.
Our lanterns shine
a bit brighter
as we travel the path,
because of the energy
of the goddesses
which is available to each
of us, every day of our lives.

What the
Irish Goddess
Told Me

# PROLOGUE

I opened my eyes and caught the sun shining full-throttle through the window next to my head. Startled, I fought for my bearings, blinking at the scene outside the glass pane – white, white puffs on light blue background. Looking out and down, I discovered a navy blue carpet – a thick, rich carpet – with gray/white flecks tossing about on its surface. And it was quite a ways down, perhaps 30, 000 feet.

Fear gripped my belly as I recalled that I was on my way across the Atlantic Ocean, hoping to land safely and then travel around the wondrous little island of Ireland. I had left New York City with its familiar winking, twinkling, spread of lights below me the night before. Hopping from one island to another would be charming if only I wasn't such a chicken about flying. From this unspeakable height, I now looked down through the clouds and studied the dark sea that plummeted to unimaginable depths, half expecting a gold and emerald isle to magically appear.

We were cruising nicely now and should be closing in on our destination shortly, but the liftoff had been as awkward as the struggling of a Canadian goose that screams and carries on as it heaves its bottom up from a rocky field. Rumbles and groans continue until it tucks its landing gear up. This was not to be the graceful rise of a swan. Oh, no, this sturdy migrator of continents inspires no confidence in its transitional phase. It is, however, a wondrous and efficient flyer once it is airborne.

And so my trip to Ireland began with a jolt. Little did I know that this was to be prophetic for how this wondrous journey was to unfold. I was completely unaware of how my ideas and my demeanor were to change – how my life was to change for that matter.

I focused on rubbing sleep from my eyes, sitting upright, putting my tray table down and considering the neatly arranged breakfast of eggs and toast that the stewardess was placing before me. I turned to the woman sitting next to me. I now said, "Good morning" to her. This was two words more than I had said last night while I was in the throes of anxiety.

I had been busy gripping the armrests and adjusting to having no suggestion of the comforting ground beneath me. As the passengers around me were settling in for the night, I was trying to curl myself into the smallest space possible, pulling my green wool sweater and my waterproof coat over me, tucking myself in as one might tuck a child in for the night. Used to comforting others for a living, I now set about to comfort myself, interpreting the small space around me as the wrappings of a cozy nest.

Peripherally, I noticed that a very old woman had settled herself with a pillow and blanket at the end of the aisle. Her glasses rested easily in her lap. Beside me, a young woman, maybe in her late twenties sat looking forward in perfect serenity. Her beautiful blonde hair flowed over the shoulders of a long green cashmere cape that fell open, revealing a gold silk blouse beneath it.

We turned toward each other at the exact same moment and her eyes held me, drew me in. Some light deep within her multiplied several times in their reflection. Their shimmering cast a haunting image. Not wanting to stare, I nodded politely and turned away.

I fished my baseball cap from my coat pocket and slid it over my head and tilted the brim down over my eyes. I did not want to dwell on my current discomfort of being hurled through No-Man's –Land at heart-stopping speed so I helplessly clung to complete denial.

As a child, I had always wanted to fly over my family's farm and so I pictured it below me – the trees and flowers and open land – as I surveyed it as a crow might, coasting on the breezes. The crows would often stuff their mouths with seeds, flying over the corn fields and open meadows, often dropping an individual seed here and there to sink into the earth and take root, starting a new growth in a new place. Watching this in my mind's eye lulled me peacefully in dreamy sleep through the night.

Now as I greeted the woman next to me, she closed a book and set it beside her on the seat as she took her tray of food from the stewardess. "Good morning to you. And what a morning it is, don't you agree?"

The stewardess asked if I'd like coffee. In the tradition of a coffee addict, I started each day with a cup and almost nodded without thinking. Then I decided I was ready for a change. After all, Ireland was known for its tea drinkers and I ventured into new ground. "Tea," I answered and held to the choice as if I was breaking new ground for my sisters who longed to be spontaneous.

"Cream and sugar?" was the automatic counter.

"Maybe some milk." The conviction was waning. I sank back accepting the cup and watched my neighbor take her mug of steaming coffee with a slight pang of envy. "I'm sorry I wasn't much company last night," I offered as we ate together. "I'm not much of a flyer."

"Oh, I love it!" she softly enthused. Her accent was New England but with a slight lilt. "I so enjoy the thrill of rising up and sailing high."

I tried to imagine what it would be like to want this experience. How would it be to actually look forward to takeoff? It didn't compute at the moment and I shook my head. "What are you reading?" I asked, glancing towards her book.

She picked up the book and held the cover towards me. "1916" was written in huge, bold block letters. "What's your name?" she leaned forward, her eyes brightly dancing in the reflected sunlight. Looking closely, I notice that each vibrant eye seemed to hold not one, but perhaps three irises, each laid slightly over the other, producing an eerie sheen.

"I'm Michelle Maguire," I answered hypnotically.

"Fidelma Siabhan Aine Quigley – Fanny for short." She settled back into her seat cushion and I relaxed. "This is by Morgan Llywelyn. Do you know much about Irish history?"

I tried to summon up what I knew. I had the impression of one invasion after another, much oppression and many rebellions of small groups of people risking their lives for their country's freedom. But names and dates escaped me and I colored with embarrassment realizing how little I knew. "Not really," I confessed.

She nodded knowingly. "This was about the Easter Uprising – Padraig Pearce, Tom McDonnagh….." I waited hoping she'd name someone I knew. Weren't these names from the movie, *Michael Collins*? "Eamon DeValera," she continued. Something was coalescing in my brain. "Have you heard of Constance Markowitz?'

My mind snapped its fingers with connection. "Didn't Yeats write something about her?" It wasn't a particularly lucid connection. It was a straw.

"Actually he did. I think that he was intimidated by her. 'Pardoned, drags out lonely years.' Sounds pathetic, doesn't it? But she was something else – one of life's true rebels. She wrote for the first women's newspaper, was a Major in the army. She was condemned to death for her part in the 1916 Uprising and was somewhat disappointed when her sentence was reprieved.

"She foiled the British from getting some damaging documents, was elected to Parliament and in true form turned it down. She worked in a soup kitchen, ran a theater company, was beaten up by police and in the end didn't even receive a proper funeral – just the appreciation of the common folk."

"What an incredible character," I mused wondering just what she might have been like.

"You'll find many strong female characters in the stories of Ireland. You won't be able to help it. Wonderful women come to life in history and in myths."

"Myths? That's funny, I had a conversation about mythology – was it just yesterday morning?"

"You're a psychologist, aren't you?"

"Yes," I admitted and went on. "Coincidentally we talked of myths and goddesses in my last session. Right there and then, I made the resolution to re-acquaint myself with the goddesses. I've forgotten so much of what I learned in college."

"Wonderful! You'll love the Irish goddesses. My parents were Irish. I grew up with names like Badbh and Macha." My untrained ears heard "Bahwah" and "Maughkaugh" – deep rich sounds that reverberated in the cave of the mouth and echoed in a hollow throat. Ancient sounds of ancient peoples.

After a moment she went on, "My mom and dad would tell me over and over again the stories of these powerful women. There wasn't one goddess for sexuality and one for healing and all that. Oh no, these women weren't going to be limited to one category, they did it all! They might fight beside you or if you angered them, they might arrange for your demise. They stood on principle and anyone be damned who stood in their way."

I shook my head, barely understanding, and she interpreted this motion as encouragement and continued.

"You'll enjoy the creative solutions these inspiring creatures came up with. I'd ask to hear the stories even when I was older, for with each age they took on another level of wisdom. These tales were the woolen yarns woven into everyday life in Ireland. No one questioned if the women in these stories were human or supernatural beings. The country people took them unquestioningly into their hearts."

I envied Fanny this intimate legacy of oral tradition I had had no storyteller to sit with me and paint these portraits for me. No words rich in human passion were passed down to me to awaken in me the understanding of universal truths, stirring up energy in my developing viscera. No one had whispered these stories of amazing women into my ears. Had my mother even known them? I sighed.

"Bawah?" My voice sounded flat in comparison. "I don't know those names. I learned Greek mythology through college texts. Athena, Aphrodite, Artemis. Heavens, the names have been buried for ages. Anyway that's my orientation and probably what I'll start with."

"Heavens, no!" I was taken off guard and turned my head sideways in question. She softened a bit. The shoulders of her silk blouse settled and she continued as if she were speaking to a misguided student.

"You'll be eating potatoes and salmon – not olives and feta cheese. You'll be walking the land of the Tuath Da Dannon and the Celts. This is your opportunity to learn first hand who makes up this complex culture. After all, why are you traveling there?"

I thought of the usual replies I would summon up over the past year as I planned my trip. I needed a vacation. I worked too long and too hard and I had to take a break for sanity's sake.

My ancestors were from Ireland. This last reason always stirred deeper sensations and questions within me. Did I still have any connection to this land? What aspects of myself had been transmitted through the generations? And were these personal elements transported on the back of a promise?

On some level, had my journey east always been in the cards? Was some contract instituted from my parents' expectations? What surfaced as the most honest answer now surprised me and I confided to Fanny, "Discovery. I don't know exactly why I'm going, but I suspect I'll find out."

She nodded firmly which gave me the sensation of having gotten a difficult oral exam question right. "Are you a teacher?" I asked.

She smiled mysteriously, her light eyes, her light hair, the creamy light skin, all gave off such a tender aura that I was disarmed and had to truly focus to keep my question in the forefront of my mind. Her mesmerizing glow, though, belied the intensity that blazed just below the surface. "I was for many years. But I'm coming over this time as a consultant for an educational project." My brows knit quizzically.

"Bringing folklore to schools through television specials," she added, moving her long fingers in a vague circle, bringing the matter to closure. She seemed so young to have such a wealth of expertise. "Anyway, the Irish goddesses will win your heart, you'll see."

"They do sound intriguing, but for now I'll probably search out the material I've been exposed to. After all, that's my introduction and I have to satisfy that curiosity first, reconnect with that model."

She sat smiling at me, not saying a word. I couldn't break her gaze and almost held my breath waiting for her to speak. After another long moment, she spoke softly, "That wasn't much of an argument, was it?"

"Not really." I gave her that and involuntarily laughed. I wanted to change the subject and awkwardly began, "So, what should I see when I'm there?"

She leaned forward. "See all you can. Walk around. See what's there, see more than what seems to be there."

"Are you saying that the society has many layers?" I asked brightly.

Her grin was slow and deep and steeped in suggestion. "I'm saying reality has many layers." Her eyes triple reflected in the brilliant morning sunlight, and I finally turned to finish my tea and look out once more through the clouds.

CHAPTER ONE

I awakened before the sun had fully risen. Thursday. This was the day I was leaving for Ireland – traveling alone, traveling further than I'd ever traveled before. Hopes and fears. Trials and errors. Joy and anxiety. This odd but familiar mix stirred once again in my belly. Leaving the realm of dreamtime, I knew to gradually insinuate myself into the compelling present. As I do most mornings to dispel the lingering ghosts of the night, shake off the smothering presence of mist's dark blanket and open my hand to the energy of a new day, I turned to the east. From the far east had come a martial art which would rein in my unbridled surge of ups and downs.

Slipping out from under my feather quilt, I set my feet squarely before me on the wooden floor and stood naked beside my bed. In that gray dawn, I could see only my outline in the full-length mirror. I pulled a turtleneck over my torso. The bottom of the cotton shirt scooped a curved line across my wide hip bones. I slipped on cotton panties. I like the look of my legs. They are shapely, long, just fine - like the legs of a horse. Big and strong and meant to run and run. I dropped into my Tai Chi stance.

As I had sunk gently into the first pose, my energy melted into the ground, my ankle joints and knee and hip joints bent slightly. I felt my weight shift fully to my left foot gradually, as if someone had just lifted a napkin full of salt and let it all slide to one side. I balanced completely on the left and the right foot popped up an inch on its own as the weight settled left. Directing the right foot lateral, I pointed it straight ahead, allowing it now to accommodate all of the weight. Feeling as if granules were shifting through my body, I swung softly to the right as my empty left foot rose and straightened.

"I am new in this moment," I told myself in the swelling, blossoming dawn. "An infant."

Both feet parallel, I stood in simple balance, a seesaw stilled, lining up at last with the horizon.

"And like an infant, I am beginning a journey by myself today." I unbent my knees, feeling my spine rise, my arms rise, my hands unfold. A balloon was rising in water. "And yet I am not completely alone."

After breakfast and a shower, I rechecked all that I had lain out on my dresser and packed everything carefully in one backpack. A pair of nice shoes and sneakers went into the bottom. I rolled tightly two pair of pants, two long sleeve shirts, two tee shirts, underwear, a dress, pajamas, socks, a scarf and last but not least – a bathing suit. You never knew when you'd need one.

A small plastic container held shampoo, cosmetics, jewelry, vitamins and batteries. I squeezed a paperback of *Ulysses*, a notebook and my walkman and tapes on top. My cameral and film went into a side pocket. I set out the clothes I would wear and stood back to survey everything. This little ceremony of order gave me the comforting illusion that I had things under control This was a feeling I needed at the moment. It was time to put on my professional clothes and go downstairs to the first floor where I had my office.

I had a busy morning planned, fitting in few last sessions. I had never taken two weeks off together from my busy psychotherapy practice, so naturally, I offered a little extra time to my patients who were somewhat apprehensive about my being away. I needn't worry about Beverly, though. She always felt she was on the edge and needed a good deal of advice, in actuality she was just fine.

She had asked me to fit her in for one last appointment before I left and I couldn't deny her for she was serious about her self-development and was open to exploration. She also had a knack for asking thought-provoking questions. In fact, near the end of the sessions she casually asked a question that wound up framing this trip that I had been planning for a long time.

She was the last client of the morning. As usual, she had chosen the hard-backed chair across from me and now sat slumped forward, her elbows on her knees, her chin resting in her long bony hands. Beverly could have passed for my sister if I had had one. Like me she had long chestnut hair, high cheekbones and a lean, tall frame. Her eyes, though, were a stunning emerald green, not a murky mud puddle brown like mine.

After we contemplated the state of the world, I asked her a question to bring her back to the state of affairs within herself.

"You won't believe how wonderful I've been," she said in a voice that had become suddenly flat.

"Oh, yeah?" I settled back, waiting for the filling to be introduced into the pastry shell Beverly had set before me.

"Yeah, I managed to alienate everyone in my family."

"Good work." I matched her casual tone and then fell silent.

"I'm so confused." Her eyes softened and misted. "Sometimes I don't like what I see."

"What did you see this week?" I leaned slightly forward.

"Well, Monday after school, I picked up my daughter from karate class. I had all these groceries in the car and when I got home, I'm dashing to get dinner together. I was trying this new thing – poulet en croute – with chicken and you wrap it in dough and my daughter's in the kitchen asking me her spelling words – that's how she learns – playing teacher – and anyway I'm lousy at spelling – ask me an accounting question for Christ's sake – and anyway she corrects me and I blow up and tell her to take her homework somewhere else and do it herself. And then I'm standing there with flour all over my arms and the table and the dough is hard as marble and my husband walks in and I tell him I'm tired of his special diets and it wouldn't kill him to eat a steak sometime and he just watches me as I throw the food in the trash and storm out of the kitchen."

"What happened then?"

"Oh, he bought Boston Chicken and we ate a bit later than usual."

I let out a long breath and sat back. "Okay, so you blew up. Can you be you and lose it now and then? Especially with pastry dough?"

Beverly crossed her long legs and brushed the hair out of her face with several half-hearted swoops across her forehead. "It's not that. I know things can get tense and it's not the end of the world to lose patience. It was something else. There was this voice inside my head that was saying, 'Why are you driving yourself crazy with cooking and spelling? You have an MBA. Why aren't you out and about in a real job? Something halfway challenging? Interacting with adults from time to time. Who is this woman up to her elbows in flour?'"

"Are you feeling a bit limited staying at home?"

"It's not just that. I know it's for a period of time. I, myself, planned to take this time and I usually get a kick out of being domestic. But when my husband walked in looking great in his pinstriped suit and I'm standing there a mess within a larger mess and cranky and shaky and well, I felt powerless and even unattractive. Was this a woman who would ever lure him to bed again? And I panicked. I mean where was that woman that I thought I was? Where did she go?"

"Beverly, you make it sound as if when you act one way, the other parts of you disappear."

Beverly opened her green eyes wide. "Other parts of me? You're not saying I'm a multiple personality or anything, are you?"

"Not at all. I mean that you are a complex person with many different aspects of your personality. Sometimes you may be one way, other times you may be another. It sounds like you need to get to know the different sides of yourself and get comfortable with them."

"So how do I do that?" Beverly asked.

"Sit back, put you hand on your stomach. Now let your mind be there now. Take a couple of deep breaths and let yourself relax. When I ask you a question, don't think too hard. Remember your thoughts are coming from your gut. Just say what seems to come to you. All right?"

"Okay." Beverly leaned her head back and closed her eyes.

"Who are you?"

A laugh escaped from her quivering lips then her brows closed together in seriousness. "Beverly."

"Beverly is your name. But who are you?"

"Oh, I see. I'm a wife and a mother."

"A wife and a mother is who you are in relation to your husband and daughter. But who are you?"

"I am a complex woman."

"A woman denotes your gender. Complex describes her. But who are you?"

"Uh, uh, uh a loving spirit."

"Loving describes how you feel." I was careful to speak very slowly now. "But who are you?"

I ,I, I..." Beverly sat forward and raised her hands from her abdomen and folded them across her breast. "I am just this." Now she opened her hands encompassing the space around her.

"Who you are – this – you can feel you, right?" Beverly nodded. "And who you are is limited by words. You are many things. And all this." I gestured to the delicate space around Beverly that she still experienced with the openness of her hands. "Take a moment to just feel who this person named Beverly is and become easy with the many parts that make up this person."

After a moment, Beverly cleared her throat. "This is good. I feel expanded. More open. Not locked in. Holding all these possibilities at once feels very light but I feel like a juggler. Too much at once. It's going to take some getting used to. It would be helpful to have some models of women to refer to as I get used to these various parts of myself."

" Models? Do you mean like references in the goddess literature?"

"Exactly! Do you think I should get a book about goddesses?" There was the question and it hit me like a water balloon that lightly bounces off your chest before it saturates you.

"A book about goddesses? That might be interesting. But I don't know if you're looking for that kind of depth with your search. I wish I could remember more from my college days. There were wonderful stories about the goddesses. One was the mother prototype – a fertility goddess who nurtured the earth and brought forth the fruit at the harvest but only if she was appreciated. One was the queen prototype. Let's see, now were they Roman or perhaps Greek? Definitely Greek – they were the ones that my class focused on. The descriptions of the individual characteristics of the women were very thorough and well-ordered."

Beyond Beverly, through the window, I could see the bird feeder in the yard was receiving a little visitor, a gray nuthatch with its long beak poking into the oily, black sunflower seeds. I recalled the course I had taken in mythology in my senior year at City College. My professor was a stern little woman whose passion in life was assigning papers. Which goddess had I felt akin to then? The nuthatch shook its head, whirled around quickly, fixed a point and took off. "You know, it might be interesting to look into the material. You see what you find, I'll see what I can find and when we get together again in a couple of weeks, we'll compare notes."

Beverly smiled and looked for a moment as if she had just caught a glimpse of the fact that the experience of her life might be more fully in her hands than she had thought. Time seemed to hang for an instant, widening out to cover the possibilities, the measures of time and there was nothing to say immediately. I wondered again about the goddesses. Which one might I feel akin to now? Which one spoke to me? Certainly not the wife or queen or even mother of the harvest. Did goddesses speak to any woman or only to a special few? How much I had to discover.

When the session had ended, I closed up the office and went upstairs. I slipped on the clothes I had laid out: jeans, a turtle neck shirt and my hiking boots which were too bulky to pack. Beside this I had set my sweater, raincoat and baseball cap to wear. A pouch with travel documents and money, driver's license, a bank card, a credit card and tissues would go around my waist.

Next I went to the phone to compose the message for my answering machine. I carefully explained I would be away for two weeks and who to call in an emergency. As I stood with receiver in my hand, I suddenly remembered that I had forgotten to call my brother last night.

I looked up Patrick's number at work and dialed. "Hello. Maguire here," he answered.

"Pat, it's Mickey. How are you? Are you in the middle of something?"

"Well, well, well, my little sis, what're you up to?" I could almost picture him leaning back in his swivel chair and tilting his curly dark head of hair towards the ceiling and closing his eyes.

"Remember today I'm leaving for Ireland?"

"Did I know that?" Was he teasing?

"I told you at least two months ago. Anyway, I'm leaving today. And so I'll be gone if you call. But you probably won't. But it's for a couple of weeks or so. You know, I did ask you if you'd go with me, remember?

"Okay, okay. Calm down. Sounds familiar. So what are you doing over there? Looking up cousins of the old man? Any of his relatives are probably locked up, you know."

A knot began to form in my stomach. "Well actually, Pat, while I am there, I'd like to try to find a relative or two, but I don't know for sure if I can."

"Check the alleys or under the tables. As I say, anyone related to the old guy's probably in a mental ward or jail!"

"Will you knock it off? You totally misjudge the guy." Here I was again defending my father. I would defend him to anyone, anytime. Even if someone asked an innocent question. I was so very sensitive -always had been. Yet to myself, I didn't dare look too closely at the anger I felt towards him.

When I pictured him, big and burly and confident, with laughing dark eyes and a constant smirk, I wanted to pound his chest and cry out to him that it wasn't me who let him down, it was he who let me down. With all his faith in me, why didn't I feel good about myself, believed in? It was the quality of his faith. It was twisted, perverted.

As a child, his encouragement translated into an expectation that I would accomplish only great things. Plain competence was somehow beneath me. Fulfilling my goals, getting my Masters in Social Work, setting up a practice - there was nothing wrong in that – if I were willing to settle for goals that were downright small.

He saw grand things for me. Things I couldn't see, things I didn't even know if I wanted. And so I felt insubstantial, incomplete. Instead of inspired by his confidence, I felt profoundly disappointed, disappointing. I felt like I had missed some large boat while wading in the shallows.

He had seen, or said he had seen something extraordinary in me and it made me incredibly angry. I had worked and worked on letting this strangling temper go. I owed him nothing. I was grown and should be unaffected by his misplaced dreams. He was gone. Gone forever. "Isn't this a bit old, Pat? He's been dead five years."

As if I hadn't said a word, he rambled on, "Actually, while you're there, do see if there isn't some rich fart we're related to. Maybe there's some compensation somewhere for being born into this family."

"Patrick, listen, I have to go. I don't know why we can't have a conversation about the family without slings and arrows."

"Aw, sis, where's your Maguire sense of humor?"

I wouldn't even know where to look so I waited a moment and asked, "Would you like me to bring you something back?"

"Irish pounds and gems from the family vault."

"Goodbye, Patrick."

"Irish whiskey then. Our heritage."

I made my bed. I closed and locked my bedroom windows. I went downstairs, had a sandwich and washed up the blue-swirled ceramic dishes I had bought at the tiny factory near my family's old farm in Pennsylvania. I sat down at the kitchen table and looked over the travel book of Ireland that I was leaving behind. While I waited for Shelly to come, I spread the tiny map open on the kitchen table.

I studied the outline of this small country that looked remarkably like a Scotty dog. It sat tethered, marooned in the middle of the great Atlantic. How would I feel there? This place surrounded by water was so north. Would I feel remote and isolated? Looking around the cozy kitchen with its blue corn flower curtains, the lovely pottery of teapot and cups on the wooden window sill, I felt at home and secure. And yet there were many evenings when this room could feel lonely, too.

Suddenly I could see clearly my family's kitchen at the farm. It too, had frilly curtains – white cotton with starched ruffles – curtains that mom had scrubbed and bleached and hung out on the line and when dry, had ironed into stiff sculptures. When dad was there, the kitchen looked spic and span. When he was away, which was often, dishes piled up, food was bought but seldom cooked. Mom rarely came into the kitchen during those times, hiding instead in the shade-drawn darkness of her bedroom. Then the kitchen was the place where I felt starved, if I felt anything. A lonely place. Patrick was the only one to talk to in those times. He was my co-conspirator, my buddy of necessity, my cellmate.

Shelly opened the kitchen door and came in, catching me staring blankly at the curtains. "Oh, my god," she said. "You're not ready, are you? You don't have ten million things to do before we leave?"

"Shelly, I really want this trip. I want to see Ireland and you know I need a vacation. It think I've been ready for months."

"Listen, hon, you know we have plenty of time. It's 3:30. We're an hour from the airport and you don't have to be there till 6 leaving at 8. Want to sit and chat some before we head out? I've got a lot of catching up to do with you, seems you're always working. And I want to tell you the latest about this little bundle I've got under my shirt. I think the head is permanently curled into my left hip." Shelly patted her huge belly and pulled out a chair.

"I'd love to Shell, but we'll catch up in the car. What if we run into traffic?"

"Traffic, schmaffic. When will you lighten up?"

"When I land on the Emerald Isle." I adjusted the answering

machine and set the door lock, put the book on the shelf and gathered up my sweater, raincoat and pack. "When I land."

"Sure, sure. Do they actually call it Emerald Isle?"

"How would I know? Now tell me about your baby in waiting."

We got into Shelly's little Honda and headed for I-95 and JFK. We didn't stop talking for the next hour. "I've got one month to go and I just may have a nervous breakdown before then!" She guided the car firmly with one hand and with other, rubbed the dome of her belly which was pressed squarely against the steering wheel.

"You're nervous?" I asked.

"Sweetie, I've never done this before. I feel like I've gotten up on skates for the first time and I'm heading for the middle of the pond. I want to give birth so bad I can taste it but I'd like to skip the actual process of elimination. I wish I could get my mother to do this one thing for me. I don't dare ask, she probably would. But I hate to have everyone standing around waiting and then I botch this cause I'm shaking like a leaf."

I ran my hand along my friend's thigh, stroking it soothingly toward the knee. She agonized through every major event in her life, but she was one of the bravest people I knew. She worried and cursed and plowed right through, confronting every last obstacle and calling them down all the while. "You'll do just fine."

"Oh I know my female instincts will kick in, they're solidly in there. The program's installed and my system's booted up. Look out thin ice, here comes an elephant!"

I made what I imagined was the trumpeting sound of a charging elephant, an apt power animal for my fearless friend. "I know you're worried I won't be here on the birth day, but I should be back in plenty of time. I have it all figured out."

"Did you purposely figure out to miss Rosh Hashanah and Yom Kippur?"

"Sorry I forgot about them. I really will miss having dinner with your family."

"Kid, you just don't know yet how much you'll miss my dad falling asleep over the decaf while Aunt Rose tells us about her latest gall bladder operation."

"Just promise you won't give birth during the apple cake."

Shelly let out a resounding belly laugh. I swear the steering wheel vibrated. "That will really give Rose something to describe to the rest of family at the next few get-togethers! Oh, by the way, my baby brother, Mark, will be there. He's moving back from Chicago, you know."

"Heavens…Mark." Somewhere around the region of my chest, a

metal gong began to vibrate. Tones as low as a grandfather clock's, bounced dizzily around the chambers of my heart, played a startling chord on my strung ribs and settled heavily into my gut. Diminishing throbs of chamber music continued to echo in my soft recesses and unsettle me.

Mark. I pictured his face, his thin face, his handsome face, with its strong jaw, long thin nose, dark thick eyebrows, long dark hair combed straight back. I saw his soft, smiling eyes. They were an incredible almond shape - smiling and penetrating, holding a soft sympathy and something much more. Something unrelenting.

As I saw him in my mind now, he looked young and brash as he had in college, when we had been so close, the sibling I had always wanted. Mark – he had been my spirit friend, so fun, so sensitive, so deep; but when he promised to be more, he had disappeared. Or had I?

I seemed to remember that the last time we had been together, we had argued. No, we hadn't argued. I had just felt threatened. With that sobering memory, the discordant energy that warned my untuned inner harp of a promising overture, was silenced and I reclaimed my composure, my footing against the Honda's floor. I tilted my head and through the side window I studied the sky and willed the weather to be clear for the flight.

Shelly slipped her right hand into one of the folds of her dress. She pulled out a delicate carving of a bear. "Here, put this little guy in your pocket. He'll bring you protection."

The bear was formed simply out of turquoise. Over the years, we had both been interested in the customs and rituals of the American Indians. We had felt a kinship with the people who looked to Nature for answers, who felt a responsibility to protect the gifts given freely by life and who respected every creature as important and equal. Together we went to lodges and sacred fires and dances to celebrate the different times of the year and to pray for health and peace in the world.

I held him lightly in my left palm, feeling the cool smoothness of his shape with my fingers. I remembered that the bear represented healing.

"What are you thinking?" asked Shelly, glancing sideways.

I tightened my grip on the bear and then opened my palm and looked for the quickly disappearing indentations he left there. "I think I'm about to learn something."

"Honestly, only you could turn a vacation into a seminar. Didn't you know that lesson number one is to sit back and let life do some of the steering for you?"

The car pulled over to the Aer Lingus terminal and I hugged Shelly good-bye. I placed the bear totem in my left breast pocket as I got out and got my things from the back seat. I stood for a moment on the curb watching

Shelly weave her little Honda back into the traffic lanes and pull away. At last I turned toward the large automatic glass doors and took a deep breath and entered the terminal.

I waited in a long line to present my passport and ticket and assure the airline authorities I carried no bags for anyone and indeed I had packed them myself and had never let them out of my sight. Feeling jumpy and uncreative at the moment, I went immediately to the gate. No one was there, even passengers were not in evidence. I set my small pack on a seat but had no inclination to sit still. I wondered how to calm myself.

I was terrified of flying. I honestly didn't know why. It was a strange concept – flying - and so I never did it, not if I could help it. I walked back and forth before the floor-to-ceiling windows that gave one a great view of the runways. This was no comfort. Back and forth, back and forth I walked, my gaze falling gradually to my feet.

My pace slowed to match the familiar Tai Chi rhythm. Carefully placing each foot, feeling the floor beneath me and the energy moving up my leg, I thought of how grounded a bear seems, lumbering, heavy with weight but light in energy. I let the impression of the bear come through me as I sampled the experience of being connected to ground. I began to feel safer within the room that looked out on the huge flying creatures that awaited their chance to carry me over the sea.

As I slowed down, I noticed the strained activity all around me. There was a constant bustle of strangers walking past in the wide halls. Passengers sat in black and chrome chairs at gates totally contained in turning their newspaper pages or talking too loudly into their cell phones. TVs blasted from bars and fast food areas where people hurried in or out or crowded around a table or a bar for a quick drink or bite to eat. I felt then, the emptiness of having no one at the moment to share my excitement with.

I had invited everyone to accompany me on this trip including my brother Patrick. I thought I was the one with the inflexible schedule but as it turned out, no one was able to make time just now. Some of my friends had urged me to wait for a future time when they could go. They told me not to go alone. They told me to sign on with a tour group.

Sometime last spring, though, I had felt a deep longing to visit the land of my parents. It was a steady urging and once I recognized it, I knew I had to go as soon as I could carve a break in my work schedule and make flight arrangements. The concept of promise surfaced again in my thoughts.I felt as if I was fulfilling a promise to someone. A promise to whom? My father? Had I actually told my father I would go someday? Or was this a promise I had secretly made to myself?

I was here now in the airport and just as I had this morning while standing next to my bed, I brought my hands to the level of my shoulders. Trying to blend into the background of the busy scenery, I held my hands out slightly in front of me, guiding the great ball of energy hovering at my chest, moving it slowly down to my pelvis. There, with an impassive face and much gratitude, I gathered it into my center and relished the warming sensation of the now tangible life force.

CHAPTER TWO

In Dublin airport, I collected my backpack from the luggage center. I exchanged $300.00 for Irish pounds at the Bank of Ireland counter then headed to the car rental desk. That morning when I awoke at many thousand feet above the sea, I looked down through the flimsy clouds for the first sign of the Erin Isle. With the sparkling rays bounding and spinning off of the gray-blue water, I recalled my Grandfather's stories about red-eared cows and the little people.

I was taking this journey and risking the seven hours or so it took me to fly across the sea because I longed to find some touchstone with my ancestors – people from long ago. I felt it as a deep draw from within my chest, like the draw to water in thirst. No matter what you turn your attention toward, the pull is always there, getting stronger by the hour. How could I hope to find people from the past? People from the far past were gone now. How could looking for them tell me something of the history that may have shaped my present?

Could something I learn there alter the story of my life being written by destiny? I didn't really believe in destiny or perhaps I didn't see it as a force separate and outside of myself. Not only were the people surely gone, but the country had to have changed also. There would be modern cities and televisions and PCs and cell phones. It was the present in Ireland as it was the present in New York. But it was different, wasn't it?

The island held the soil and contours of the lives of the people who shaped certain aspects of our present way of being. That inheritance lay far below like a treasure chest, closer to the people who lived there. The story of the people lay beneath the story in the news. Could the truth of the story be understood by physical proximity to it? I didn't know. And if it turned out to be just a lovely trip across a lovely land, I'd be satisfied. The call, however, came from within me and I was trying to get closer to the source that spoke the words to me that rose and fell like a whisper, a hint, a tease.

At the car rental desk, after I had signed the papers and got the key, I studied carefully the map that they gave me. The city of Dublin was a good half an hour away and I traced my route over and over with my index finger. I had booked a room in a guesthouse in the Georgian section of town, just across the street from St. Stephen's Green.

I had heeded the travel book's warning that driving in Dublin was impossible and infuriating at best and so had made sure my lodgings had parking. I would leave the car in the lot from today – Friday – until I headed west on Sunday. Everything that I wanted to see and do was easily in walking distance in the "quaint, intimate, European capital city,"

In the lot, searching for the row with my car, I noticed many posted reminders to remember to drive on the left side of the road. "I must keep my right shoulder at the middle of the road," I told myself over and over. "Right shoulder/ middle of the road." I climbed into what I expected to be the driver's side and found no wheel.

Moving to the passenger's side, I located the steering wheel easily. The controls for the gears were on the left. This felt as awkward as having your shoes on the wrong feet. This would never feel natural. Heading out into the main road, I had to make a left turn and as I guided the little car into that left lane, my body involuntarily tensed for a head-on collision.

I drove for a good while on the main road that was full of cars traveling extremely fast and with much open space on both sides of me. Then suddenly, the city of Dublin appeared before me. I was able to watch only the cars as the lanes were narrow and cars zipped in and out of small spaces at record speeds. When I was able to look up, in the very middle of the town, I could see it was as charming as promised with old buildings of many sizes, shops close together and many people walking quickly along the boulevards.

I found the Georgian House after driving around St. Stephen's Green at least three times. If you're going to make a move like turning, you had to be clear and decisive and quick here. It was a two-story building connected directly to other guesthouses on either side of it. The man at the little desk in the hallway greeted me warmly. His desk, like a desk in a home, was there as soon as you pushed open the tall narrow door from the street.

He handed me two keys, one to the front door that was locked at midnight, and one to my room which was a tiny room on the first floor. Breakfast would be in the Dining Room from 7:30 to 10:30 and I should let the desk know if there was a problem with the hot water. And would I have any idea what time I'd like breakfast? I had no idea. The room wasn't locked.

It was very small and the furniture was all pushed together with a narrow space in which to turn around or perhaps stretch. The window was open a crack. But it was cute and I quickly unpacked and then took off all of my clothes and lay down on the bed. In long slow risings and fallings, my body was breathing in the fresh air and my mind was finally exhaling. "I'm here, dad. I'm really here in Ireland! I don't believe it, do you?" Suddenly I realized I was very uncomfortable picturing my dad there when I had no clothes on. I crossed my legs and folded my hands over my eyes. But the serene moment was gone.

Why would I be uneasy being simply me in a room with a man who knew me most of my life? Will there always be parts of myself I will want to keep hidden?

I set off from the guesthouse at a little after 11 and began walking toward the center of town. Passing the elegant Shelbourne Hotel, I crossed the street. I walked around a tall gate, past a modern statue of a family and entered St. Stephen's Green. This was a huge park filled with the greenest green grass and trees. Benches faced a lake with geese and ducks surrounded by flowers and curving walkways.

I walked to the north end of the park and left the peaceful oasis. I crossed the busy street and started down Grafton Street – a busy shopping area with no cars. The cobblestone streets were full of people walking past quaint shops. Two ladies sold colorful flowers that they had arranged in huge bunches all across one alleyway. A man standing on a curb played folk music on a guitar.

Further down the street, three high school age girls played a classical piece on violins. Near the bottom of the street, I stepped into a large bookstore. I browsed through the great selection of Irish literature. In the travel section I found a comprehensive guide to Ireland. There was something else to be found.

I passed a history section, and anthropology section and came to a women's study section. In the middle of the top shelf, a book stood out, *Goddesses in Everyday Life*. I smiled, slowly took down the book and began to leaf through it. Near the front was written, "Goddesses are with us today. They exist now as much as they did in the ancient past. References to them are evident in our modern culture. In essence, they live within each woman's soul."

Buying both books, I headed back up Grafton Street to a very busy but charming café – Bewleys. I sat at a little wooden table, a pot of tea and a fruit scone before me, my travel guide open, a book of goddesses on my lap, when a little lady came over and asked if she could join me. Like the unassuming notes of an orchestra tuning up, there was little warning that a great piece was about to begin.

The small woman in a neat flowered dress and a tiny felt hat seated herself across from me. She nodded and smiled, looked quickly around the crowded, bustling room and back. "You're a tourist, then? Visiting?"

I set my guide book down. As yet I had had no true conversation since my arrival that morning. "Yes, I am. Are you?"

"Oh no, dear. Oh, no. I live here. Well, between her and London. I split my time, you know. Live in both places."

"You do?"

"Oh, yes. You see, my father was English and my mother was Irish, so I've always lived both places."

"And which do you like best?"

"France."

"Huh?"

"Well, I like France. Of course I've only visited it. Not lived there. But if I had my choice, I'd pick France. Very nice. And you're from America, are you?"

"Yes, I am. How can you tell?"

"Not hard at all," she smiled. "Are you driving about here?"

"Yes. I rented a car. But I'm slightly nervous about driving on the left."

"You're nervous, are you?"

"Yes, I guess I shouldn't be."

"Oh, yes you should, dear. Be nervous. Every summer it's one crash after another. It'll be a tourist. Terribly dangerous."

"Really?" The lady nodded hard, her eyes closed. "I guess I should worry then."

The little lady looked into my eyes, thought for a moment and shook her head. "No, you'll be just fine, dear." She reached over and patted my arm. "I can tell. Just fine."

"But do you think it's safe?"

"Well, it's not unsafe." She shrugged her shoulders and went on, "What have you seen, then?"

"Nothing yet." I held up the guide book. "I'm deciding now."

"What you see will guide you," she confided with no explanation and then as an afterthought added, "Well, first, though, you'll have to see St. Pat's. St. Patrick's cathedral. That's first. But if you want my opinion, St. Mary's is nicer."

A few minutes later, she touched the corners of her mouth with her napkin and set it under her tea saucer. She slid out from her seat somewhat stiffly and slowly bushed her thin hands over the front of her dress. Then she nodded to me, wished me God's blessings and left all in one wave of motion. I sat still wondering what "unsafe" meant.

I tore little strips of the paper napkins and slipped them into the pages in the guide book that detailed places that interested me and then took out the other book – *Goddesses In Everyday Life*. I stared at the cover for a moment – the frame of the work within – and framed my own efforts that brought me to acquiring this body of study. I had opened a dialogue about myth with one of my clients and now I was half-way across the world holding a book on the very subject.

Even with all of my work with women, I hadn't considered studying goddesses since I has been in college. The archetype each represented could be a real key to understanding the hopes and fears, goal and trials, pleasures and sorrows of a woman in many moments of her life.

The opening section was the overview of the six Greek goddesses profiled in the text. I was utterly entranced, dropping buttery scone crumbs across the pages. With each general description of a goddess, I wondered which of her aspects were reflected in the personality of people I knew or even in myself.

I really wasn't so much like Athena, the woman of the city, who with her cool reserve conquered in business dealings as much as in war. No, that would be more like Queen Elizabeth I or Margaret Thatcher or perhaps Beverly. But at times I was logical and organized, so there was some connection with Athena.

Demeter, the selfless mother, the fertile Earth ruler, wasn't quite reflected in my hand mirror either. I was reminded more of my friend Shelly. When Demeter's daughter who had been kidnapped in the winter, was away, Demeter withdrew her help and the plants withered. Her daughter was finally returned to her, but only for the spring and summer seasons. During that time, Demeter celebrates and shows her joy with living plants and flowers in abundance.

Now I have nurtured my clients while maintaining clear boundaries. I didn't retaliate on those who harmed them. I didn't fix things for them. I did feel for them. Nurturing, but hardly a mother. I wondered how my own mother had embodied some of these goddesses' traits. I can't picture my mother causing something so dramatic as fall or winter if I had been spirited away. Perhaps a cold shoulder. More like a withdrawal herself, leaving an empty nest desolate.

When it came down to it, I was probably most like Artemis whose name means "bear." I did enjoy solitude, loved to walk in Nature and looked for natural solutions first. I didn't quite take things as far as Artemis did, who in honoring the natural process, hunted animals with vigor, killed them and then danced in celebration of this balance of life and death.

The tea tasted completely cold as I read further, contemplating Hera, the Queen Mother who ruled the gods with her husband, Zeus. This would be the type of woman who organized and executed great programs or social events. This was not my m.o. at all. Maybe Queen Victoria's and of course, my own grandmother's, the matriarch of the Maguire's. I was completely mystified by Persephone, the daughter of Demeter who had been kidnapped by Hades and rules the Underworld a part of each year.

I had always had a hard time understanding that psychic realm, that descending into darkness and death to find one's power. There was a woman in my practice who was teaching me quite a bit as we negotiated her psyche in our sessions. As I supported her in the present physical world, she revealed to me layer under layer within where she was compelled to travel but could not manage alone.

Next Aphrodite was described. I wished I were more like Aphrodite, the goddess of love. Created from severed genitals and born from the sea, Aphrodite is beautiful, sensual and comfortable in the expression of her sexuality and passionate love. As I pushed my long chestnut hair out of my eyes, I savored the sensation of their silky texture along my high cheekbones. What was sensual? Was it also attractive? Was it necessarily sexual? From where is our sexuality truly born?

Suddenly, it began to rain very hard. Then just as quickly, it stopped. Through the café windows, I saw people in the street shading their eyes, looking up at the sky. Was there a rainbow? For some reason, I got up, crossed the large room and looked through he pane of glass, catching the fading streams of yellow and red above.

When I returned to the table, it had not been cleared, but the book on goddesses was missing. On the seat was the travel guide. I looked around and then under the table but no book. Straightening up, I caught sight of a blonde woman in a green cape walking out of the front door. The figure seemed so familiar. The lavish green cape, a cape like a cape I had recently seen, was captivating as it flowed out in a gracious swirl and trailed elegantly behind the tall woman.

I walked back down Grafton Street past the gray stone structure of Trinity College and past the massive Bank of Ireland. I crossed the O'Connell Street Bridge and saw the inspiring statue of Daniel O'Connell. I walked a block east along the River Liffey and turned left. At the Abbey Theater *St. Joan* by George Bernard Shaw was playing. The window was open and I was able to purchase a ticket for tomorrow night's performance, in the center left, for fifteen pounds.

I then continued down Marlborough Street, off of the main thoroughfare to St. Mary's Pro Cathedral, the only Catholic Cathedral in Dublin and noted the mass times. I looked into the peaceful space and the weight of serenity settled in my lungs. Back outside, I passed the General Post Office. A fierce struggle ensued here between the rebels and the British, in the Easter Uprising of 1916. The structure was completely destroyed by fire. Later, the beautiful neoclassical building was rebuilt in its original form.

I meandered along the River Liffey, feeling a sober appreciation for the simple, neat, low, concrete walls and walking paths that ran alongside of the gray/brown, slowly moving river. Crossing a little footbridge, I wandered into the Temple Bar Area. People were crowded closely together in the narrow, twisting odd streets of this upscale, offbeat section of the city. Here, hippie clothing stores flourished beside expensive wine bars, with gift shops sporting giant cardboard cutouts of celebrities such as Captain America interspersed along the block.

I traveled around the intimidating City Hall and was charmed by the quaint Dublin Castle, built in the 13th Century. I was becoming accustomed to the sensation of awe as I took in one more architectural wonder. This time, I stood before the majestic Christ Church Cathedral. In this small city, this beautiful early-Gothic style structure seemed to magically appear.

At last I reached St. Patrick's Cathedral, serenely surrounded by flowered walks. This was the national cathedral. I walked to a side entrance and looked in. It was huge, with cool air and muted light. Gratefully, I sat outside for a moment on the stone steps. History, architecture, friendly faces, all swirled together in my mind creating a collage of this lively city.

Being near St. Stephen's Green, I headed in that direction. I would find a pub serving an Irish Stew – shouldn't be too challenging – and fall into bed at an early hour, surely falling right to sleep.

CHAPTER THREE

8 a.m. Saturday morning. I rolled over, parted the curtains and looked up to the sky. A misty dome of gray-brown hung over the now quiet city. During the night I had half woken, aware of the sounds of people talking and walking by on the street, double-decker buses braking and accelerating, and music spilling out of various establishments. These sounds of life and interaction wrapped about me and comforted me as I lay peacefully in the little bed.

I took a quick shower. Very quick. I played with the dials until I arrived at a good temperature. Once under the spray, I longed for more warmth. I turned the knobs, first cold hit me then a trickle then nothing. I panicked and wildly manipulated the metal dial past red and blue, alternately burning and freezing my chest. By the time I made it to the final rinse, I had figured out how to work the foreign dials. If only I could retain this understanding of the system in the future. At any rate I was wide-awake.

I was alone in the dining room that had been all set up for breakfast. A cheerful girl brought me a glass of orange juice and a pot of tea and a pitcher of milk. Next, from the kitchen, she brought a bowl of cereal, a banana and a container of yogurt. I placed my hands lightly over the fresh food and bowed my head gratefully for this nourishment, trying to be aware of and open to the good energy it would bring me.

I finished the cereal and was beginning to feel pleasantly satisfied when the girl brought out a plate of two fried eggs, two rashers of bacon, two sausages, a black pudding and a fried tomato and set it before me. Beside that she placed a basket of toast, soda bread and scones and beside that, set a plate of butter and jams.

"What's this?" I asked.

"Your breakfast, ma'am," the girl answered and retreated to the kitchen.

I was able to just stare for a while at the mountain of food. This was my introduction to the "Irish Breakfast."

After a walk in St. Stephen's Green, I was glad to spend a good part of the day at Trinity College with its lawns and cobblestone quads. In the Treasury I studied the display of the Book of Kells. I could almost picture the Iona monks in the 880's laboriously copying the four gospels in Latin.

I could see them in their plain rough robes decorating the writings with elaborate pictures of people and animals and then escaping from the fierce Vikings with their lives and their precious manuscripts. I followed the lines of a huge Greek letter "X" in fancy scroll on one page and saw angels gradually emerge from its side, while rats appeared eating bread in the lower left hand corner.

I had a late lunch and spent the rest of the afternoon in and out of the shops on Grafton Street. Going through the change that was accumulating, I realized I had at least one of each coin: a punt, 50 pence, 20 pence, 10 pence, 2 pence, 1 pence. These were the markers of a changing world and would all disappear with arrival of the Euro. I thought of my nephew, Evan – Patrick's son – who was eight and loved to collect coins. I knew he'd get a kick out of these for they were individual, had interesting markings and good weight to them.

Evan had thick black hair like his dad. He was shy, though, and calm. He did not have the dark, explosive temper of my dad., his grandfather. Both of my parents had had a problem with drinking. My mother had kept her own supply close to her at home and each night drank quietly and slipped out of reality.

My father, on the other hand, was the control guy, the public performer. He cajoled and drew people out or waxed eloquent about the hardships of life while he enjoyed his whiskey. He would joke that he didn't trust the water so he had to drink the distilled and spirited variety and anyway, whiskey was really "uisce beatha" which translates to "water of life" in Irish. Besides, he could quit anytime he wanted. Didn't he give it up every year for Lent?

He would talk of Ireland, sing Irish lullabies to me, promise he'd take me one day to County Clare where his grandfather came from and on to Donegal, and at some point, we'd kiss the Blarney Stone together. His talk was big. He painted pictures of greatness, especially my own to come. I always felt I had let him down. Never in my young years did I turn it around and sit with my own let down, my own loss of the kingdom that had been painted large and promised me. It was a bittersweet bit of comedy.

Inside Davy Byrne's Pub were lovely wooden tables and soft lighting. Behind the bar, a wide, stocky man in a dark shirt and dark cotton pants was constantly in motion, servicing the bar, washing glasses, wiping surfaces, working the register. He turned back and forth with grace as efficiently as a player on a soccer field.

He came to the end of the bar where I was standing, setting plates in a plastic pan on the floor, stacking coasters on the inner edge of the counter and then leaning forward, resting his weight on his hands. "What'll you have?" he asked earnestly.

"I guess a Guinness."

"A pint, then?"

"Oh, no. That's too much."

He smiled a slow smile. "A glass, then?

I was guessing that a glass was somehow less than a pint. "Yes, a glass would be fine." He filled a narrow glass that held about a cup of liquid, about ¾ full and then set it aside.

I saw him pick up waiting pint glasses and top them off, handing them down the bar. A creamy head floated over a dark brew while flecks of cream dived downward into the abyss. When the pints were set before the patrons at the bar, they didn't touch them. Each was aware of the grand arrival and would look straight at this minor masterpiece with anticipation, but none would go right to it. Instead they watched the lighter bubble of the top settle before they ventured to bring the drink to their lips. Even then, they didn't gulp or rush the experience. This was a reverent ritual in progress in the sanctuary of the bar.

After a moment, the bartender topped off the little glass that I then paid for and took to an empty table at the back of the bar. At a table next to me, two young women sat with pints before them, smoking. Their heads were close together as they talked. In a short time, they were laughing loudly and I looked over at them. They had been looking in my direction, but now they turned away. A minute later they were laughing again.

I began to wonder if my pants and long shirt were inappropriate or if my long straight brown hair falling to my shoulders was a mess. I'd finish my beer and leave.

The girl at the next table, a blond, leaned over and tapped my table. "We're sorry, dear. We're just a couple of girls out for a good time while the hubbies watch the kids. You're visiting Dublin, aren't you?"

I nodded.

"Come sit with us. We'd love to talk to you."

I shook my head. "I couldn't…"

The girl stood up and dragged the chair across from me to their table. "Come on then. My name's Mary and this here's Adele." I stood up uncertainly and walked towards the table. A girl with an apron walked by and Mary said, "Give her another glass," and pointed to my half-full glass of stout.

"Oh, that's okay…" but the girl had walked to the bar.

"What's your name?"

"Michelle." I sat down beside Adele.

"What a lovely name," said Adele. "My boy's named Michael or I might have named one of my girls Michelle. A nice strong name, don't you think?"

"Where're you from?" asked Mary. "Oh, let me guess. The States."

"Yes." Once more I was amazed at the easy recognition. "Is it written on my forehead?"

"On your forehead?" murmured Adele quizzically. "Uh, where's your husband, dear? A woman out on her own tonight?"

"Actually, I am on my own. I mean I'm traveling alone."

"Oh, you're not!" said Mary. "How can you do that?"

"Well, I know where I'm going. I'm careful. And sometimes I like to explore things on my own. So, your husbands are baby-sitting? Probably giving the kids a bath right now, huh?"

Adele and Mary looked at each other and burst out laughing. "Oh, right," said Mary. "Sure I can see Dan up to his elbows in bubbles and drowning babies." The laughter subsided and she continued, "No, love. I'm sure they're all cozied up to the telly about now. But they're wonderful lads, all the same. If me and Adele didn't get out once in awhile, we'd go through the ceiling, wouldn't we? Here Michelle, have a cigarette."

"No thanks, I don't smoke."

"Oh, go ahead, it's your night out. Have some fun." She held the pack out to me.

"No, really. I don't like it."

"Aw, no one'll know." Mary lit a cigarette and handed one to Adele. The waitress brought my glass of Guinness and Mary and Adele ordered two more pints. So, how can you afford to travel on your own, if you don't mind my asking?"

"She must have a good job," Adele offered. "What's your work, dear?"

"I'm a psychotherapist."

Suddenly Mary nodded. "Oh, you mean where people come and tell you their troubles and you tell them what to do, right?"

"Well, I don't tell them what to do. I listen to people and acknowledge what they're going through and then I support them as they figure out their own solutions."

"But you tell them what they're doing wrong and how to fix it, don't you?" asked Adele.

"Well, Carl Jung once said that therapy was like coming upon a lost horse. If you pick up the reins and walk with the horse, he will lead you to his farm even if you don't happen to know where it is. And if the horse wanders over to some flowers on the edge, the therapist gently encourages him back to the path home. That's what therapy is in a nutshell."

"But you're not working with horses," said Mary.

"And you can't really talk to horses, can you?" asked Adele. "Unless it's Mister Ed." The two girls laughed loudly. I also laughed, but lightly. I knew it was all very funny, but the laughter felt hollow like the empty echoes of heels on a wooden floor in an empty room. I couldn't get past the fact that I had strong convictions about psychotherapy and, after all, this was my life's work.

"Oh, Wilbur," Adele mimicked Mr. Ed's slow, low, neighing voice. "I've totally mucked up my relationship."

Once again I laughed half-heartedly. Mary offered me another cigarette. "We're just having fun. Are you okay? You know what you do sounds awfully gripping. I'm sure it's good work. Ever so often my Dan'll push me to take a course in TV repair or something. I tell him, 'You take the course. You're the one always breaking the set trying for a better picture.'"

Adele crossed her legs and gestured with a lit cigarette. "Oh, Mary's always saying how when her kids're all in school she'll go back herself and finish."

Mary frowned and shook her head, her blonde hair falling over her small brown eyes. "I don't know what I'll do, but I don't want to end up like my poor ma. God rest her soul. Took care of sufferin' sots all her life. And nothing to show for it. Raised ten of us and not much help from my da. At her funeral instead of dirt, they should have covered her box with potato peel. Just a mound of potato peels."

"And what a mound it'd be. What with all the potatoes she peeled," Adele put in.

"A right mound," agreed Mary. "Up to the sky. But we didn't think to do it."

"It's too bad you didn't," I said, trying to look serious. "What a tourist attraction – the Irish pyramids."

"Pyramids?" Adele looked at Mary. For a moment they were silent then they collapsed in peals of laughter.

Mary slapped me on the back. "We'd no idea you had it in you. You've got to lighten up more often. Why if the music was starting soon, me and Adele'd teach you set dancing. You know set dancing?"

"No."

"Well, before you leave the isle, you've got to try it. And hear some good music, too."

"Where is there good music?"

"Oh, everywhere," answered Adele. "All these little bars have sessions – live music – fiddles and tin whistles and bodhrans. Might even see a flute or accordion or banjo. It's all good. We love it – lets us escape our insanity from time to time. Our therapy. We adore the music and the craic."

"What exactly is 'crack?' I asked.

"Just jawing," laughed Mary. "Here we are, the girls, talking about anything in the world. Good craic. We'll show you a good time tonight, you'll see."

"I'd love that," I said. "But I've got to go. I have tickets for the theater." I appreciated how fully they had accepted me even though they didn't know what to make of me. I wished I could in that one moment, meld into the simple, uncomplicated image that they reflected of me in the plain appreciation in their eyes, asking me to be no more than that, expecting no more than what was perceived. "Can I buy you a drink before I go?" I asked them.

"Oh, no." Mary smiled. "You go ahead and don't be missing your play now. Plays are grand. You just come on back when you're done with it. We'll be here."

Mary reached into her pack of cigarettes and pulled the cardboard insert out. She fished a pen from her purse and on one side of the cardboard wrote numbers. "Here's my number. If you don't hook up with us later, give me a ring sometime. We'll go out again. Anytime you're around. See how you're feeling."

Outside I headed towards the bridge. Sitting on the corner against a building, huddled a woman holding a small child against her. In her hand was a paper cup with a few coins in it. She looked into my eyes with hope, saying nothing. I walked quickly past, uncomfortable. Who was she? Why was she here with a child? Why did she have a child if she had to beg? What would she do with the money?

When I reached the foot of the bridge, I turned back. Why was I judging this woman? I felt the loose coins in my left pants' pocket, coins set aside for my nephew, Evan. I took them out. When I came upon the pair sitting on the ground, I looked into the woman's eyes, dark and unfilled as the interior of the vessel she held. I dropped the coins into the cup and turned back towards the bridge.

CHAPTER FOUR

After the play, I wandered along the quiet street, passing small groups of people now and then. I felt too sleepy to do anything further this evening and couldn't possibly meet up again with Mary and Adele. So with slow, uninspired steps, I made my way sluggishly towards my little guesthouse and my little bed. As I passed the bar I had been in earlier, I noticed a small collection of people standing outside. I paid little attention as I passed through their midst. Suddenly a hand was on my shoulder.

"Here she is! I told you she'd come back, Adele. And you said she'd walk all the other way around Dublin to avoid taking up with the likes of us." Mary laughed easily and began to speak to me. "I knew you'd come back. We were keeping our eyes peeled for you. Just getting ready to head over to Ellen Glory's, we were. And now we're all here, let's head out."

I wasn't sure if she was referring to a person's house or a pub. I started to protest, appreciated the gesture, if they indeed had been watching for me, and as a little group of about five of us started to walk, I found myself caught up in the migration, curious where we were going.

We walked for some time in the brisk, clear night air. Mary introduced me to two men and a woman who walked with us and we talked some about the news of a boy who had fallen down a well that day and had been rescued. At the corner of a dark street was a great house. We walked down some steps towards a basement with a wide wooden door. Mary rapped sharply and in a moment, we heard someone unlock the door and open it inward on a room filled top to bottom with a virtual sea of people.

We squeezed our way in and I still did not know if it was someone's home or a commercial establishment. Everyone seemed to be crowded around a group of musicians installed, closely together, against the far wall. In an easy chair sat an older man with an accordion. Next to him, on a couch sat a woman with a fiddle and next to her was a young man with a tin whistle.

On a low stool, pulled up close to the couch was a large woman keeping time on a bodhran – the treated skin pulled tightly over a round frame and sending out the low base tones of the drum to wake the lower regions of your body in the ancient voice of a pounding beat . The room was alive with the cheerful strains of a jig. People were packed in closely around the musicians, some even standing on various chairs and benches.

From the back of the room, I saw no place to move to. Mary

propelled me forward to a bench and leaning herself directly between two people, she non-verbally encouraged them to make space. She had me sit and took off a jacket and asked me to hold it. "I'll get us some cider," she said. "I'll be right back." I loved apple cider and was cheered by the prospect. Adele had moved to the front of the room somehow and was leaning over two guys. They were all deep in conversation.

Although many separate conversations were going on all at once, there was a general cohesiveness to the crowd, a general connection. The rhythm of the talking, the movement of heads and shoulders, the direction most people were oriented to, all reflected the central pulse of the live music. The propulsion of flowing notes formed the core of the room, the heart of the experience. Though people come here to get together with friends, it was this sentiment, the feeling of motion woven through the beautiful strains of melody, the emotion lying deeply beneath the sound that drew them, held them.

This tradition of simple instruments, played throughout the island, over the years, was a way to connect, soothe, enliven and express the deep stirrings of the composer and the player and the listener. Music was the colorful thread that ran through the day-to-day fabric of the social tapestry, the artistic touch that lifted the mundane in to the spirit of celebration.

The jig ended - was literally up - as Mary came back with a glass of amber liquid and pressed it into my hand. "I guess we won't get a chance to teach you the dancing tonight," she said. "Not a flat bug's space to turn around in." She shook her head and raised her glass. "Slainte."

I took a long drink of the cider, thirsty from the body-heated room. "Not unless they pull the fire alarm and clear the place." I joked.

"I don't see a fire alarm. What are you talking about?" The cider hit my stomach and the back of my eyes at once. This wasn't apple cider. This was hard cider and it definitely started me reeling.

The group began to play a soulful ballad and I watched the room switch with the lamenting, slow tones they played. Their voices softer, their movements slower, their hearts more open. I felt like I was in the belly of a large beast. We were its intestines, all crammed together, all responding as a unit. New material traveled in and through us and continued down the line.

Now we were carried away on the notes of the soul-searching tin whistle. We were looking for his long gone, one true love. We all kept watch for her, lost hope and mourned the loss, this loss and many others in our collective lives. I hadn't seen the bar that Mary had gotten our drinks from. It must have been off to the side and in another room, perhaps a kitchen. But soon she was off again and I found myself just listening to the music and nursing my drink.

Next to me sat and old man who coughed violently from time to time, then seemed almost to nod off, his head bobbing lightly and sometimes resting on my right shoulder. Next to him sat a much younger woman with yellow-frosted hair. At one point she got up and, though he appeared to be asleep, she announced, "I'm getting your coat. It's time to take you home." She set off to the other side of the room.

He sat up, adjusted his eyes to mine and asked. "Where did Niamh go?"

"Your daughter? She went to get you coat."

He laughed lightly then coughed harshly. "She's my wife is Niamh of the golden Hair. You know Niamh of the Golden Hair?"

"Golden Hair?" I asked confused.

"Well her hair's many colors now," he said frowning. "But once t'was golden like the goddess."

"The goddess?"

"Niamh of the Golden Hair. As I said. But of course you know that story."

" Actually, I don't. Would you tell it to me?"

"Oh, heavens, it's an old story. Now how does it go?" His eyes studied the deep recesses of mine as if the answer was there. His skin was very wrinkled and grayish. With each breath he struggled, and I worried that I shouldn't have taxed him by asking for the story. But I was intrigued. He smiled a wide, crooked smile and a brightness came into his little eyes as the story came back to him.

"Let's see now. Niamh, she was from the Land of forever Young – the Tir na n'Og. She was quite the enchantress with long golden hair. She lured Oisin, the son of Finn, to come and live with her. They were happy for quite some time and had their little brood – at least three little ones. Now Oisin was having a good life and all, but he was longing to return for a visit to his homeland, his lovely Ireland. Can't hardly blame him, can we?

And after he went on and on about it, Niamh says to him, 'Okay, I'll give you a horse to ride in on, but don't get off. Don't let your feet touch the ground. You see, to him it was the blink of an eye that had gone by when in reality, three hundred years had passed. So you know in these stories something always goes astray. Now, I'm not sure if his horse tripped and Oisin fell off or he just forgot himself, overcome by seeing his native shores, but he dismounted and as soon as his feet hit the ground – ah! –he turned to dust! What with three hundred years catching up with him all at once. Poor man. Can you believe he'd walk away from lovely Niamh of the Golden Hair?"

"I liked the story," I told him.

He nodded and asked, "What's your name?"

"Michelle."

"No, that's not it. Something else."

"My family calls me Mickey."

"Yes, that suits you." He coughed again. Then weak, he closed his eyes. "These are my last nights of going out, I'm afraid."

"What's wrong?"

He tapped his chest with a withered forefinger. "The lung cancer's got a hold of me. Got a hold and rung for the priest, I suppose."

"I'm so sorry. Are you getting treatment?"

His eyes lit up. "Oh, you mean going to the hospital so I can hang on a few more months? Hah!" He cleared his throat with a prolonged rasping and drew a shallow breath. "Oh, I do take some things my doctor gives me, just to please him, mind you. When your ride pulls up before your door, you just go out and get in. That's all there is to it."

"People do a lot of alternative therapies: visualizations, massage, macrobiotic cooking," I offered lamely.

His eyes twinkled and he smiled showing large gaps between discolored teeth. "God bless you, Mickey. You're a fine girl, you are, but in truth, I've smoked most of my life, my ma had the weak lung, too. It was bound to come for me. I take my turn. And now the fighting's over. Do you know what I mean?"

I wasn't sure I did. I looked into his tired, small eyes still shining with life. I wished I could gather this old bag of bones up and comfort him like a baby. Make him well. He struggled to cough and struggled to breathe. I thought he was done talking with me, but he sat up and continued.

"I've had a good life. Beautiful children, all grown. Had a house, took care of my parents till they passed. All my life I've been a scrapper and made my way, the hard way maybe, but my way in the world. Now, thank the Lord, I can relax – relax once and for all. I do know when to take myself out of the game. When to stop fighting. I'm sure not going to be fighting myself along with everything else. My ride's just about at the front door. I'm just sorry to leave my Niamh – Niamh of the Golden Hair."

The air round us was thick and heavy and still. "When Niamh calls…let's see…Yeats it was that said, 'The winds awaken, the leaves whirl round. Our cheeks are pale, our hair is unbound.'" He began to cough again, violently now, his rib cage rattling.

He squeezed his eyes shut and it almost seemed quiet until he spoke again. "She brings me here, makes me go out, trying to fill me with the music and people. Gives me one more time. Tries to fill me up with life, she does. So I'll have no regrets. But I'll tell you, Mickey, I'm very tired. She's the one with the life ahead. I want to tell you about all the projects that woman's got going, but I'll spare you. She tells me, 'Don't touch ground yet. You're in your flyin'.'"

He cleared his throat and tapped his chest with a crooked, yellowish finger. Bringing up a ball of phlegm, he deposited it in his stained brown handkerchief. Blinking back moisture gathering thickly in his eyes, he looked straight into my eyes which also blinked hard. "Now, now, don't look so sad," he said. "You like a kid who's lost her puppy. I'll be just fine. Fine."

I shook my head trying to make some sense of this tragedy. I put my hand on his thin arm. "I thought I was so brave to travel here by myself. You seem to be the brave one, though."

He lifted his chest, looking rather proud of himself and nodded. "It's the one journey we do have to take alone, isn't it?"

"I don't think I could be so strong." I thought of how much I'd resisted leaving my friends and family and work behind.

He patted my knee and leaned very close. I could feel his labored breathing on my neck. "You're not supposed to yet. You've got a lot of life before you. Of course you're not ready. But it's the years, the experiences. They all get you ready. You get used to the idea. You look back on your life and it's set. That's when you're glad to move on. What were you so scared of, you ask yourself."

He tapped my knee – his attempt at a hardy slap. "Now isn't that funny? What a fun one that is. What are we scared of? A good night's rest? God's in his heaven having a good laugh over that one."

I laughed too and agreed. Life was funny. And such a dear little man. I thought of Dr. Charles, a lovely man, a professor whom I'd felt close to in college and who had died in his middle age. Such a loss then. And who knew what this man was like when he was middle age, when he was young. This was him now. This is what with all his trials and travails he had come to. No matter what he might have been, this was the finished product, the man. What was his name?

Niamh came back, wrapped his coat around his shoulders and helped him to his feet and led him to the back of the room. He just looked straight ahead as she guided him to the door and out. She, however, looked back, caught my eye, tilted hear head and nodded to me.

When they had gone, the crowd promptly filled the space they'd occupied and very soon it was hard to imagine how they could ever have fit in there.

I focused on listening to the music again. Watching the people move easily with the music. I felt like I was being rocked to sleep. I went over to

Mary and told her I was worn out. She somehow found Adele – I couldn't locate her for the life of me. We worked our way through the crowd which would probably be there long after we left. Gratefully, we spilled out onto the pavement. When the door closed behind us, the music fairly disappeared and faded into a muted universal memory.

"I'm not sure where I am," I told Mary.

"Where you are? Well, here's just around the corner from my place. Come along now. Adele here's staying over and so can you. There's the couch."

"Oh, no. I've got to get back and be in my own bed." How quickly the rented bed had become mine, my safe harbor, my place of rest waiting for me through the long night. "I couldn't. Not at this hour. Can't I get a cab? I'm sure the transportation's not running."

The two women looked at each other and broke up laughing. "What's not running? It's not so late, Michelle. And besides, Dan'd love to take you I'm sure." At this they laughed again.

At Mary's little house, set close to the houses on either side, the scant front yard was full of toys and kids' bikes and a scooter. Inside, Dan was on the couch, a beer beside him. He was watching TV with a child curled up in his lap, the child's head on Dan's leg. Dan looked sleepy but roused himself as we came in. He said he'd be glad to take me and got up and placed the child on the wide, soft chair seat.

He snatched a white fisherman's sweater from the back of the chair and pulled it over his head. He finished his beer and fished his keys from his back pocket. Mary picked up the sleeping child whispering "good night," and "grand time," as she carried the child up the stairs.

I followed Dan outside and to the car parked on the street. Sleepily, I went over to the right side and tried the handle. Dan came up behind me and stood. "Will you be driving then, Michelle?"

I looked in through the side window and caught sight of the steering wheel. "Oh, my god, I'll never get used to everything being backwards!" When I'd see a car coming down the road, I'd automatically look to the left side of the car for the driver and flinch finding no one there; or worse, a child or a dog, and I'd notice them looking out the side window, not watching the road.

I stepped backwards and collided with Dan and lost my balance. He caught me, his large hands squarely on both of my shoulders and steadied me firmly. "There you go now." I turned and looked up at him.

He was incredibly good looking with long, even features and the suggestion of a dark beard. A big guy with big hands and wide shoulders. I could picture him as a rugged fisherman or a sea captain.

I took a step sideways, away from him, and went around the car and got in. The interior light glowed softly on his attractive face, his thickly lashed, bright eyes fairly glowing, his smile wide and warm and welcoming. "How was your night out with the girls?" The warmth and welcome continued to radiate even in the tone of his voice.

I told him in detail about the music and the people and about the play I'd seen earlier. I was animated as I talked to him, talking a little too much, trying my best to entertain him so he wouldn't be bored while being kind enough to drive me to my guesthouse.

All the while I felt him listening and I felt he was watching me closely between glances at the darkly lit roads. Outside of my lodgings, I turned to thank him. He still held me closely in his gaze. Before I could say anything, he said, "Glad to have seen you home. Seems you've had quite a night. It'll be hard to settle yourself down to sleep after such an affair."

"I'll be fine." I felt myself stiffen. I touched his hand as if to shake it goodnight but it was still wrapped around the wheel and I pulled it back, setting it in my lap as I reached for the door handle. For some reason I kept looking at him, watching him as I fumbled to open the door.

"Such a liberated woman you are. Let me get that door for you. I'll walk you in."

This threw me. I was completely ruffled. "Are you kidding? Absolutely not!"

"It's fine now. I'll just make sure you get in all right."

"Why would you say that?" But he was outside and around the car and opening my door. He reached his hand in toward me and I pulled back, my back smacking against the gear shift. I must have had a look of fright on my face. He broke into a grin and took my hand and helped me out. "Just a couple of steps then, Michele and you'll be there. You know, if I didn't know better, I'd say you were flirting with me."

I could hardly speak with the shock of his words. I felt as if I had just swallowed a paper napkin and could hardly get the incredulous words of my own out. "Flirting? What? Well, you don't know me. You obviously don't know I would never flirt or anything with a friend of mine's husband!"

I raced up the steps, and at the top I turned and looked at him standing calmly at the bottom on the pavement, his hands crossed in front of him. "I'm glad to hear that Michelle." He actually seemed peaceful, non-aggressive, even polite. In a moment I felt rather silly and wished to fly through the front door, but I had to fish for the key and fumble around fitting it into the lock.

All the while he stood patiently waiting. I swung open the door and turned around. He had to have been very cold standing so still in the crisp night air, but he smiled and touched his brow slightly bowing towards me.

"Thank you for the ride," I mumbled, and let myself inside.

CHAPTER FIVE

On Sunday morning at 11 am, I found myself at St. Mary's Cathedral. Mass was being said in the musical language of Gaelic which rose and fell in an engaging lilt, the words being almost sung in an entrancing rhythm which stayed in the higher registers of intonation. Even the men's voices sounded soft and high and light.

The words themselves were difficult to decipher for just as I would begin to recognize one or two, they would turn up again but changed ever so slightly. The language seemed to be having a good laugh at my complete confusion. Perhaps this was the intention of the original speakers – to keep non-native speakers from easily understanding them. Allowing the rhythm and pitch and sound to drift enjoyably by me, I was able to sense more deeply the underlying spirituality wending its way through the ceremony.

The hour passed in the familiar ritual, but I had new appreciation for the formal forms that everyone moved through together. Seeing it through newer eyes, I tried to picture the mass as if for the first time.

I remembered one Christmas eve when I had taken Mark to Midnight mass. Matthew, my partner, who was Catholic and whom I lived with in my junior and senior years in college, was supposed to have gone with me.

During an afternoon get-together with friends he had had too much to drink and was sleepy and didn't even beg off, he just crawled into bed and wished me Merry Christmas. I loved midnight mass, though, with all its singing of carols and the beautiful church decorations, the incense and the fancy vestments. As a child it had taken on such magic because we could stay up so late. There was also the promise of gifts later at home, the possibility of snow and the exquisite joy of everyone being together for once.

I was crushed that night and then Mark dropped by with a gift and he offered to go with me. I didn't believe he'd truly want to go, him being Jewish and all, but suddenly I wanted to show him what it was like, share with him the fascination I found there.

I talked all the while we walked in the cold in our scarves and mittens and heavy wool coats, preparing him, building up the experience as if his life had been leading up to this point.

With all the briefing, you would have thought I was prepping him to say the mass. We kept warm by walking quickly and I teased him that he didn't know the seasonal hymns. I remember laughing and saying, "Frosty the Snowman is not a Christmas carol!" When we went into the huge old church with all of the lights and candles, everything gold and red, a hush came over us.

Mark seemed interested, or maybe he was just very patient, but he stood and sat and knelt reverently when everyone did even though there didn't always seem to be obvious cues for these positional changes. He sang the songs from the hymn book we shared and when we wished each other "peace," he took my hand and looked into my eyes and for a moment I really felt as if there could be peace through the world.

When we walked home afterwards, we walked much slower, almost dragging our feet in the light snow cover that was accumulating. I was so tired but also so curious about what Mark had seen. "Was it boring for you? Too long?"

"It was long, I'll grant you that. I liked it, though. The up and down was a bit much, but it was pretty and it was nice to hear an organ playing. And it was a wonderful choir. I'm used to simple but long services and there isn't usually much musical back-up. It's rather singsong and it's easy to nod off."

"So you're happy you came? You're not, are you?"

Mark looked at me and shook his head. "Actually, I am. You know we were raised differently, but we're not so different really. I think we see things very similarly."

I had always enjoyed discussing politics and laws and morals and anything else that might come up at the student union and often as not, Mark and I had been on opposite sides of the issues. We'd had some pretty heated discussions and this familiar banter was actually a comfortable connection for us. I felt our constant debating made us like siblings who would always be competing, unlike parents who were supposed to be united on matters.

Now when someone challenged a point of view that Mark and I shared, we would become rather fierce, especially if it was an issue we believed would change the world. In college it's easy to get somewhat gung ho about saving civilization and even though I was basically shy, together we could become rather intimidating to the point of obnoxious to those who opposed us.

I thought one time he and Matthew would come to blows because Mark told him the death penalty was just a simple solution for those who wanted to play God. Matthew tightened his fist and faced Mark, then he looked over at me realizing that I had taken the very same ideological position. He just turned and walked away from us both.

That was typical of my relationship with Matthew. We never seemed to argue. We had such a peaceful, comfortable way of being with each other. We shared an apartment while I got my advanced degree in psychology and he studied for the bar. Of course, much of our time was spent in our individual studies, but when we went to dinner, usually we'd agree to go to whatever place the other had suggested.

The meals would go smoothly. We'd each talk of our day and the other would listen and be supportive of any difficulties. The same was true for films. We'd easily go along with each other's choices and spend the time we had together enjoying the movie and seemingly having seen it from shared eyes. I felt very lucky to have so early in my adult life found such a perfect relationship. I almost wanted to go to my parents and say, "See, this is how it is done. It's not so hard."

My father's angry quarrels, my mother's withdrawing, haunted me but I never confronted them with the proof that things didn't have to be so difficult. I just contented myself with the understanding that someone in the family had finally healed this battered and worthless trait that had been handed down over the generations. They hadn't needed to argue. And so in an intimate relationship, I would never allow myself to argue.

"This is different," I told Mark on that snowy night. "This is about beliefs and I think we couldn't be farther apart."

"Are you kidding?"

"You don't believe in heaven and hell and missing mass being a sin and that Jesus was the savior."

"Mickey, just a minute here." I turned and he brushed snow out of my hair and led me to a closed storefront doorway to escape the flakes coming down now heavily. We huddled under the darkened overhang of a giant hotdog whose neon lights had been turned off.

"Fundamentally, I think we believe much the same thing. We both believe there's a God and that basically He/She is good, right?"

I nodded. "Right."

"And we believe that Jesus said some powerful, true things. He being a rabbi and all…"

"Well, I don't know about that…"

"Anyway, no matter how many commandments God handed Moses, Jesus said that the most important was to be excellent to others."

I laughed, "I think Bill and Ted said that."

"The sentiment is the same. Anyway, afterlife or not – and I suspect there is - we both believe you lead a good life, do well for others, take care of your family. Don't we?"

His beautiful almond-shaped eyes were wide with question, searching mine for confirmation, searching mine for a connection to him that stretched from his eyes to his heart, from his heart, to perhaps, his soul. "Mark, do you believe in a soul?"

"I don't know if I'd call it one, but there's definitely a spiritual side to us. Would you like me to prove it?"

I was laughing, "Yes."

"I can't." He touched my nose with a corner of his mitten. "But I'm touching it now. Oops that's a nose, oh well, close." He looked very serious again, almost earnest and yet confident. "You don't suppose that the spirit that runs through me is so different from the one that runs through you, do you? It doesn't know religion, it know us. It knows us from within."

I was very quiet for a minute, watching the snow whitening his shoulders, sinking into the material of his coat, the same snow falling on him as on me, indiscriminate, cold all the same.

"It's kind of funny, isn't it?" I said. 'The one thing I felt separated us the most is actually something we have in common. What are we going to fight about at this rate?"

"There's nothing to fight about." He gathered up some snow from around the store's window panes and shaped it into a ball. "And you know you guys got the first part of the bible right – I think you call it the Old Testament." I snatched up the ball and tried to throw it at him but he caught my hand. "Boy, everyone's ready to take up arms against us poor Jews. Where's that peace on earth, goodwill to men?"

"Goodwill's closed till after the Christmas holidays. You'll have to wait. " I don't remember much more of that night. We walked home, I slipped into the apartment quietly and the next day I headed home to spend Christmas with my family. I think it was a very high volume snow holiday that year.

After the mass in Irish, I returned to the guesthouse, checked out, retrieved my car and began the journey westward. It's funny, but I had learned that the word for "westward" in Irish also means "backward." The further west you go in Ireland, supposedly the further backward you find things. Was I traveling backwards? Perhaps in time, but in as far as I knew I had never been this way before.

Last night when I had gotten back into my room and had calmed down, I finally saw some humor in what had happened with Dan and spent a good five seconds laughing to myself. As I replayed the moments we had together, I got the impression from the perspective of distance that Dan was a friendly guy and I hadn't really been in danger or even compromised.

I know that I am very quick to jump into a defensive stance and I'd probably have some insight if a client did this. I'd explore her past relationships and try to uncover who or what had instilled fear in her close interactions with others. Her feeling less like the child caught up in the past could help to subtly diffuse a sticky situation happening in the present. This process of discovery was much harder to do for oneself, but there was no therapist here for me now.

I suspected my combined love and fear of my father had surfaced so fiercely because I was alone in a new place. It made me skitterish of a man being close just now. My father had had big energy. It was intimidating. It was also seductive. But what do you do when the most attractive man is your father? I had wished more that anything he'd think me pretty or at least alluring. But what if he had? Would he have kissed me? I could almost faint in terror at the thought. But that was from a long time ago. That was me as a child.

I had also been close to my brother Pat as a child and teenager. Pat would often get the best of me, especially when I was most trusting, like when he borrowed money and bought baseball cards and then paid me back in crummy baseball cards he had doubles of. Or telling a boy at school I had a crush on him. I stayed out for a week that time.

I loved Pat, but didn't trust him. I wanted a brother so much to share things with and not worry there'd be any romantic/scary entanglement. A brother. That's what I'd hoped Mark could be, but I couldn't control what Mark wanted.

I thought about the play I had just seen. It told of a modern St. Joan. As a young, bold woman, she had somehow convinced the military to let her take charge. Devising a strategy, she had won the physical war but not the war of the sexes. I lay awake for a long time.

Were some women born to lead or did they propel themselves into the fray? Were they answering an inner call or did the plea come from those who needed help? And so is their disposition to fight born of a masculine urge or is it truly a feminine instinct?

Did one have a duty to assume leadership and in turn, did they deny it if they withdrew from action? Or did one foster peace by displaying inaction? At what point did being uninvolved mean running away and when was it simple self-protection?

I loved solitude so much, walking by myself, the hour of reading in my bedroom. Saturday mornings I'd drive alone out into the country. Often I avoided encounters.

Was my quietness merely covering timidity? Or was this my nature – to explore intimately what lay within my own breast, chart my own stirrings, and so be able to understand others who are wandering lost in their own sentiments, their own lives, lost to themselves? At this moment I felt I was only beginning to understand myself, only beginning to map the journey, only beginning to travel now.

What lay within, if gathered in strength with awareness and acceptance, would nourish me, help me to grow, eventually lead me to the way out. Where was the action to be? Was it within? Didn't we truly understand ourselves through relationships? The battles took on new forms as they summoned us today.

The temperature that morning was in the mid-sixties and the sun continued to shine strongly on this corner of the earth. Was the wind at my back? "All I need now is the road to rise to meet me and God to hold me in the hollow of his hand," I told myself, "and I will have completed the Irish blessing."

The road didn't exactly rise in greeting, but it did meet me half way. I found the N7 and traveled southwest out of Dublin and cut straight across the width of the country.

I entered the Lower Shannon area of Ireland, with lush green fields running alongside the Shannon River. Rising mightily out of the Tipperary Plain was a gigantic limestone outcropping called the Rock of Cashel.

I parked the car in the gravel lot, walked up the hill to the ruined abbey. I wandered through the roofless gothic cathedral with its carvings in stone, the Hall of Vicars Choral and the tall round tower. At this fortress, kings had been crowned.

Everything here seemed to be for the purpose of instilling in the people of the surrounding countryside, a sense of protection. Historically the region was often under attack from warring local kings or foreigners. Did the people here ever actually feel safe?

I drove through Limerick, a good-sized, industrial city that seemed very busy. Coming into the Kerry area, I pulled over at a rest stop at a break in the mountains called "Ladies' View" which looked out over the breathtaking forest and lakes of the Killarney National Park. It brought to my mind my family's property in Upstate New York – the uncleared woods surrounding the planted fields.

This was the first area in Ireland where I found the trees close together, shading the paths and creating a cool, solemn atmosphere. These trees, thick, full, lush with leaves, rustled in the wind and carried me right back to the woods of the farm. What a cool and dark refuge they were for me on a summer day. On a winter's day, they were a warm windbreak as I walked in their darkened chapel, my footsteps crunching on the crusted snow, echoing loudly through the serene chambers.

Here at the tearoom for "Ladies' View" I had my standard pot of tea and scone. I took my cup and plates outside and sat at a little table to take in this lovely view that many ladies and men must have cherished in their arduous trek through these narrow, winding steep roads through the Irish mountains.

Following the narrow road that wound down into the valley, I drove until I found a clearing for cars on the side of the road. I continued on foot, down the road to a skinny path that wriggled through an opening in the trees. As I entered the shaded hush of air between the thick trunks, I looked up through the brown limbs and branches and green leaves, allowing the gray-blue of the sky to form a reverse picture created from what wasn't there.

My foot slid across a twig and I lost my balance for a moment. "This is not the way to walk through the woods," I told myself. Mindfully I placed my foot on the ground and felt my sole conform to the irregular surface of the earth. A subtle energy rose from my foot and leg into my center and then continued upward. I felt a solid balance that adjusted to each step. I felt strong and sure within myself, an integral part of the setting.

At my family's farm, I had had a special tree near the region of the woods where I would go alone. I would step on a large rock at the base of the thick oak tree and swing up to the first big limb. Maneuvering around and around the tree to the sturdiest of the branches, I would climb to a place far above the ground. At a high point, three separate parts of the original trunk came back together and formed a comfortable shelf with a horizontal arm.

Here I could stretch out and hide out, far away from the confusing and distressing politics that came from living among people. To a child, it seemed people always had rules and opinions about what you should be doing.

The loud shriek of a bird pierced my chest, and I laughed at my surprise. I felt a breeze on my cheek and almost tasted the moisture of near water. The odor of the soil mixed with occasional decomposing leaves rose and filled my nostrils. Once again stirred in me the familiar sentiment that I could stay here forever.

The path opened to the still waters of a natural lake. I walked carefully to the edge, noticing a tiny corner of algae forming on this water that seemed caught in a still-life mode. Leaning over slightly, I was able to see the outline of my long hair and the top of my broad lean shoulders in the shadowy mirror.

Moving closer still, I could define the frame of my silhouette further. The soft suggestions of large brown eyes, a short thin nose and a full mouth began to appear. "Could I fall in love with this person?" I wondered quietly. "Could I see this person as if for the first time and be intrigued? Could I love what I found there?" A laugh surfaced and my throat felt wide. "What's not to love?"

I felt light. I was a loving and caring person. Yes, but what about the times I withdrew into myself? Times I was tired or distracted and didn't care or want to hear word one from a friend or a client. Sometimes I wouldn't answer the phone or even check my messages until late at night. And how about the time I had finally had a free night and a client had asked me as a special favor to come to her recital, and I had said I was working all evening?

But then there was the time I gave up my lunch break to sit with an elderly patient on the porch and talk to her about gardening while we waited for the woman's granddaughter to pick her up. Yes, I supposed I was a mix of many elements. And yes, I could love this flawed yet sensitive person, could even encourage her to flower. And basically wasn't this what my work was about? Getting people to know themselves and appreciate what they found.

The hardest part was acknowledging the dark, animal aspects of one's nature. Too many times a person wanted to rise above the basic drives of sex, aggression, survival or pleasure, and conform to an image they had of the "healthy, well-adjusted, morally superior" person. And they were wretched when a basic trait surfaced and played havoc with their neatly plotted life.

The night school adult who lusts after her professor can't just embrace this diversion and accept it, perhaps even enjoy the jolt of energy they're getting. The stockbroker who would just love for once to abscond with a fortune, instead of chuckling about the urge, may beat himself up with guilt and resolve to be more disciplined. He may try to excise this ugly deformity that presented itself as part of himself.

But even the dark qualities are a part of nature. In the mystery of this delicate balance, life surely and excitedly thrives. Balance. Light and dark. Male and female. Birth and death.

"What's not to love?" Love is an emotion. Emotion is the bridge, the middle layer, the agent that connects mind to body so that they may heal. I somehow leaned just a bit further forward, and the little bear totem in my shirt pocket slid into the water.

I rolled up the long sleeve of my shirt and reached my bare arm into the water. The wet surrounded my elbow before I could touch the bottom.

My fingers combed through silt and mud, catching soggy leaves and then a stick, but coming up empty. Through what was once a telling portrait and now only a cloudy smear, I searched until my hand came upon the cold shape of a bear. My thumb and forefinger, still submerged, rubbed the water and mud, clearing off the surface of the little animal.

As in the principle of homeopathy, it would from now on, no matter how well I cleaned it, carry molecules of this place with it. I lifted the bear out of the lake and when I opened my palm, I was startled to find it was actually beautiful black and gray stone with fine lines etched into its surface. I turned away from the lake and dried it off with the corner of my shirt.

"It's enchanting, isn't it?'

I almost dropped the stone then and turned quickly. But there was no one there. All was still. I couldn't shake the feeling I had that someone had been standing there, perhaps had been standing there for a long time. What was this presence? In the delicate, fading light I began to see the outline of woman standing at the edge of the water.

Her image became clearer and now I got the impression of a stunning, wide-shouldered woman with fiery red hair before me. I could see now that she wore a long green skirt and a simple white cotton blouse. She seemed to project a serious look but then it immediately softened into a smile at my bewilderment.

"How long have you been here?" I closed my hand around the wet stone and stood up.

"Let's just say I've been here since the dawn?" Her voice was soft and musical as the lapping of the waves upon the shore, hypnotic.

"The dawn?" I didn't quite understand. Did she mean this morning? "Who are you?"

"Who are any of us?" Her answer came on the heels of my question almost before it was asked. The words rang round and full in golden tones then settled into silence like a pebble dropping into the lake. She opened her long, fair arms wide. "I am this. And I am all this. I am Ireland. I am Eriu."

I moved backward to where the grass grew in thick clumps but then I wasn't able to see her clearly any more. The edges of her seemed less distinct. I sat down on a grassy mound and closed my eyes.

Suddenly I saw people in a field, rough people, dressed in rugged clothing, perhaps from a time long ago. Other people were overrunning the area, tough, fierce people frightening the first people off. A young woman stood to one side, angry and frustrated. With tears running down her cheeks, she cast about for something, perhaps weapons and finding none, she picked up handfuls of dirt.

She clumped the dirt into tough balls and began throwing them at the attacking people. A funny thing happened. The balls did the trick. They held off the assault and as if bearing a special power, these mud missiles drove the attackers into full retreat. They ran away madly the way they had come. The woman was ecstatic. She had won the battle. It was inspiring and I was about to open my eyes when I got the impression there was more.

I saw frames and frames of later skirmishes, until finally the fierce assailants had retaken the field. I now saw the girl standing with the attackers, clearly on their side. What had happened? I began to understand that she wanted them to believe she was now on their side and would remain there no matter what her original affiliations were. She seemed a bit older now, a bit weary, but to me it was obvious where her heart lay. She was biding her time, planning her moves, all the while thinking of the people she had first fought for, yearning for their freedom.

The first scene showed a case of winning a battle but losing a war. In the last part I saw the war being waged below the surface. She was demonstrating very plainly for me that when one adapts to a loss, if one is patient, there can eventually be a tremendous gain and a measure of peace.

The vision reminded me of a time at home. When I was eight and Pat was ten, he was much bigger than I was. He would push me around from time to time. And then sometimes, like late at night when we'd already said our prayers and had been sent to bed, he would creep down the hall and into my room. We'd talk and play and make up stories. It was so secret and exciting to be comrades in the dark.

One night he told me he had just heard mom and dad arguing and dad was going to leave. He was so mad at him, he said he'd like to "punch his lights out." I told him that dad was a pretty lonely guy and mom always said things that made him angry. People just never understood dad so of course he'd want to get away, be by himself, not stay here just to be hurt. Pat called me "daddy's girl" and asked why I always stuck up for him. Didn't I know he was a "goddamn son of a bitch?"

I don't know what happened. All of a sudden I just hauled off and punched him in the nose. He stood looking at me, amazed for the longest time. Then he came at me and we just rolled around and he fell off of the bed. Well, we made such a commotion, that my parents came in and of course we both were in trouble. But no one, especially me, could believe I had bested Patrick that one time.

That too, was a hollow win. For later that night my dad did leave; he was gone at least a month. And my brother never stole into my room again to share those private moments with me. I waited but he never came. Could we ever be such good friends again? I didn't think so.

I opened my eyes and could see the woman again. I watched her tilt her beautiful face up to the sky, her strong features stark against her creamy skin. With large green eyes, looking through the spaces of the branches, resting her gaze on the great blue dome above, I knew she held me carefully in her peripheral vision.

Somehow I knew she was looking out for me in this moment. I could imagine her understanding me, maybe even seeing my own small battles. She reached down beside her and lifted up a small harp that she cradled before her and began to strum. Lovely notes that soothed the soul floated freely about us with the gentle stroke of her fingers across the strings.

I wasn't sure how long I sat there. The wind lifted ripples lightly on the lake and I watched the wisps skid across the surface until all blended into the smooth sheath once more. I followed the play of evening light as it filtered and ebbed to mellower lengths.

I had seen the movie, "The Horse Whisperer," and at the time I had been willing to bet I couldn't sit in a field all day as Robert Redford had, waiting for the horse to finally come to him.

But here I sat, peaceful, having no immediate plans, I felt I could wait for whatever was to come, for however long it would take. I closed my eyes. I felt alone and yet not alone. Time was standing still for me.

All was in order, I thought, as I listened to the lake water blithely lap the sandy shore. I opened my eyes and could no longer see the woman. I opened my hand and there lay the totem of the bear.

I was losing the light and soon it would be dark. I needed to head back to the road or I would be unable to make out the trail and might have to consider spending the night there. The thrill of staying in these woods in the dark, sharing the space with nocturnal creatures here and weathering the falling temperatures sent suggestive shivers through my bones.

An interesting idea, but I really didn't know this place that well. I quickened my steps to the car.

CHAPTER SIX

It was almost completely dark as I approached the town of Dingle on the Dingle Peninsula. I was tired and getting very hungry. I kept my eye open for a Bed and Breakfast with an available room but every little house with a sign denoting "B&B – Board Failte approved" had a "no vacancy" one as well.

I was in the town proper now and still no room materialized. The narrow two-lane road was very crowded with much traffic moving both ways and both sides of the street were heavily lined with parked cars.

Passing restaurants and shops with no place to park, I looked up to see a rather wide truck coming quickly toward me in the opposite lane. I was sure he would hit my car on the right side and instinctively veered left to protect myself. My little red Peugot smacked into the back corner of a green Range Rover with a resounding crash.

I was past the car. There were cars behind me. I continued down the street until I came to a parking lot and pulled in. Still sitting in the car, holding tightly to the wheel, I closed my eyes. I waited a moment for the pinball crashing around inside me to come to rest.

Suddenly the car I had hit pulled in directly behind me. A man and a woman jumped out and ran up to the car. Calling in through the window, the woman yelled. "Do you know what you just did?"

The man right behind her shouted, "And where were you going? Running off?"

I slowly opened the door. They stepped back and I stood up, my legs shaking. "I'm sorry," I began. "I couldn't stop there." My breathing was coming in short gasps. "Is your car damaged? I'm really sorry."

"It's all right," the man said. The couple, who were in their thirties, looked at each other and then at me. "Just the reflector panel of the brake light's smashed a bit."

"We were sitting in the car," the woman spoke gently. "You gave us quite a start. Are you okay?"

Was I okay? I couldn't believe that here they were standing peacefully and I plowed into them and now they asked if I was okay. I took a deep breath and nodded. "I was looking for a B&B and I couldn't find one and I guess I misjudged the…Listen, I'll pay for whatever damage there is…"

"You're from America, aren't you?" asked the woman. I managed to smile wanly. "We're from the North. Up by Omagh. We're here on holiday. We come down here all the time. Don't worry about the car, we'll take care of it." The man moved his head up and down in agreement.

"We're staying at a B&B down this main road here, second turn on the right and around the bend, a big yellow house. There may a room there for you and it's nice. Or if not, next door's a little one, or you can take the coast road out of town and you'll see some turnoffs with B&B signs. Do you want me to write this down for you?"

I shook my head. "Thank you. I appreciate your help. I'm just a bit out of it right now, but I will take care of any –"

The man smiled. 'Wouldn't hear of it." He turned back to his car.

The woman touched my arm. "Listen now, get yourself a bite to eat and a room and don't worry about it. If you want, you can follow us to our place."

"Thank you."

The couple got in their car. I got into mine. They waved and eased their car back onto the busy main street. I watched them go in the rear view mirror and then focused on the large brown eyes there looking back at me. They had filled with tears and the scared face that framed them began to blur.

The tears rolled down those reflected smeared cheeks and the tops of the shoulders below began to shake. For once I hadn't known what to do. Many things could have happened. I had done nothing to handle the situation. And yet, I had survived nicely thanks to the grace of other humans.

I was too tired to look for a B&B now. I had lost sight of the green truck ahead. Earlier in the town, I had passed a hotel and I headed back to it. I secured a room for the night and had an Irish Stew in the bar downstairs. Settling into my room, I opened the windows and heard the soothing sound of the surf nearby. I curled up under the covers, the lamp by my bedside lit and read the next part of *Ulysses*, "A cloud began to cover the sun wholly slowly wholly."

The next morning, I awoke with a rush from a powerful dream. It was not daylight yet so I turned on the bedside lamp again. In the grayish dawn, in sleepy awareness, the yellow light was soothing. Separating myself from the realm of dreams slowly, I felt as if I had just come down from flying. I managed to gather my notebook and pen to record the dream.

I had been swimming in the ocean and playing with many little animals. When I waded to shore, a mean-looking dog had been waiting, his teeth bared. I had been terrified and then realized he was only lost. Unable to read his tags and discover who he was, I said I would find help for him.

The dog became a bear of a man with hairy arms and a thick neck.

Although he had been grateful, he still appeared very scary. From a briefcase, he pulled out treasures from his past and photographs and news articles that proved he was a very famous man. Vowing to buy me a fancy dinner, he headed off to make the arrangements. I was relieved when I realized he was not coming back. I set the case up on its wheels, sat on it and rode it to the bottom of a hill, fairly flying on my own.

It was too early yet for breakfast to be served when I checked out. I asked for an envelope from the desk. I got in the red Peugot and drove back down the main street. After a while, I made a right turn, went around a bend and came upon a big yellow house. In the parking lot was the green Range Rover with the cracked reflector panel. The lot, the house, even the road was quiet now. I put a twenty pound note along with my business card into the envelope and placed it under the windshield wipers.

I drove back to the main road and headed on to explore the twenty-five miles or so that covered the Dingle Peninsula, a languid arm stretching out from the mainland in county Kerry. Yellow orange streaks of a rising sun broke through the predawn sky, lighting up the narrow road that wound around and around, following the playful curves of the coastline.

Traveling between seascapes and mountains, I came to Dunbeg Fort dating from the Iron Age. Close to it were beehive huts that were built for the early Christian pilgrims. I traveled around Slea Head and saw the roadside sculpture of the Crucifixion of Christ.

At Dunmore Head, the mainland's westernmost point, I looked out across the rough dark blue waters of the sound and in the distance, could make out large shapes rising out of the water. They looked like the backs of ancient animals carved in stone. These were the Blasket islands.

I drove a further north towards Dunquin. There, at the Blasket Interactive Center I learned about the islanders who had lived many generations on these harsh islands until 1953. Three rough miles across Blasket Sound, these islands were only accessible with primitive wooden boats – curraughs.

Living close to the land in this bleak existence with no modern conveniences and no form of entertainment, the islanders looked forward to the end of their hard workday when they would sit around the hearth and listen to the storytellers – master word-crafters in the Gaelic-speaking oral tradition.

One such gifted storyteller was Peig Sayers, who held residents and visitors spellbound with stories of fairies and death, and antics of the weather. She drew from ancient verse and recent stories. She recalled dramatic events such as when her son had been brought home to her dead after falling from the cliffs.

She received his broken body with his skull broken into pieces. She dressed him for his burial, but first she put the little pieces of his skull together like a puzzle to give his head its proper form. Telling stories was her family tradition. Her father had told stories until his death at 98. In her own old age, she spoke of her words living after her, quoting the proverb:

Is buaine port na glor na n-ean

Is buaine focal na toice an tseal.

"A tune is more lasting than the song of the birds, and a word more lasting than the wealth of the world."

Early in the afternoon, I continued on to Tralee and then to Talbert, where a ferry would carry me and my car across the River Shannon into County Clare. There I hoped to find the land my father's family originally came from. The ferry would save me 3 or 4 hours driving time. I skirted the river and followed signs to the ferry and then got into the long line of cars at the dock.

When the ferryboat came, men efficiently directed the cars to be driven onto the huge deck. Three cars in front of me, a man signaled the cars to stop. Another ferry would not come for an hour and I anticipated the people in the cars in front of me complaining about the wait, perhaps insisting that they squeeze a few more vehicles on to the ferry.

A man in the first car got out as I expected. But instead of approaching the ferry, he began to walk past my car and down the road the way we had come. From the second car, a man and a woman got out, stretched, fussed with putting on sweaters and then also walked down the road. The car directly in front of me was abandoned by a family of four with two young children.

As they made their way past, I began to wonder just what this ritual was. I rummaged through my daypack and pulled out my book to read as I waited. Then on an impulse, still holding the book, I also got out of the car. I stood a moment watching the line moving down the road, then locked the car door and fell into the line. After about a quarter of a mile, I saw where everyone was heading.

In the middle of nowhere was a little pub. I followed the crowd into the cozy, dimly lighted establishment with people ordering pints or tea and snacks or sodas for the kids. I sat at the small table in the corner – not the best light there – but cozy. I ordered an iced tea. After a bit of negotiation, the bartender agreed to make a hot tea and pour it over ice for me. I pulled out *Ulysses* flipping through it, looking for my place.

"Nice book. Mind if I sit?" A dark woman in a dripping, black trenchcoat came over to the table. I motioned for her to join me and she draped her coat on the back of a chair and went to the bar. She returned setting two pints on the table. She sat down across from me and pushed one of the pints my way. "Glad I caught up with you."

"Do I know you?"

The dark woman, her jet black hair wet and slicked straight back, looked deeply into her pint and then slowly around the pub. When she spoke, her voice was low and clipped. "Not at all. But I saw you from the river out there and you reminded me of someone. Eerie. Well, nice to make your acquaintance then." She appeared to wear no makeup, yet her eyes seemed to be fully outlined in black eye pencil. They were dark and laughing, suggesting humor that stung like sarcasm.

"Is it raining out there now?" I asked.

Once more she looked around, then taking a large gulp of her stout, the woman answered. "It was wet the way I came. That seems to always be the case. It's probably cleared up by now. Drink up."

I nodded to her in thanks. "So, I don't know you?"

"You do now. That should do." Her words resounded low and deep, filling the space between us with strong vibration. It commanded attention.

"And your name?" I asked brightly.

"I don't think you could pronounce it."

"Really?" The nerve. But I pressed on. "So what should I call you?"

"You should call me Sonny." I almost chuckled for the image of someone "sunny" that the name conjured up was the last one I'd have picked for her.

"Just Sonny?" She nodded. "I'm Michelle Maguire."

She nodded again and said nothing. I felt obligated to keep up a conversation. After all, this strange woman had just bought me a beer even though I really didn't want it. "Are you from around here?"

"Up north a bit and west."

"Could you be anymore vague?" I said exasperated.

"Could you be any less?" How annoying, but then my style in dealing with people seemed to contain very little mystery. It was quite different than her manner. I laughed and continued, "So, what do you do for a living?

"Such questions! What do you do for a living, ask questions?"

"As a matter of fact, I do. I'm a psychotherapist."

With that, she smiled. "Same field as me almost. Give 'em survival tools and send 'em back into the fray. Only I don't talk 'em to death first." She laid both of her hands out flat on the table. They were wide with long fingers, strong hands with prominent veins, painfully short fingernails, and no jewelry.

"I teach the fighting arts, you know – martial arts, self-defense. I'm running a program now that works with teenage boys who get into trouble. It's through the schools and sometimes the courts. It sorts 'em out. Very challenging. So much is in the head, don't you agree? Attitude."

"Do you only work with boys? How about girls with behavior problems?"

"Mostly guys work with the girls. That's the old way and it works well. A woman trains guys, a guy trains women. The boys are characters, trying to impress you, trying to overpower you, finding they can't do it with brute force alone. In the end, they come to respect a woman. One lad I'm working with is quite the handful, always trying to catch me off guard. I had to floor him three times this week. Fancies himself another Cu Chulainn…and perhaps there is a resemblance."

"Who's Cu Chulainn?"

"You're kidding, no?" she shrugged. "He was a pretty famous guy in his time. An old fashioned warrior. I thought everyone knew of him." She folded her hands around the near empty glass, her fingertips meeting each other in a solemn symmetry. "So, how about you? Have any of your patients challenged you?"

"They're all challenging in some way." I waited a moment and asked, "How is that for vague?"

"By Jove, I think she's got it," she quipped in a mock English accent.

"Seriously, I did have a teenage girl last year that I truly didn't know what was the best way to help her. Her mom brought her because the girl was angry much of the time. She had a brain tumor and was dying. At first when the girl would come, I'd get her to talk about her family, school, anything, and the whole time I could hardly concentrate thinking about what a tragedy the whole situation was.

"I saw her struggling very hard to handle going to school - she was exhausted from all the drugs. But she managed to keep playing some basketball even when her balance was going. She'd try to do her reading assignments even though she developed double vision. She was working so hard that she forced me to work hard too.

"Together we were trying to find some understanding. She was coming to terms with her life and it was inspiring just to be there with her then. It was a discovery that you couldn't design. Much of the time I was baffled, moment to moment baffled, as to what to do."

"Sounds like she did just fine. She was evidently something of a warrior herself."

"Yes, she was." My eyes softened as they drifted back to look into that lovely teenager's face with her determined eyes and jaw. "In my work

I'm usually focusing on someone improving their life. As much as I liked her and wanted to help her, I couldn't change the one aspect that was cutting it short. I felt somewhat powerless."

"You were powerless. It was her fight." The dark woman, bent her elbow on the table, drew her long fingers together, made a fist and let it fall squarely on the table.

"Like I tell my students, 'you don't have to look for fights, the important ones come to you.' Fighting is a part of each of our days. You did your part, your struggle was with yourself. She did hers, living each moment throughout her illness. She was winning and she had someone beside her as she fought. Still wondering about it, are you? What a piece of work you are, but I guess that's the major part of learning – once you have the technique, wearing the confidence."

She stared far past me, looking as if into another dimension. "Well, the ferry's due back. Time to leave."

"But who do I remind you of?" I leaned forward earnestly. In retrospect I must have seemed desperate to understand who this woman was and what our connection could have possibly been. In all honesty I might have seemed somewhat hyper.

"Did you ever study martial arts?" Her eyes seemed half-closed as she addressed me.

"Not per se. I studied Tai Chi, a form that was originally used for fighting. Why?"

"You could stand to embody the essence of it. You know what I refer to?"

"Being centered – that seems to be the main point. Or being grounded." This wasn't what she wanted. "Letting the energy move through you?"

"Essence." She looked like she would nod off if I didn't come up with something quick.

"Oh, I know, the whole intention is that when the energy moves through you, you are able to heal. Are you saying I need to heal something?" What was she getting at?

She drew herself up and looked squarely at me. She was going to pull this answer out of me. "For the healing to take place, the energy has to move, what allows the energy to move?"

She stood up and put one foot in front of another, sunk into a low posture and easily extended her arms before her thigh as if she were about to ward off a moth at about the level of a kick.

"Let's look at this another way. Say you're in a stance, a defensive posture, ready to fight. Someone is attacking you and you have to react.

Perhaps you want to block their blows or you may want to land a punch or kick. In your case, you may just want to get out of the way. So, what's the first thing you have to do?"

I was silent trying to picture a particular technique. She went on, "Before you can move to do any of these things," she made as if she was trying to lift her arm. "Before you can move one muscle, what do you have to do?" Her arm was so stiff, it looked like it had been set in concrete. It wasn't moving unless she softened it.

"Oh, I get it - relax."

"Like pulling teeth." She eased out of her stance as she brushed her hand across her leg at lightening speed and with a tangible force that would have repelled any physical attack.

"Relax?" I said brightly, like a student who locks on to an answer to reinforce it.

"Relax and know." Cleverly revealing her riddle, she smiled. Her flexible arm now swung down to the table, picked up her glass and finished the pint.

In a quiet, non-aggressive tone, I asked again, "But who do I remind you of?"

She tilted her head at me then straightened up. "Just a resemblance. Someone long ago. The hair's different though." She seemed to dismiss the subject as she slipped into her slicker and tucked the collar up against her throat. Then she turned abruptly and walked away. Stepping through the door, I lost sight of her.

The ferry ride was smooth and easy. With all of the cars parked close together on the large barge-like structure, it felt no more unsettling than crossing a bridge, only it was the bridge that was moving. People sat in their cars or stood beside them as we crossed. Some went to upper decks for the view of the river flowing gently between two green bands of land. And if some people chose to have a snack, they had to contend with the large birds begging mercilessly.

CHAPTER SEVEN

I drove into the quaint sea town of Killimer. I drove past a lovely marina in the heritage town of Kilrush and with the help of the map, I headed towards Cooraclare, a tiny rural town about fifteen miles from the ocean where my great grandfather had grown up, and from where he had left to come to America. Because it was the in the center of County Clare, and in French, coeur meant "heart," I easily imagined it meant "heart of Claire."

The countryside was open and uncomplicated. Except for the scarcity of trees, the rolling green fields reminded me of my family's farm in New York State. On the outskirts of Cooraclare, I saw a riding school and stables. A hearty woman in knee-high rubber boots was walking a quarter horse on a lead near the fence by the road. My father's family came from this area, and as I tried to imagine how they felt living here and what their life might have been like, I thought of my mother.

When my brother and I were little and our father was around a lot, my mother was always cooking wholesome meals, snapping and steaming fresh green beans, boiling and mashing potatoes, making a roast with gravy from flour, salt, water and pan drippings. She would roll dough and boil blueberries, reducing them down to a luscious pulp and adding sugar to make fresh, nourishing pies.

She made her own curtains, bright flowery patterns with ruffles and valances that she starched and ironed. She took care of the small animals who were part of the household. She spoiled the dogs, each of which was named "Lassie" or "Laddie" and she considered each to be a member of the family.

She participated quite often in town affairs, setting up craft shows and church bazaars and fried chicken dinners with biscuits, even bake sales for the Grange. She would sew clothes for us kids and make every one of our fancy Halloween costumes.

My mother had a vegetable garden and many flower beds around the house. She would feed the birds and make sure the little pond was cleared out each spring.

It was funny, usually when I thought of my mother, I thought of the later times when she withdrew deep into herself. But when my mother was in her glory, hers had been a very full and rich and largely unappreciated existence.

At the edge of town were two B&Bs , but they did not look welcoming. The entire town seemed to consist of a main street with a bar with public rooms about it, two smaller bars, a post office/convenience store/video store, a church, a hardware/small items store and a laundry.

I parked in front of the post office and went in. I asked the woman at the counter if she knew of a place where I could stay the night, perhaps a local B&B.

"Oh, I'm afraid the B&Bs are closed for the season, it being late September and all. About now we don't get many people coming through. You should come back in June, July or August," said the middle-aged woman with big dark-framed glasses.

"But if you want to stay on, there's the bar here in the middle of the block. Dan and Ann Kelly own it, they could put you up. They have rooms upstairs and a dining room and all. You can just walk right down there and someone should be about."

I thanked her and went to "Kelly's," a bare bones establishment, and found a teenage boy behind the bar watching TV and another boy, perhaps his younger brother, at a pinball machine next to the bar in the dimly lit barroom. "Can I help you?" The teenager stood up and picking up a white towel, he began to wipe the bar down.

"I'm looking for a room for tonight." I smiled at the boy and looked around the small room with its rectangular bar and mirror and four wooden tables with wooden stools. There were some sports pictures on the wall and a banner hanging from the middle of the ceiling, "An Clare!" I did not know then that this signified a cheer for County Clare in the upcoming finals hurling match.

"I'll get my mom," the boy said. "She's upstairs."

Several minutes later, a tiny woman stood in the shadowy entranceway to the bar wiping her hands on her apron. "One night, then?"

I nodded and the woman turned, talking over her shoulder. "Follow me." I followed her up the narrow steps and down the hall, stepping over a vacuum cleaner cord. The woman talked with the nonstop energy. Her voice, like the constant rhythm of the Hoover itself, rushed forward without a break or a breath.

"I have a nice little room, it's over the bar but it has its own bathroom and a shower with hot water - if there isn't enough hot water, let me know in the bar, or better still, let me know a bit before you need it. We don't get many people out here this far into September, you know. It'll be 12 pounds and that includes breakfast. What time will you be having breakfast?"

When she paused, I was surprised and hesitated. "How about 7:30?"

"7:30's fine," the voice was resigned.

"Is 8:30 better?"

"8:30's much better." The little woman smiled. "And will you be having dinner? I'm planning on making a nice beef stew, ready anytime after six." I nodded and took out my wallet. "Oh, don't pay me now, dear. Don't you worry about it. Now do you need help with your cases and all? I'll bet you're from America. Am I right?"

I laughed out loud at what was becoming the standard joke. I seemed to be the only one surprised that people knew it automatically. I declined help with bags but asked for a phone book. The only family in the area named Maguire was on the road coming into town. I got directions for the address and also to the rectory, which was outside of town in the other direction.

Ringing the bell beneath the sign, "Father Bergen," at the modest one-story building, I waited several minutes. Then the woman next door, a religious sister, came over and told me that father was away at a match - a hurling match - in Dublin and would not be in until the next morning. I thanked her and drove back through the quaint one street town with no stop lights and no theater or library and few cars.

I headed out past the small, tidy farms that began at the edge of town. At a mailbox with 'Maguire' written in white paint, I turned my red car into the dirt driveway and passed a couple of sheds beside a small farmhouse. An older woman, her graying hair tucked under a hand-knitted woolen cap, wearing short rubber boots and a dress with a long sleeve shirt over it, was making her way through the muddy drive with a black and white dog at her heels.

She was carrying a bowl of feed and walking in the direction of the chicken pen. When I turned the car off, the dog ran towards me barking madly. The woman called the dog back and walked over to the driver's window. "Can I help you? Are you lost?" She bent down close to the window and cradled the feed bowl to her chest.

"Is this the Maguire's?'' The woman nodded. "My name is Michelle Maguire and as you may have guessed, I'm from the United States."

"Oh, are you really? I'd never have known. Well, come on out of the car then and come on into the house a bit," the woman stepped back from the car door. "Come here, Rex! None of your shenanigans. Be careful, he'll jump up on you. But he just likes to be friendly, don't you?"

When we got inside the drafty kitchen, the woman put a kettle on to boil. "I'll fix us some tea." On the refrigerator were taped pictures of drawings made by very small children.

Very soon the panes of glass in the cozy little kitchen steamed up. "What brings you to Ireland?"

"Well, my father's family came from around here a long, long time ago, the late 1800's. I've always wanted to come and see Ireland and see if there's anyone here we're still related to. That's why I stopped here."

"Oh, that sounds very exciting!" The woman looked at me intensely and smiled. "What a wonderful trip you must be having. And have you have enjoyed it so far?"

A boy and a girl ran into the kitchen from the living room. They were between four and five years old. "Can we have tea?" they asked together.

The older woman took off her long outer shirt and hung it on the back of the chair. She took off her cap and hooked it over the corner of the chair. Her gray hair was flat against her head. Her eyes, which looked very tired, were afloat in the many ripples of weathered lines. "Of course you can. Now where are your manners? Say 'hello' to our guest."

"Oh, that's all right," I began, a bit surprised by the appearance of these two young ones.

"This is Jesse and Donna," the woman broke in and then addressing my surprise, she added, "They're my grandchildren. Both of their moms, my daughters, work during the day and the kids stay with me till dinner. Next year, though, Jesse's going to miss his cousin, aren't you, when she goes off to kindergarten for the day."

The children ran back into the living room, where I was now aware that a television was on. "That must be a lot of work for you, taking care of grandchildren and the farm and all."

"Oh, they're good kids," the woman took out cups and plates, cookies and milk. "I've been very blessed. My daughters live nearby and they have good work. My sons are in Cork and Limerick but not too far. No, I've been blessed. The kids get in my hair from time to time and tease our Rex or worse try to ride on the poor old fellow, but they're a joy to have around.

"I don't know what I'll do when they're both in school. Probably learn what to do with a few minutes strung together is what. But for now I'm glad to have them. So, do you have children, Michelle is it? Lovely name."

"No, I haven't had children yet. At this point I'm not even married." The older woman looked at me and tilted her head. "I don't know if I will ever have children. I worry that I won't be able to keep them from developing problems. I'm nervous about what gets passed on to them through the genes. And nervous about how to raise them. So much can go wrong."

"Oh, heavens. With such thoughts, no one'd ever bring another babe into the world. Making mistakes is as natural as the birthing. Children are a gift, to be sure. But we shouldn't fret over 'em and we shouldn't coddle 'em, or they'll never grow up fit. Don't think so much, dear. You'll get yourself crazy."

The girl, Donna, brought a page from a coloring book and some crayons and set them on the table. "Grandma, will you color with me?"

"I'm making tea now." She put some of the boiling water in the teapot and swirled it around and then dumped it out.

"I'll color with you," I quickly offered.

The girl took up a crayon and began to color. "Grandma, I'm making the sky green."

"Now don't we have enough green on the ground for sure? What about a blue sky?"

The girl continued to color. "It has to be green."

"Why does it have to be green?" I asked softly.

"Because it wants to surprise the birds." She handed me a red crayon and pointed to the birds. "Won't the birds be surprised?"

"They'll probably be so surprised they'll fly in circles." I colored a couple of birds.

"Yeah," the child laughed. The older woman brought the full teapot to the table and began pouring, adding sugar and milk to the two small mugs. The child picked up the picture and held it toward the woman. "Here, grandma, this is for you."

"Oh, it's grand! Just grand. We'll just have to see if we can find a space for it in our gallery," she said nodding towards the refrigerator. "And this is for you." She handed the child a plate of Vanilla Wafers. "Now take some in to Jesse."

She carried the two mugs into the living room and came back shortly and sat down beside me. "Now where were we? Oh, you're having a lovely holiday. And have you found any of your family so far?"

I put some milk in my tea and took a cookie from a plate on the table. "Well, I couldn't help but notice your name is the same as mine. The phone book says Thomas Maguire. Is that your husband? I thought maybe there was a chance I might find a connection there."

"Oh my, no. Well, Thomas is my husband. He's off getting a part for a machine in Ennis. Won't be back till later. And I'm sorry, I didn't tell you, I'm Fran. But Tom's family - oh, they came from Donegal, let's see when Tom was just in high school. Got this property from an in-law who died, when was that? Well, anyway they're Donegal people.

"Most of the family's still there. But I don't think there's a chance we're related. All the same, I'm sure Tom'd love to meet you and all. Why don't you stay and have dinner with us, he should be back soon."

"I told them at the hotel I'd have dinner there." I now regretted my commitment.

"Hotel? Oh, the pub. Well, Tom's off early for Dublin in the morn to pick some stuff up. But why don't you give me your address and all. I'm sure he'd like to have it."

I wasn't at all sure why in the world this guy would care about someone from across the world whom he wasn't even related to. But I took out my wallet and from a pocket extracted a card with my name and address and the title, "Licensed Psychologist," and handed it across the table.

"Oh, my, isn't this impressive?" Fran read the card.

"It's just easier with a card." I sipped my tea.

"Of course," she agreed.

Later, as I sat in the bar over the remains of a hearty and filling beef stew, the bar began to fill up with a good number of people. They were returning from the match in Dublin. County Clare had won a fierce game and everyone was just as fierce to celebrate the victory.

At about one a.m., with the bar full of smoke and a crowd loudly singing "Rhinestone Cowboy," I made my way out of the bar and sat on the curb in the dark, deserted street. The air was comfortingly cool with a touch of moisture, perhaps carried from the coast only fifteen miles away.

A stray puppy, whose owner may have been inside in the core singing circle, came up and nuzzled my pant leg. I sat there for a long time, petting the pup, and telling him my musings as they came up to me in this dreamy, magical town, a stone's throw from the sea.

"We're all small players, aren't we? Pulled and pushed by the great dreams, and all we need is this little touch behind the ears, right?" He licked my hand and readily agreed.

The next morning, after breakfast, I took a long walk through the town, turning down side streets and following them to the end. I studied the farm fields and pastureland, rich in rolling green grasses. Some fields were enclosed with stone walls or heather. The grazing areas were comfortably populated by sheep or goats.

The yellow Marsh thistle and raspberry-colored meadow vetching grew wild. In the cultivated areas, birds swooped down, resting on the great bales of hay to get their bearings. I wondered what it would have been like to grow up here. Would it have been much different a hundred years ago?

I walked until I came to the rectory. Now a little black car was parked there. I rang the bell. A small man in a dark suit and white roman collar answered the door.

"May I help you?'

"Father Bergen?"

"Yes."

"I see you've returned from Dublin?"

"Ah yes, right. Sister told me you were here yesterday. Please do come in." He stepped aside and when I entered the simply furnished house, he showed me into his office. He switched on a lamp, pointed to a chair and went around his desk to sit at a swivel chair behind the desk. Floor to ceiling, three walls were lined with books of all sizes and ages.

"I must apologize to you. I just got back this morning and everything's disorganized. So, here we are. And what might I, in my small way, do for you today?" His voice was soft, comforting even while he made light chatter. He had a gentle way of leaning forward with his question and then leaning far back to give you all the space and time you may might to answer.

"Well, Father, I came to ask you if you might help me with the parish records. My great grandfather left this area in about 1890 and came to the United States. I was hoping to find some record of him and also to see what happened to the rest of the family, whether they stayed in this area or not."

"Ah, the parish records...well, I can tell you they're not in the best of shape. I mean, I'll be glad to help you. We'll look through them together, but at best, they're incomplete and the older ones were handwritten and hardly legible."

He went over to an old metal file cabinet that stood before one of the bookcases and pulled open a drawer. He pulled out a great sheaf of papers. "Now the later ones were transcribed and retyped but these older ones, well, we haven't gotten to them yet. Someday, God willing, we'll have it all on computers, and of course the current ones are on disk, but you can see these are literally falling apart." He leafed through the bottom pages. "1890, 89. 80...What was your great grandfather's name? "

"Maguire. Patrick Maguire. His wife, my great grandmother, was Katherine Naughton."

"Naughton. No, I don't see that name here at all. Probably from a different parish. Don't see their marriage record. Maybe married in her parish. But here, here's a baptism and it's a son, Daniel, born to Patrick Maguire and Katherine Naughton, baptized April 13, 1887. At least that was when it was recorded."

"That was my grandfather, Daniel. So, he was born here."

"They must have left shortly after that. I don't see his name again. There are some other Maguires, a baptism in 1888 under Thomas Maguire and Mary Kathleen. Just says 'son' and no name. And a marriage later of Seamus Maguire to Mary Rose Hanrahan. But that's it. No other Maguires in the 1900's that I see. Here we go over into the typed records. But still nothing. So, either things didn't get recorded, and that happened. They were busy making a living off the land, I'm sure. Or they went to live on land elsewhere in another parish. Or went on to America or Australia."

"Australia?"

"Oh, sure. Many's a family was poor and couldn't support themselves. They were given passage for their families and guaranteed a job and they would have to work a certain amount of time to pay it back. It was a good solution for some. I'm sorry I can't find more relatives for you to track down. But let's write these names down for you to take with you."

We copied the names and he wrote down the address of the library in Dublin if I wanted to do further research. We sat again at the desk facing each other. "So, what else can I help you with? What else would you like to know?"

"Gee, I don't know. I guess that's all I can learn."

'Well, this I can tell you. Your family was here during the Hunger. They didn't leave then. Many did, a million at least. And many died; also at least a million. Your people had to be very strong and brave to have survived that time here. They called it the Great Famine."

His perspective was one I had never considered. He stood up and went to the bookshelf behind me. He took down a book and opened it. "It started in 1845. The whole potato crop failed. And the people were very poor. Their lives depended on the potatoes they grew. And then, it happened the next year and so on. People outright starved and little was done to help.

People were losing their land and many people were fighting for independence. A terrible time. Ireland lost almost half of her children when all was said and done, what to death and immigration. So the ones that pulled through were very sturdy of spirit. I have a wonderful book, let's see...." He replaced the book he held and continued to look over his shelves. "I must have loaned it to someone."

On a piece of paper, he wrote the name, "*The Great Hunger: Ireland 1845-49*" by Cecil Woodham-Smith. Below that, as a second thought, he added, *"The Silent People"* by Walter Macken. "That will get you started. Answer some of your questions for you."

He sat back down and folded his hands in his lap and was quiet, smiling over to me in sweet acceptance of whatever might come. Then he leaned forward and asked, "And what else can I do for you today?" He leaned slowly back and waited with the patience of a modern saint.

"Nothing. Thank you. I appreciate your time, really."

The doorbell rang. "Just a moment." He stood and went to the door and let two men in and pointed them towards the kitchen. He came back to his office and sat down. "I'm so sorry. Plumbers. Today is the day to get everything done. I apologize for interrupting you"

"Oh, no, please. I didn't even have an appointment. I should leave." I stood up but he motioned for me to sit.

"Now don't feel you have to rush off, all right? I would like to say one thing though. I am sorry that we did not find relatives for you into this time so you could have known them. I'm sure you wonder what they were like. Well, I can tell you this: they were good people. The people from this area were poor. They were farmers with small farms, working the land as best they could.

"But above all they took care of their families. No matter what happened, they provided for and protected their families. They may have fought or had a drink now and then or had bad luck with the crops, but they were decent, good-hearted people. Of that you can be sure."

I told him how much I appreciated his time and rose to leave. He gave me the paper with the family names and dates, the names of reference books. At the bottom, he wrote his name and number in case I thought of something later I'd like to ask him.

I walked slowly back towards town. The fields looked different now. Before they had looked rich and luxurious. Now I knew that every square inch of this land here probably had some sad story to go with it. But then, the land also held some heroic tales of kindness.

I drove into Ennis, a much larger town in the center of County Clare and parked next to a cafe. I went into the noisy establishment, and a heavyset woman with a lilting Irish accent greeted me immediately. "Good afternoon to ya. Will ya be havin' lunch?"

"Yes, please," I said making my way to a little table in the middle of the room. "What's good today? Do you have any soup?"

The big woman began wiping the table. "The split pea with ham. I helped make it. So, where are you from?"

With grateful pleasure, I fairly announced. "I'm from the United States."

"Oh, I know that, dear. What part?"

"New York."

"No kidding. I'm from Philadelphia."

"But you don't seem - I mean you don't sound like you're from Philly."

"No? Oh you mean the brogue? Oh, I've been here five years. You pick it up. Can't help it."

"Do you like living here?"

The brogue abated as she confided, "It's wonderful. I just love it. I mean it's a slower pace and all. Very slow at times. I visit the States but then I love coming back." She pulled out her pad and pencil and put them together to write. "So, the pea soup, then?" The Irish accent was right back. "And maybe you'll be having some brown bread with it?"

After lunch, I walked around the crowded town. In a small bookshop, I found an audio book of Lady Gregory's stories of the Irish myths and many of the goddesses. I couldn't wait to listen to it. Near the checkout, I found a Gaelic/English dictionary. Hoping to verify that Cooraclare meant "the heart of Clare," I looked up "coora." It meant swampland.

CHAPTER EIGHT

At 1:30 p.m. the sky clouded over and a light rain was expressed from the sky as mist, dampening all from above to below. Soft weather, as the Irish called it. I checked the map and took the N85 towards Ennistymon with its shop fronts painted gaily in bright colors. In Ennistymon I picked up the R478 and drove along the coast to the dramatic Cliffs of Moher.

I parked and walked up to where the path began. No one was charging admission today. A hand-written sign explained that the person who sold the tickets was at a funeral this afternoon. I climbed up the steep slope and suddenly was able to take in this breathtaking sculpture of Nature.

From the serene green hills around us, shot this great long arm of rock out into the sea. The top of this narrow peninsula was flat. You could easily walk out towards the end of this treacherous promenade and just as easily slip and fall straight down the 650 feet to the sea that surrounded you on three sides. The jagged cliff face of sandstone and black shale fell dizzily down into the rough waters that beat themselves against its stone base.

I watched sea birds swoop dangerously down the sides of the cliffs in a sharp arc and magically land on a tuft of moss or a crack in a rock, balancing continuously on the razor-thin ledge. They perched precariously for a moment's rest before catching the powerful updraft and taking off again.

Intrigued by these dangerous and wildly beautiful rocks, I continued along the path, following it as it angled upwards and downwards, following the line of the seacoast.

I had put the first tape of the Irish myths into my portable player and as I walked along serenely and quite alone, I listened first to the "Cattle Raid of Cooley" and Queen Maeve. Next I heard the heartrending story of Cliodna. Walking along these cliffs, looking down the long drop into the rocks and pounding surf, any story seemed believable.

I tried to picture this goddess, Cliodna, with her long blonde hair, who hailed from the Otherworld, a place of spirits beyond this world, a place she was not allowed to leave. When a young man, Ciabhan of the Curling Locks had been rescued from the sea, he had been brought to the Otherworld. She fell in love with him the moment she saw him.

There had been a big celebration that night, with entertainers and much music. She convinced Ciabhan to take her away. More than anything she wanted to escape to Ireland and live with him there. He stole her away in his curragh and banked on a southern strand. He left her there while he hunted a deer for their provisions. A sea god, Manannan, who believed the world of people should never mix with the world of the fairies, sent his people to go after her.

They found her and played music until she lay down in the boat and fell asleep. And then a huge wave came and swept her back home. Since then she has not been allowed to set foot on the land. It is believed that some of her spirit comes in with each ninth wave. In the Otherworld she continued to help heal lost people and even sent birds to the land to heal people with their song.

I turned off the tape, took off the headphones, and sat down not far from the edge of the cliff. The roar of the surf below, the cries of the birds, the wet spray in the wind, all engaged me, all touched me and kept me anchored in this moment.

No signs of anything modern broke into this present that spoke of timelessness. Across the span of ancient times to now, the elements tear and blow and wash and shape and recreate the landscape. The landscape is the backdrop for our daily dramas, shaping our lives in its own image.

I recalled a small moment in my life that faintly paralleled the disappointment and loss of Cliodna. When I was in junior high, I had a mad crush on a boy in my class. One day in the park, I saw him coming along, holding hands with a very popular girl. I climbed a tree quickly to hide.

Unbelievably, they stopped under the tree. I think they were going to kiss and I was leaning over and bam! I feel down, landing almost on top of them.

The girl ran away, frightened. But the boy thought it was funny and was impressed with a girl climbing a tree and all. He walked me home and came into my house. We started to watch TV and he held my hand. I was so excited, I slipped away to my room, lay on my bed and began writing in my diary. I might even have drifted off for awhile. When I came back downstairs, he was gone. And the next day, I saw him in school with the girl again. I went far out of my way to avoid them. I was confused and deeply embarrassed.

I stood up and started back along the path. As I came to a sheltered curve in the rock, I stopped and looked over the edge. Far below, standing ankle deep in the surf, I swear I could see a blonde woman. The image lasted only a moment. She did not move any closer to the shore but seemed to look longingly towards the bank. The woman was gone, but I found myself counting the waves - seven, eight, nine. Lovely Cliodna.

I drove on, through the town of Lisdoonvarna, which was once a spa town, but now in September it was known for its ongoing Match-Making festival. In the past, farmers would come into town, the bulk of their work done, their pockets a bit fuller from harvest profits to pursue the business of finding a wife.

In present times, the town has a month long festival and people come from all over to meet potential mates. It was quiet this afternoon in the town, things probably got livelier at nightfall. I told myself I should stop, go into a pub, have a drink, and see what happens. But the prospect of almost announcing the intention of meeting someone, putting one's self "out there," was gutwrenching. And this crude ritual would only slow me down.

Besides, what did this have to do with my quest? I was in the process of just discovering. The scenery and the local people in their own element was what was happening. I slipped over the speed limit as I pressed my foot to the pedal to emphasize the enthusiasm for the newly-acknowledged mission. I glanced at the speedometer. So what, kilometers registered much higher than miles per hour - 60, 80...My little red car and I fairly sailed through the town.

I was coming into the region known as the Burren - 193 square miles of limestone and shell thrown up from an ancient seabed. Rocky underbelly, ravaged by the glaciers, was gradually smoothed over by ice and rough weather. Rivers run haphazardly beneath the surface. Tunnels and caverns sprawl extensively in all directions.

Neolithic Man built dolmens and burial cairns and stone forts. Unique is the Burren where plants from all zones of the world grow. Plants such as gentians and mountain avens and many types of orchids growing side by side, are landing pads for some butterfly species found only in this area. The Irish hare, Whooper swans, and the hooded crow all abound here at different times of the season.

I was enthralled driving along between great outcroppings of rock with deep fissures and herds of wild goats making their way on the rugged stone slopes. Great fields of rock; it was as if limestone were the crop here and the patches of flowers growing between the cracks were only decoration until the harvest. Walls and walls of stones piled on top of each other, in many different designs, many of them built during the famine, marked the fields.

I drove past a sign that noted the Aillwee Cave, and I turned down a dirt road to investigate. There was a cave that became a tunnel that then opened into a number of caverns. The first cavern was called Bear Haven, and it was here that bears in the area had hibernated for many years.

Their scratches on the wall may well have been their communications, their own hieroglyphics. The darkness, the quiet, the simple home carved by nature had slowed me down more that I knew. And when I pulled back on to the main road, the R480, it was in a contemplative mood that I surveyed this area of the Burren.

I remembered that in the 1640's when Cromwell had banished many of the northern Irish to this area, it had been described as, "a savage land, yielding neither water enough to drown a man, nor tree to hang him, nor soil enough to bury." It was savage and stark, this land, but in its bleakness was a raw beauty - the great gray rocks, the patches of green, the dots of purple and yellow breaking from the gashes in the rock and the lone crow diving here and there, a solitary sentry.

I passed through Ballyvaughan on Galway Bay, a fishing village where one could see slate-roofed cottages, and the Galway Hookers - the traditional wooden sailing boats. I picked up the N67 and drove through Clarinbridge where each September the Galway Oyster Festival is held. Tempting, but I continued on to the N18 and Galway.

When I reached Galway, I secured a small single room in a large hotel in the city's center. They were currently serving a high tea in the lobby and so after taking my bags to the room, I returned to a low table in the lobby and ordered a 'full tea'.

A waiter brought the tea and milk and sugar, a plate of many kinds of sandwiches, cookies, scones with butter and jams, a turnover, and slices of fruit. "Well, I guess this is dinner," I thought, surprised at how hungry I was and how much I was able to eat. I finished my turnover with a cup of Earl Grey tea and felt that were I to disappear right now, like the cat in *Alice in Wonderland*, my contented grin would linger a long time.

Although I was tired, I was so full I needed to walk a bit. In the still damp air and fading light, I strolled the lively city of Galway. It had been a trading center for the West since the 1300's. It had gone downhill after the Battle of the Boyne but since the 1970's, it has been beautifully restored.

The River Corrib ran right through the center of town and I crossed its banks several times, walking past the university and the cathedral and the large downtown shopping mall. As it was getting dark, I returned to the hotel and got into my bathing suit.

On the top floor of the building was a large swimming pool. Glass walls made up the area around the pool and you could see over the whole city. I took a sauna and then swam and then floated in the pool. The edges of me disappeared as the water buoyed me up. The day-to-day struggles of life were gone. With no effort to being at all, I felt like I was melting into the water, into all I saw about me.

Wrapped in a big white towel, I sat on a chaise lounge and looked at the active city life going on at ground level. The magical lights of the early evening glowed golden from the shops and restaurants and street lamps.

Lights from cars and buses streamed throughout the gilt grid below and lit the fantasy side of the observation room with its constant little light show.

I took out the book I had brought with me to this rooftop lookout and opened it slowly to a dog-eared page and began to read. My eyes began to close of their own accord.

When I opened them again, a tiny, old woman sat sideways on a plastic chair beside me. Her skin was covered with sores, her face deeply lined. She wore a long-skirted bathing suit, nylon stockings rolled down to her ankles and a large bath towel over her shoulders. The rooftop oasis was fairly deserted now.

"Don't be alarmed, my dear, I'm not contagious."

"Oh, my, what are those sores?"

"Leprosy."

"Are you kidding? In this day? Are you getting treatment?"

""I chose this condition, Dearie."

"Oh, no, you don't believe we create our illness, do you?"

The old woman tilted her head back and laughed a bit maniacally. "This one I did. I choose how I want to take human form and over time, I've come in a variety of ways."

I sat up now and looked at the woman closer, dismissing what was being implied, I asked, "Are you talking reincarnation?'

"I'm talking worlds overlapping. What's your name, dear?"

"I'm Michelle. And yours?"

"That's a bit complicated."

"I thought it would be."

"A smarty are you? All right, try this one on. I'm part of Morrigan. Now Morrigan can be a person in her own right and she can be three of us, Badbh - she's the furious one, Nemhain - she's the crazy one, and me, Macha - the crow, who picks at the spoils of the battle. We all hold the power of destruction, sexuality and prophecy. We are three. We are one. How does that fit into your neat little picture of the world?"

"As well as any of my other dreams."

The woman curled her lips in a wry grin. "Well, if it helps you to believe this is a dream, go right ahead. Dream on. But you don't know who you're dealing with here." She chuckled deep in her throat and then began to cough as if she would choke. "If Morrigan had chosen to come, she wouldn't let you off so easy. She's a doozy, she is. Would you like to hear about her?"

"I would."

"I'll give you the overview. For awhile, she was always helping Cu Chulainn while throwing the battle against his enemies."

"Cu Chulainn? I know that name."

"No kidding. He's a rather famous hero from ancient times. Anyway..."

"He was a warrior. By the way, how was he trained?"

The woman thought a moment. "He was trained to fight by a woman name of Scathach whose name means 'Shadowy One'. A shady character, that one. She wasn't a close friend to me -- nothing of the sort. So, getting back to the story, if we can keep on track...

"Let's see, after one of his battles, Morrigan appeared to him as a beautiful lady. She said how much she admired him and would like to show that affection in bed. He said he was all fagged out. She said there was no one could equal the pleasure she'd give him. What a come-on, huh? Well, he says he's still not interested and she just cracks, whips out a sword and says from now on, she's fighting against him.

"Well, she disappeared and reappeared and fought him as an eel, a wolf and a white heifer with red ears. He was incapacitated, but managed to blind her with a sword thrust. Later, she appeared to him as an old woman milking a three-teated cow. When she gave him the warm milk to drink, he gratefully blessed her. This happened three times and so she was healed of her injury.

"Once she foresaw his destruction and tried to prevent it by breaking his chariot shaft. He went into battle anyway and realized his doom when he saw her washing his armor in a stream before his final fray. She was with him to the end, his enemies realizing he was truly dead when they saw her, as a crow, perched on his shoulder.

"I must not leave out the part about her and cattle and the tricks she did play. I've always said, 'if she hadn't snuck a bull in here from the Otherworld, that whole Cooley Cattle Raid would never have happened.' On one hand, she caused chaos, and on the other, she prevented chaos as when she helped the Tuatha De Danan triumph over the evil Fomorians. What a woman, no?"

"She sounds delightful." We laughed. "She does sound incredible. I'd hate to be on her bad side."

"Oh, my dear, who wouldn't? Meet the original bitch on wheels!"

"How about you? You, as Macha? Were your experiences different or were they always about combat?"

"You must understand that I am in the same group as Morrigan. But if you want to prolong your bitty dream another minute or so, I'll tell you a story of mine."

I nodded and watched the old woman's eyes light up as she warmed to her memory. "You'll get a kick out of this one, hon. One time, I came into life as a beautiful peasant girl. I met and married a lovely man, Crunnchu. We were so happy and nothing other than our love would give him more pleasure than to have a child with me. We took care of our little farm.

"I was strong and healthy and could run like the wind. I ran everywhere at great speeds. He was so proud of me, but once in a pub, when the king's party was scheduled to come through, he bragged that his wife could outrun anyone, even a horse, even the king's horses. Well, the king's soldiers didn't take kindly to his boasting and arrested him. They were going to kill him if he couldn't prove his words. I was distraught, I can tell you.

"I went to them and pleaded for his release. They'd have none of it. Only a race would free him. I was pregnant with twins and hoped the soldiers would show mercy. Only the race could save his life. So, the great day came. The king's horses ran sharply, but I ran a better race and won, thank you very much. But it was too much for me. At the finish line, I went into labor. That day, I delivered two strapping boys, but I lost my life with the effort."

"How horrible. How did you ever manage to forgive those soldiers?"

"There was nothing to forgive. I set things straight then and there. I put a curse on that army so that they would be as helpless as a woman during childbirth, five days and four nights, just when it was most crucial for them to be strong. Hah! It worked out just fine, turned a battle against them. I felt a virtual waterfall flowing through my innards with no hard feelings left to wrestle with. You look surprised. Think back to some time when you've set someone straight and finished the matter just like that." She slapped her palms together loudly.

I shrugged. "I can't."

"Think aways back. Family? A father, maybe?"

"Mostly I was trying to understand him, feeling sad often. As for my mom, I spent the first half of my adult life trying to forgive her, and the second, hoping she'd forgive me. I lost my temper with my brother when I was young. But no, I can't think of an instance when I just balanced the score and moved on."

"Someday, you will. Not vindictive-like, just spontaneous. And when you do..." She threw back her head, almost cackling with delight, "it'll be a world of fun!"

I smiled, watching this mysterious creature, looking so decrepit and sick, yet so full of life, ready to jump into a conflict on the spot.

"I'm going to jump into the pool," she said softly as she leaned forward and touched my arm. Her scarred face was just inches from mine, and though still grotesque, it took on a familiar sweet quality.

"You just go right on with your dream, dear. Dream on and on..." her voice, so heavy, so soothing, trailed off. My eyelids dropped shut and I breathed very slowly, very deeply, very peacefully.

CHAPTER NINE

The next morning, in my hotel room, I awoke slowly from a deep sleep just as the first streams of light began to paint in watercolors at the topmost corners of the window. The heavy floral drapes were open and artistically framed the impressionistic scene that was evolving with muted grays and browns melting into gold and silver streaks as the sun climbed higher and into a position of more prominence on the horizon.

Faces of people from my past danced in my head. I had had so many dreams. A strange old woman with incredible stories was the first one I recalled. It had been so vivid. Next I dreamt of old friends and forgotten family members.

It had been a long time since I had thought of the dog I took care of when I was six. I had only had him a very short time, but he had become my best friend and then had run away. I had wanted to take my allowance money and advertise a reward for him. My mother had said, "No, people would return him out of the goodness of their hearts." He was never brought back and I was sure on some level, it was only because I hadn't paid the price.

In my dream last night, there he was, lively and affectionate and again running off. But I saw him go and I chased his little brown tail down a street and around a corner where he bounded over a vendor's cart and promptly disappeared. I was standing in a European square, maybe in Italy. It was sunny and everything seemed very white and warm. At an outdoor cafe sat Mark, having a cup of espresso. A large white cat sat on the table sleeping. "Come join us," Mark called to me. I sat down and had an espresso also. "They are preparing to have the World's Fair here at any moment," he told me.

"The World's Fair? The World's Fair?" I repeated. "Since when is the world fair?"

With this we both laughed so hard, we fell off of our chairs. We frightened the cat, who jumped down off of the table and scampered away. From the shadowy space under the pushcart gradually appeared the cat's eyes. Then a second pair materialized – the puppy? Then emerged mysteriously a third pair of eyes before everything faded away.

Why had I thought of Mark? He never used to come to my mind, but lately he was popping up a lot. I thought back to college. I went back over this time again looking for what I seemed to be missing in my sense of closure here.

During that time I had dated only Matthew, assuring everyone who would listen that we were soul mates and lifelong partners.

Yes, Mark had been my buddy and my debating partner. I thought of myself as his little sister. We had played pool together and bridge. We'd meet on Friday afternoons after class to have coffee or a beer and discuss the upcoming weekend. I would tell him of my struggles to understand Matthew and my even more desperate struggles to make Matthew understand me. I would tell him of my strategies for romancing Matthew and getting him to fall passionately and unreservedly in love with me.

With most men, I was conscious of how I looked. When these men looked at my thin small nose, my very blue eyes, my broad shoulders, my small square hands, my long strong legs, when they assembled this assortment of traits, I wasn't sure what their final verdict would be. To myself I felt like an attractive, healthy woman. But I worked hard to maintain that impression when I was with others. I was conscious of how they responded to little movements and casual remarks.

At times I'd catch myself holding my waist in as I talked to a group of people, totally uncomfortable and totally discouraged with my efforts. As I would talk with some guys I'd find my thoughts drifting, wondering if this one perhaps didn't care for fine brown hair, maybe if he saw it in a different light, some golden tones would shine through. They were poses, I knew that, poses not unlike those of the other women in my class.

They seemed to drop away around Mark, though. Probably because I didn't see him in the role of a date, I was comfortable putting my head together with his and not focusing on the outside world. We'd toss ideas around and around, surprised at each other's point of view. We'd hang on the other's words, intent on either finding a point to contend with or even a common ground there.

I had the latitude to be comfortable with diving down inside to find how I felt or thought about a particular subject. I'd surface with awe, presenting what I found almost as a gift for Mark. I was sharing a part of myself at these times. And it wasn't always easy. Sometime he might have introduced the question of human rights or what we were doing to the environment or the burden of his mother's over-protectiveness and I would be moved to search for what it meant to me.

He might disagree. He often did. But he never tried to change my mind. And I trusted him. At least I felt I did. And this trust was my true gift. I was trusting someone completely - him.

But that trust only extended within safe boundaries. As long as he sat across the table from me or walked with me in the snow or occupied my sofa with Matthew between us, things were fine. Only once did I cross that barrier and afterwards I was shocked and confused.

In the end, it was Matthew and I who turned out to be more like brother and sister. Even after we had begun to live together, I don't think I ever noticed that there was no deep curiosity about each other's inner workings. Not from Matthew and not from me. There was no great yearning to explore our histories, our feelings, our dreams. I was very happy, or so I thought, having this smooth togetherness, sharing times and spaces together.

I suppose I told myself there was no need to talk all the details out for we must certainly, deeply, already understand the intricacies of each other. And we were on the same path, the same wavelength, meant for each other. Why rock this smoothly sailing ship? I was completely mystified when I came in one afternoon and found Matthew in the living room, holding a piece of mail he'd just opened and he was truly grinning ear to ear.

"What? What's the news?" I asked, setting my books on a coffee table and pulling off my coat.

"This is great, just great, it's all coming together. The job of a life time."

I was excited for him and hugged his arm as I looked over his shoulder. Our plans for the future had seemed to be evolving naturally. I had come to understand that when I got my doctorate in psychology, I'd do my clinical training in New York. Often, in our travels in the city, we'd evaluate a particular neighborhood as a potential place to live.

We'd gotten acclimated to the hustle and bustle of the city together. Matthew was considering a professorship teaching law or going into a law firm in one of the groups he already knew well. Things just seemed to be flowing along. The return address at the top of the letter was Portland, Oregon.

I couldn't really make out the text of the letter but Matthew was ecstatic and began to explain. "I've been talking off and on to Ron Harley – you remember him from undergraduate school – anyway, I didn't think anything would come of this. I didn't think he'd get the backing. But it's all here and ready to go. He's opening an experimental firm in Portland, and I'm going to head it up."

I was flustered, my head felt clouded, like the language coming through my brain's verbal center had been scrambled and mixed with foreign words all of a sudden. "Matt shouldn't we talk about this? I mean this is so out of the blue."

"It's not really new. As I say, it's been in the works. I just can't believe it's all worked out. Of course, we'll probably have a fine time deciding on the firm's name, but that's a minor-"

"Matthew, I didn't, I mean we didn't talk...." I was getting confused. "Matt, are you talking about moving there?"

He nodded as he got his briefcase from the hall and set it on the dining room table and opened it, searching for some papers or something. I just followed him around, trying to stop his motion, trying to stop the motion of time that was slamming me into the wall and tearing the future from my grasp.

"Matt, I don't understand. I mean we plan to live here. I – I'll be finishing up here, working here. Didn't we plan on staying in the city?"

"Not really, sweetheart, nothing definite. I know this must seem like a shock, but I'll tell you it's going to open things up for us. We're going to make the big figures. You and I, baby. Eventually, we'll have a major office in San Francisco and who knows - LA. This is the moment to take the bull by the horns."

"I can't leave now....I don't know that I-"

"It won't be for a while. And anyway, you don't have to come right away. I'll get settled. All my time will probably be tied up at first. I've always wanted to locate in the Pacific Northwest. You'll love it. And you'll come when you're ready." I was trying to feel my feet on the floor. Trying to feel some support. Was there anything beneath me? I felt like I was standing on wet sponges. "I can't wait to tell my parents," he continued. "My dad's always been after me to take him fishing around Vancouver. Wait till he hears this."

"What if I don't want to go? I live here. My family's in this state. My friends are here." I couldn't think of anything else to say. I was about to repeat these sentences again like a mantra when he pulled a letter out of his case and then another paper and laid them on the table. Was he was going to write something in reply right then?

Not looking up, he said something that shook the whole etch a sketch pad and whisked away the rest of the lovely picture I had built up in my mind of our relationship. "We're such good friends, Michelle. We want good things for each other, right? You'll go along with this won't you, like you always do."

"What if I don't want to?" My lip was quivering, my hand shaking.

"I respect what ever your wishes are, dear. I deeply appreciate how you feel. But we'll work it out. We'll find a great house, we'll plan great weekend trips. The area's got incredible places to explore. We'll put it together and it'll be your dream come true."

"This is a bunch of crap, Matthew." I spoke softly. I wanted to scream, to say much more. To say how ridiculous everything he had just said was. I wanted to tell him that he didn't seem to know me at all, let alone what my dreams were. And how dare he just assume I'd go along. But I couldn't say anything else. I didn't know how to argue with him. He hadn't seemed to hear what I'd said anyway. He had started to make notes on one of the papers.

I picked up my coat and opened the door. "Are you stopping at a grocery store?" he called to me as I stepped outside and softly shut the door.

I walked, got cold, and put my coat on. I wasn't sure where I was heading at first. I didn't want to go to the student union and run into anyone. I'd be damned if I'd go to the store. I vaguely knew where Mark lived and I headed in that direction, getting turned around a few times. By the time I located his apartment, it was getting dark out. I rang the bell and when he opened it, I just stood there probably looking bedraggled, definitely looking forlorn. "What's wrong, Mickey?" he said ushering me in.

I looked around at his apartment. It seemed cozy, warm. He was alone. "I think I just broke up with Matthew."

I felt stiff as a statue as he closed the door and guided me to sit on his futon covered sofa. He sat down beside me and asked, "Want to tell me about it?"

I shook my head. I felt silly being there with nothing to say, my coat on, my head pounding. What could Mark do? Then very simply, he just put his arm around me and coaxed my head to his shoulder. Feeling the warmth there, the shoulder to cry on, I began to cry and cry. When I slowed down for a moment, Mark said, "I'm so sorry. I really am, but I'm not surprised you two broke up. I am surprised how broken up you are. I didn't know you were so deeply in love."

I began to cry again and shook my head. "That's not it?" he asked. I shook my head again. "Then what?"

I shook my head and out came a jumble of sentences. "My professor, Dr. Charles." My words were slurred and I could hardly get them out I was so choked up. "He's been diagnosed with liver cancer and they can't treat it. It's too far gone." I had meant to share this with Matthew when I came in but hadn't gotten to it.

"He's so nice. I think he's gay and I think his partner left him a few months ago, but then he came in at the end of class today to get him. Dr. Charles had just spoken to us as a class and told us he didn't know how long he'd be able to teach us. He is so wonderful, so full of life. It's such a tragedy. He is so involved in life and it's almost over. He said for us not to feel bad, that he is lucky to know how long he has. And his partner came in to get him - you could see how much Dr. Charles meant to him – it must be breaking him up too. So maybe he'll stick around and help him. But the whole thing's so sad. I think I love him and now I'll – we'll all – lose him."

I stopped for a moment, swallowing, wiping my coat sleeve across my face. I'm not sure to what the reference point was when I said, "Something beautiful will be gone forever."

Mark just sat there with me. After a while he asked, "What can I do for you?"

"Hold me." He stood me up and took off my coat. He threw it on a chair and then lifted the futon off of the couch and laid it on the floor. He disappeared into another room and came back with a quilt and a pillow. He settled me on my side on the pillow and put the quilt over me. Then he turned out the light and crawled under the quilt behind me.

He held me all night without saying a word. I lay there quietly for a long time. It was hard to relax at first and then I began to appreciate just the embrace that asked for nothing from me. The embrace that traced for me my edges and kept them secure, secure for now, for as long as I needed.

The next morning I said goodbye to Mark and went back to my apartment to pick up the pieces of my life and survive a very uncomfortable and long but final end to my partnership with Matthew. I lost the web of contact with Mark after that. I knew he'd become a successful journalist. At some point I'd heard he'd moved to Chicago.

I saw him one time at a family dinner at Shelly's parents' home. There in the comfortable cushion of many friendly people, we caught up with each other and talked of things going on in the world. In the world ourselves and caught up in our careers, we didn't manage to get to the depths we had had when we'd gotten together at school on Fridays and shared a coffee or a beer. I didn't see him again after that for years.

CHAPTER TEN

The next morning I dressed and went down to the lobby of the Galway hotel and into the formal dining room, which was set up for breakfast. It was funny to see many businessmen in suits sitting before the starched linen table clothes with lace trimmings and teapots and creamers. There were also women in business suits and couples and families with young children. We were all beginning our days and sharing these moments together in separate rituals.

Today was Thursday. It had been a week since I had touched down on this enchanting island. And since then I had been up and down and in and out of many different places. I was beginning to feel at home here in Ireland even in the midst of moving around.

For one thing, I had begun to eat more than cereal in the morning. I had learned to pace myself with the Irish breakfast, looking forward to the eggs and a second cup of tea and there was always room for a home-baked scone. At my little table in the elegant dining salon this morning with fresh flowers in a glass vase and crystal chandeliers lit overhead, I read the tour book. Initially I had thought my next stop would be the Connemara peninsula and its famous ponies, but something else caught my eye.

At the scene of a vision, craftsmen from each of the 32 counties had built the great Basilica of Our Lady. On these grounds, where healing had occurred over the years, also stood the Knock Folk Museum and a Marian shrine.

For some reason, I felt drawn to visit this shrine. I didn't feel I was desperately in need of healing, I was healthy and fit, but then, what exactly is healing? On a deeper level, don't we always carry wounds within us that we may not have healed at the time they happened because we had to carry on, get on with our life?

At the most inopportune moments or at opportune times in close contact with another soul, weren't we likely to open up only to find what we thought were hardened scabs were actually festering wounds? And amid the tears or stormy words, the thought comes into the back of our minds, "I am not yet healed."

I believed that I'd come to terms with my relationship with Matthew and I felt a certain tenderness toward myself for being so naïve. But I didn't think that I could ever fully heal my friendship with Mark.

After the last time I saw him, something had broken between us, and there were little pieces of something vital that lay crushed underfoot that kept us separated even now. I couldn't even imagine how the pieces could fit together again after all this time.

Once, three years ago, when I was 33, we had been on the verge of a real date. I ran into him when I was going into Central Park. He was cutting through the park, heading to the museum. We began to talk and quite naturally began to walk and talk, and we walked and talked for 2 hours. I told him the 'unofficial' story of the break-up with Matthew and how we were never serious partners and he told me he hadn't believed it could ever work out. What I had assumed was compatibility, he'd seen as indifference. Why didn't he tell me before? He said it would be like someone suggesting you give up coffee because it isn't good for you. I wouldn't really hear it.

"I hear you now," I told him.

"Good, then hear me now as I ask you to have dinner with me tomorrow night."

"I'd love it," I said honestly.

"I should make you promise," he said half-jokingly.

"I promise and I'll hang on every word. Now walk me back to where I met you and we'll finalize the plans."

On the way back to the park entrance, we continued to talk. We quite naturally began to talk of our dreams. I was very surprised when he said he'd like to settle down and start a family. He'd always pictured himself with kids and dogs and station wagons full of soccer balls and picnic baskets.

This middle-class American image began to frighten me, but I let him talk and even asked what names he liked for children. We had fun considering names like Alexander and Emily and then went too far with Seigfried and Constantina, and Geronimo. He told me he wouldn't have let me be so complacent with him if he'd been in Matthew's shoes.

He told me that he felt a healthy relationship was interactive, kept people on their toes and forced them to be honest. You confronted your mate. You played a part in how they treated you. This made the bond strong. He thought I could have handled challenge but Matthew had his head in the clouds and was probably afraid of his own shadow confronting him.

Mark said I deserved more in a relationship and that I would be great in a partnership. Maybe Mark saw more in me than I did, but he didn't see my wavering confidence when he said this. When Mark left to get to the museum before it closed, he told me where to meet him for dinner the following night. I agreed and we went our separate ways.

I never met him. We never had our dinner. And shortly thereafter I had heard from Shelly that he had taken a job with a paper in the mid west and in his new office had met a woman Shelly was sure was "the one." Why hadn't I met him?

Oh yes, my grandmother had called me that night and commanded my presence at the hospital in Chicago where my grandfather was dying of cancer. 'You'll take the 7:15 a.m. flight tomorrow morning. Your ticket will be waiting. Now please let me get off of the line. I have a thousand things to do. Oh, and call your brother, Patrick, he's to fly with you. See you then."

I had left a short message for Mark, saying only that I couldn't make it. The next morning I flew into O'Hare airport where I met up with a great number of family members. At the hospital, my grandmother had orchestrated a virtual family reunion.

I stood shoulder to shoulder with relatives I hadn't seen for years and watched my unconscious grandfather, who had always been physically strong but who kept most thoughts to himself, now lie there struggling to breathe with still nothing to say. I stood there, against my will, but as expected, to witness him take his last troubled breath and rattle it angrily into eternity.

The grand funeral and the reception were outstanding and elegant, having been planned down to every detail with as much precision as one might have given a wedding. All this, my grandmother had done in graceful stride with the composure of a mother of the bride. A great deal of Chicago's society was present. Because of her close involvement in the family business, she knew intimately many of the business figures. With studied subtlety, she had commanded their presence much as she had commanded mine.

In the past, she had been active in women's rights and was close to the many political personalities who came for the service. Because of her charity organizing, she naturally invited the simply wealthy to share this experience with her. The reception was a gala. And there I was, standing in the corridor, outside the great hall filled with family members and notable people, only three days after the death of my grandfather.

How flabbergasted I was when my grandmother had come up to me, elegant in her black silk designer dress, appropriately solemn and sincerely a bit sad, and whispered in my ear, "Last month I sent you a check and you still haven't cashed it. Could you do that when you get back so I can balance my finances?"

When I got back, I didn't call Mark. I don't think the thought came to me. I just became very busy. Now I realized that with all our closeness and caring, that path that we walked that day in the park was probably taking us directly to intimacy. Perhaps it was suggesting just the promise of it. And that promise threatened to change the friendship I had with him – a friendship that I cherished.

I couldn't fathom what that change would mean. Would I be setting myself up to lose something dear again? And for all his assurance of my capability in a relationship, I wasn't very convinced. I wasn't even clear about how I felt. When I thought of Mark, a knot would tighten my whole solar plexus. Actually, I felt no emotion – just pressure.

Now, in Galway, in the wake of last night's dream, I read again this page from the past. I was intrigued that when I thought of the plans for Mark and I to share more than a discussion, I still felt only breath-stopping pressure in my belly.

The N17 had looked like a major roadway on the map, but like most of the "major" roads in Ireland, it was a simple paved road that easily led in and out of the villages and towns. Not exactly like the Interstates and city bypass routes of the States. It amazed me how after leaving a city such as Galway, that one was very soon in the lovely rural environs, the constant green setting always there in the background of one's travels.

I pulled into the small town of Knock and found it slightly congested with pedestrians crossing the street and cars crawling along. There was a main strip of stores and then very soon, a large enclosed area with a great gray steeple visible over the stone wall. This must be the shrine.

I was amazed at the many different peoples here, some well-dressed, some poor, many from other countries, old and young. I followed where the main stream of them was going, looking for the entrance. Outside one of the gates, a man stood with a bucket on the ground and a sign propped up behind it. He was collecting for relief for people with MS.

I was glad to stop for a moment, fish into my pockets for coins and generally get my bearings. To the right of the gate, stood a middle-aged woman seriously frowning. Before I could pull out a pound and a few 50 p.'s, another woman hurried up to her, visibly rattled. "Oh, my God, that was horrible. I'm so sorry I'm late. I couldn't find any road signs and had to stop twice."

"I've been waiting an hour. This is so irresponsible and just like you. I know you love keeping me waiting."

"No, really. It's not like I could call."

"And what time did you leave?"

They had turned while arguing and were now walking through the entrance gate; the threads of their conversation spread out and blended with the crowd's voices, becoming part of the general litany. But I stood very still a moment longer. Their interaction had stirred something.

The week before I left New York, I had been on my way to my acupuncturist's. It was getting dark early and my acupuncturist, Janine, had recently moved. I wasn't sure if I had gotten off at the right subway stop and I began walking in a direction that someone had suggested to me earlier when I was asking for advice.

Very soon, none of the streets seemed right and I was sure I was getting farther and farther away from her new office. I was the last client of the night. Although, Janine had little patience for someone arriving late, I had even less tolerance for my own lateness. I suspected I was walking in circles and so when I came to a convenience store, I went to the counter and asked, "Which way is Madison?"

The man behind the counter, a dark small foreign sounding man said, "Just a minute." He sold cigarettes to a woman who then wanted change for her five dollar bill that she'd gotten in change. Then he sold a newspaper to a man. Then he counted his one's and bundled them. Finally he turned to me. "Madison? It is the next street up."

I was peeved but I would not be delayed by being annoyed. It was getting dark which meant it wasn't safe, it would be harder to read the street signs and Janine might just leave to get home at a reasonable hour. At Madison, I wasn't sure which way to turn, assumed it was right and very shortly, realized once again I was lost.

At this point, I was 15 minutes late. In business time, in New York time, this is significant. I looked up and down the street for a phone booth. On one corner, I spotted a phone and deposited 35 cents. It was the old number for Janine and I was told to dial again. No change was returned. I found the new number and wrote it down. I walked down to a hardware store getting ready to close and begged for change for the phone.

I went back, put all of the change in, coin by coin, as the phone kept upping the ante, "Please deposit 15 more cents for the next 1 minute." When I had deposited all of my change from the dollar, the phone went dead and the change return stayed jammed. I was late, I was lost and I couldn't even tell anyone. "I put the damn money in!" I yelled into the phone but it was dead and uninterested.

I dropped the receiver and kicked the pole holding the phone. Nothing. I kicked it again and yelled. What if someone heard me? So what. Tears came to my eyes. I wasn't giving up. I walked back into the hardware store and raised my voice. "I need to use your phone, it's an emergency."

"Is it a local call?" a manager type asked. And then seeing my registered rage, didn't wait for my response and set the phone on top of the counter and turned it towards me.

I dialed and Janine picked it up immediately. When I heard her soft voice answer, I almost burst into tears but I stopped myself. "I'm lost but I don't think I'm very far."

Janine had been very understanding, told me to come right over, gave me directions - I was only 3 blocks away. She was very soothing when I got there. She told me my pulses were very elevated, especially the liver and gall bladder ones, ones that got agitated in times of anger, and I had said I didn't want to come there to get work to deal with the trauma of getting there.

Janine had tittered, looked at my tongue and then proceeded to put needles in various points to balance the liver and gall bladder meridians. She left them in for 15 minutes while I thought about how I could have handled it better, have become less upset, and I wondered just why I had lost it. It wasn't because I was afraid of Janine's wrath. I was still agitated. Why?

I hated being late. And I had made a major effort, planning my route beforehand. I had asked directions - something I hated to do. I had tried to be on time and I couldn't avoid being late. No one would acknowledge my trying and totally absolve me from blame. No one would let me off the hook and reverse the impression I was a screw-up. No one, no one, not even me.

When Janine came in, she lifted my arm and felt the tissue on the underside of my wrists for the quality of my pulses. "Not much has changed," she said. "We better leave them in a bit longer." She left the room and once more, with needles in my feet and ankles and abdomen and hands, I was left to look at the ceiling and ponder the recent frustration.

"I'm not changing. I'm still upset. Why don't I give myself a break? Why, when Janine has forgiven me, am I still beating myself up? Because I'm not really forgiven. Was this because my dad had never really forgiven me? How many times as a child did I try and yet mess up and with no recognition for trying, hear, 'Once more you've let me down. I guess I shouldn't expect anything of you.'

I would be devastated, trying to explain what had gone wrong, but before I could hardly begin, he would silence me and say, 'Don't make excuses. Make things better.'" I couldn't bear someone not knowing how hard I was trying. How much I wanted to please someone. How much I wanted to hear that my non-successes were not my fault.

It was childish and hard to believe I felt this way, but I did. And right now I needed someone, even if it was myself, to let me off the hook. A tear rolled from my eye and I involuntarily took a deep breath. "So be it."

Janine came in and felt my pulses again. "Good work. You're cooked." And then, "Take a deep breath," and she began removing the needles. I felt calmer and more balanced, and I committed to memory the names of each intersection as I made my way home that night.

I went through the shrine's front gate and found lines of people walking together. A husband and wife in their sixties said the rosary together as they walked. A group of religious sisters walked together in silence. There was an overpowering air of serious prayer here. The chapel was lovely and the Basilica was enchanting as I walked all around it.

At the glass shrine to the Blessed Mother, I looked in from the outside. A mass was being said and the church was filled with the faithful praying together fervently. I almost went in - it was the early part of the mass - but then I stopped. Watching the ceremony from outside, it seemed complete and self-contained. With its pointed glass roof, it could have been a missile that had already started it journey to heaven, fueled by the faith of the celebrants.

There was no way I would interrupt this process, and I watched the mass progress as if a movie were being shown with the volume turned down. How surreal to see the priest move, come forward, go behind the altar and the congregation rise together, then sit, then kneel with no noise whatsoever. All a beautiful dance, all together, all with faces upraised or looking down into a book and every so often looking up at the magnificent statue of Mary the Queen of Heaven, their expressions bordering on rapture. Who would dare to interrupt?

I waited for the communion service and then left to walk around the spacious grounds. There was a large section of well-cultivated gardens, and I began to walk back and forth through them.

As I walked, I felt a gathering of heaviness. A stirring there. I fell into a rhythm with my walking. Step. Step. Step. Each time I made contact with the path, a shock wave traveled up my leg and into my pelvis.

Sometimes I wished I could spread out the blueprints of my being before me on a table with trusted friends around me. And they would hover over it as if it were an intricate painting or a treasure map that had been folded and refolded and stuck into a back pocket until now. A treasure map nonetheless. Ah, there is the king's throne, there is the vault of gold, there is the queen's bed chamber.

My essence would be there in one piece before my eyes, and I could see it and come to terms with it. Nothing hidden. No surprises. No secrets. No confusion. But that was never the case. Sometimes I had to work so hard to bring some of the parts forward to figure out what was bothering me.   As I remembered how angry I had gotten two weeks ago looking for my acupuncturist, I felt deeply upset.

All had ended well but I hadn't forgotten about it. Afterwards I had gotten very active with work and had put it out of my mind. But now as I recalled the rattled feeling - I could have slugged someone - I couldn't help but wonder how this peaceful, understanding, mindful person had lost it and so quickly.

It bothered me to no end. I felt I was losing control. So what? So what? That was the scary thought - I was losing control. A familiar feeling took hold. A squeezing of my diaphragm that curled up through my esophagus and burned the back of my nose. I hadn't felt this way since high school, since early college. During that time I had suspected I was going crazy. Somehow I feared I'd make a break and be forever lost and apart and misunderstood. How terrifying. And what had really made me feel I was crazy? Was it just the curse of being young, feeling I was different from everyone?

No, that wasn't it. Was it my dreams that were haunted and grotesque? I would awake shaking with images of people appearing and disappearing. Places and things dissolving? No, dreams never really haunted my waking reality. It wasn't the dreams that made me feel as if I was going crazy.   And it wasn't how I struggled with the religious questions, and I did so struggle with them.

I agonized over believing that someone was sent to earth, tortured and brutally murdered and it was all for the love of us.   How could I understand this was the act of a kind and forgiving God? And what was eternity, that sensation of never coming to an end that tied my stomach in knots. And what was this part of myself that lived through eternity? And where was it?

Surely my personality could not continue on and on. But what about my memories? Oh, in truth I had turned my mind inside out. It was discouraging, upsetting and quite often I had to get up and go out and take a walk, call a friend, and just stop thinking about anything for awhile. No, that wasn't crazy; that was just a part of my growing up.

There had been a real, sustained feeling that I was insane. That someday I would say something and they would come and get me and take me to a locked ward and tie down my arms and give me medication and feed me tapioca pudding and creamed spinach and macaroni and cheese. And I would get very fat and think that everything was funny and never have an authentic connection with another person.

What had made me feel this was the direction I was heading in? And why now, was I being so careful in exploring this subject? Why when I asked myself the question, "Why do I feel I'm going insane?" did I automatically calm myself? As if on some academic panel, why did I quickly make logical excuses for this mental state? What really terrified me?

My family. There was the alcoholism, the hiding of the bottles, and the tempers and misplaced time; the forgotten PTA meetings and the mean words that were said. No one was as each seemed, not for a minute. And in the midst of that chaos, I had tried to make sense of things, had tried to call people on things.

Yet I was made to feel that I had misunderstood everything. My parents thought they had produced a very functional family. They were loving. They were caring. They did well in society. Their kids had everything they could want. They went to church. They voted. And each one of their children, though they were individuals in their own right, had a very happy childhood.

What was wrong with me? What truly was wrong with me? I had tried to see things in their light. And then, later, I would try to alter the pictures that sprang spontaneously into my mind. Eventually, I did get a bit mired in the unreal. And I even tried to become different personalities, going along with the program at some times, rebelling at other times.

I lost the thread of who I was during all this time. And when I went to look for the thread again, I found there were many threads and none of them, not a single one of them could sustain me. And I knew if I kept on in this way, witnessing, commenting, trying so hard to make it all make sense, I knew they would come and take me away. And I would be lost. I would have relinquished that future chance to someday sort it out. And so I had surrendered. I had rolled the stone in front of the tomb.

I became a therapist. My work became sitting with others while they looked into their own depths, while they took me into their psyche or they allowed me to communicate with their soul. And I was comfortable with this work. And they did their healing.

My comforting, my understanding was their encouragement, their catalyzing force. And who was I in all this? Wasn't I someone who hoped that by being comfortable helping others in their healing, that I could be as comfortable in my own healing? And the many stories of so many of the patients did teach me that many of us had difficult childhoods, many of us were struggling, and many of us were fine in the end.

I walked on and on past the red and blue and yellow flowers, past the cultivated shrubs and the wooden benches. Step. Step. Step. There was no map, but the territory was all here and each step took me further in, each encounter told me more. Each step felt clearer, more comfortable.

I visited the Folk Museum. There I saw life-size reconstructions of what life in 19th Century rural Ireland was like. There was a schoolroom and a cottage and a display of what happened at the time of the vision. Outside, near one of the walls, I saw a fountain spouting Holy Water. Someone told me I could buy little plastic bottles at the local store and fill the bottles there.

I went out to the store and came back with ten little bottles, all for 5 pounds. I removed their caps and one by one held them under the stream at the fountain. I decided I would give one of the bottles to my grandmother - whether she liked it or not. I would give her the little bottle and tell her it was good for her.

Although my grandmother generally did things with the position and the welfare of the family in mind, underneath all the contrivance, I knew she appreciated little gestures. I also knew she truly loved me. I remembered the time when my mother was in one of her depressions and Grandmother had sent for me and took me to Florida for a vacation - and at the start of spring!

When we arrived at our hotel, my grandmother had begun to unpack the little suitcase that my mom had carefully packed. The clothes were clean and ironed but when she opened them out, she shook her head, refolded them and repacked the suitcase. "We'll keep these here so they stay fresh for when you go back," she told me. I wasn't sure what was wrong with the clothes, but I felt embarrassed.

Shortly thereafter, grandmother had taken me shopping in Ft. Lauderdale and bought for me fashionable shorts and pedalpushers; tops, dresses and a white sweater, a blue bathing suit and wonderful patent leather shoes with hard soles. She had taken me to lunch by the water and introduced me to the taste of lobster and sorbet.

I loved my new shoes and couldn't help tap tap tapping them. My grandmother had frowned. "A young lady does not tap. Now sit up straight and cross your feet at the ankles." I pushed my shoulders back and tried not to move my feet. Before I knew it, though, I was tap tap tapping out a rhythm under her chair. My grandmother would frown and I would hold my breath and push my ankles together. After several times of correcting me, my grandmother had finally smiled and said well, if I must tap, then she supposed I must tap and that was that. And she never said another word to me on the subject. I knew someday I would be just as gracious as my grandmother.

As I had almost finished filling the bottles, a short round man with hardly any hair on his head - he could have been an off-duty friar - leaned forward towards me and confidentially said, "I think I saw Mary MacAleese here, I did. I think it was herself."

"Mary MacAleese?"

"Ah, you know. The president of Ireland. I think it was herself, I do."

"What does she look like?"

"Ah, you know, she's thin. Thin and has the bangs all the way down to the eyebrows. Brown hair, brown eyebrows. She wears the glasses, you know. I think it was she, herself, standing there."

"Did you ask her?"

"Oh no. I thought I'd get my bottles full first." He leaned forward once more and lowered his voice. "Then I've a mind to ask her to bless them for me." He nodded his head at the grand idea.

"But the water's already blessed."

"Well, it wouldn't hurt it to give it a boost, now would it?"

I wished him luck and walked to the gate. Then I turned and looked back over the enclosure. Here was a warmth, a tangible security that filled this area. Here was a place of prayer, a place of healing, a place of miracles. Anyone could come here from anywhere and ask for help. Here was a place where power gave rise to hope. And I breathed in that hope, the sacredness, before walking through the gate and back into the secular world.

CHAPTER ELEVEN

I was very quickly on the N17 heading north and slightly west to Sligo. This was Yeats country. Although he spent a lot of his time in London and traveling, he loved to return to this area and he often wrote of it: "Sligo has always been my home." Although he died in France, he is buried on the outskirts of Sligo in Drumcliff. In the early evening I pulled into town.

I was delighted to find a jumble of streets crossing over one another and lined with shops at the center of this good-sized town. I parked the car outside of a newsstand. Inside I bought an Irish Times, some mints and looked through a B&B guide. I noted a nicely rated one, "walking distance to Yeats's Society" on Rose Hill Lane and memorized the number. Outside, I walked to the corner and dialed the number. A pleasant voice said, "Good evening."

At the edge of town, up a hill, a little development on the left was Rose Hill. Here I found a delightful little cottage painted bright white with flowers in boxes under each window and rows and rows of flowers and shrubs all around the house. It was like walking a maze to get to the front door. The door was immediately opened by a thin older woman with very short hair wearing a big bulky green sweater. "Please come in and welcome. I'm Mary Ann McBride."

She showed me into the kitchen where I could have breakfast anytime and then took me upstairs to a room with two beds with hand-sewn coverlets, a night table with a lamp, a small dresser with a lace cover and lace curtains at the window. All this was crowded into a tiny room and there was barely room to turn around, but with the crafty touch to the decor, it didn't seem crowded as much as cozy. She showed me the bathroom with the tub and shower. "If you'd like hot water, you tell me and I'll turn it on for you. Takes about 40 minutes. In fact, I'll turn it on now and you can have it later. How's that?'

"Perfect," I said. "The décor is lovely."

"Oh, my, it's little things you know, something made here, something bought there. You're from America, aren't you?"

"Yes, there is no way I could hide my nationality here."

"Now, why would you want to do that?"

"I'd just like to surprise someone sometime so they'd have to guess where I'm from. You know, have some mystery about me."

"Now, dear, I bet you guessed right off I'm Irish. No mystery there either." We both laughed. I settled in and then began to walk into town to have some dinner. I walked down John Street, past the Catholic Cathedral of the Blessed Sacrament, and the Protestant St. John's Church. I passed a few pubs and then came into the center of town. I passed many shops now closed and even saw an Italian restaurant. At the end of the street was a sign saying "Tea Room Upstairs - serving fine meals all day."

I walked up the steps to a rather busy dining room overlooking the street. I sat by a window and watched the street below. There were few cars but a fair number of pedestrians. I ordered the inexpensive special and a waitress brought me chicken breast in gravy, three kinds of potatoes, steamed vegetables, cold sliced vegetables in a vinaigrette and a basket of brown bread. Almost content, I ordered an apple tart and a cup of tea.

Afterwards I walked through town passing the Silver Swan Hotel perched on the town's churning, rushing river. With its dark molasses color and off-white foam, I was willing to bet that this was the source of Guinness. I crossed over the bridge, walked past an art gallery and the Library. I hadn't reached the school, or hospital or the abbey before I headed back. A creamy yellow moon was rising as I reached Rose Hill Lane.

I had a bubble bath and then curled up under the soft bulky covers in the doll house-like room with no space wasted. I had the bedside light on and the copy of *Ulysses* resting on my chest. I read the second chapter. I read slowly, trying to digest Stephen's thoughts about his father, his physical father and his spiritual father. I felt empathy for Stephen who is haunted by the memory of his mother's death, recalling the image of her green bile that had risen to her lips, and the smell of wet ashes. He had worried about her destiny but was unable to pray for her at her bedside. He wrestles with his Catholicism.

He realizes that one of his students, though inadequate in many ways, must still surely be loved by his own mother. I wondered if some of Joyce's comments weren't about Ireland in general, but I didn't understand most of the references. I was amused at the answer to Stephen's riddle of a complex scene that turned out to be "the fox burying his grandmother under a hollybush."

The next morning was a bit drizzly and Mary Ann apologized not once but at least three times for the weather. "It's not your fault," I kept saying as I ate my toast and eggs and fresh baked scones and fruit and tea. But Mary Ann went on and on about how it was worse this week than usual and she was sorry for the inconvenience. "I saw the Yeats Society building in town last night," I said, hoping to change the breakfast conversation.

"Oh yes, Yeats. Don't you love him? Now this summer we had a fair crowd here, couldn't get a room to save your life. You see each summer for two weeks, end of July, beginning of August, people come from all over - professors, students, writers - and they have the summer school. Next year is its 40th year. So many people and everyone gets along and so much to do. Lectures and poetry readings and then the school puts on a play in the Hawk's Well Theater."

"There's a theater here?"

"Yes, and this weekend, there's a play. Now let's see, what was it? Oh, my how silly, it's "At the Hawk's Well.""

"The theater?"

Mary Ann crumpled up laughing, having to set her jelly-topped toast down on her plate. "That's the play, the Yeats play, 'At the Hawk's Well.' Oh isn't that a riot and a half?" Mary Ann told me I could get tickets at the door and the theater was only two blocks away. "Make a left at the Cathedral. It'll be on your left. Me and my husband and my daughter and her husband are going tonight. Eight sharp, it is."

I got in my car and set off to explore the outlying areas of Sligo. I turned on the car radio. I loved the Irish stations, playing a love song one time and then maybe a rock song and then following it with a country western song. At noon and six, I might hear the chiming of the Angelus being played on air. People called in to the station and talked about any subject at all: bulls, farming, the latest in recorded music, an outing, politics and of course the weather was always popular.

Sometimes people would tell stories and once an older man was reciting a rather long poem from memory. Just before the last stanza, he blocked on the words and was quiet all of about 5 minutes. No one interrupted him or spoke and valuable air time or no, all waited till he picked up his lines and finished with a flourish. I know I breathed a sigh of relief, but no one at the station seemed a bit perturbed. I listened to Johnny Mathis sing "Misty" as I drove to the north end of the town and took a left turn out to Rosses Point.

Rosses Point was a quaint seaside village. Yeats had spent many of his boyhood summers here. I parked the car and began to walk a path along the water where there was a pier with a number of small fishing and recreational boats. The sunlight began to break through the clouds playing gold and pinkish fingers over the surface of the water.

Gold folded into brown and then into pink rolling back and forth on the ripples of the wet surface like someone shaking a tablecloth only slightly to unsettle the crumbs. The warming action of the sun's rays sucked up the extra moisture towards itself and created a steamy curtain that rose and disintegrated as you watched it. The beaches along the point were clean and white and taupe with fine sand.

As I came near a bench facing out to the sea, I noticed a young couple, a guy and a girl, sitting close together, their heads together, holding hands. They were speaking low and I thought, "They must be making plans. Planning something. Sharing ideas. Talking about what they would do together." Suddenly, from nowhere, I felt so alone, so lonely, off and apart from the rich warmth of human intimacy.

I breathed into the pain, almost crying. I breathed deeply again and the hurt was less. Now my breaths came slower and I exhaled the heaviness and gray cloud of loneliness and began to breathe in the lightness and sunny rays of freedom. For now, I loved being right here at the crossroads of making my own decisions. The pang of missing the closeness of another became a little melancholy ache under my heart, a little morsel not so much painful as sweet, that I would save for another time.

I moved away from the young couple on the bench so as not to disturb them. Let them make their plans - grand plans, small plans - it didn't matter. It was their moment of sharing and my moment of solitude.

I left the point heading back to the main road from Sligo and once more turned left riding now towards Drumcliff. As I drove on the two-lane road, in the distance I saw the dramatic rise and domineering presence of a mountain, Ben Bulben. This dark imposing head with the crewcut top was the mountain in whose shadow William Butler Yeats had wished to be buried.

I saw the small sign for Drumcliff, turned off of the highway and pulled into a little car park. It was empty except for an old black car. A woman sat in the front seat with the door open. She was knitting. The back door was also open with sweaters lying across the back seat. I walked past the car and then into a tree-filled graveyard that lay on either side of the elegant Church of England.

I passed a carefully sculpted high cross, a Celtic cross, carved with scenes from the Old Testament and saw further on, a crumbling round tower in the churchyard. To the left of the church, under the branches of a large tree, lay a flat limestone slab into which had been engraved Yeats' words, his epitaph: "Cast a cold eye on life, on death. Horseman, pass by!"

I wandered into the great church, with its austere texture. There were finely-carved, plain wooden benches and a choir balcony, high windows and a simple platform in the front with a pulpit carved out of wood. I could almost imagine the church filled with people listening to a forceful sermon. The lesson of not being tempted by the flesh was reflected in this simple, plain though lovely decor. I pictured it also at dusk, voices rising together to sing Evensong, filling this bare, pristine air with round, full notes of joy.

Outside again, I noticed there was a tearoom on the grounds but it wasn't open yet. I would have loved a cup of tea. I walked back over to the parking lot. The woman was still there, though now she was rearranging things in the back seat of the car. I walked over to her and looked at the sweaters she was refolding. "These are lovely. You made them yourself?"

"Oh, yes, thank you. A lot of work. Not many people today will take the time to hand knit them."

"May I?" I picked up one of the white cardigan sweaters and felt the thick close- knitted yarn organized in a rather complex pattern, and the hand stitches binding the pieces together. "You're selling them?"

The woman nodded. "Twenty five."

"That's incredible," I said. "Are you sure? Are you sure that's enough?"

The woman nodded and smiled.

"Do you happen to have one in my size?"

"That one should fit you. Try it on." I did and felt the softness and the close- knit fabric immediately warmed me. Why, I could be warm in this even in the "soft" wet weather, even on a fishing boat in a gale. I laughed and gratefully paid cash for this handmade piece of artwork. My first Irish sweater. "Oh, what's your name?" I asked. I had noticed there wasn't a tag inside and felt I should know the brand or name of my purchase.

"It's Madelene. Madelene O'Brien, Maddy to my friends."

"Thank you so much." And I got back in my car.

I drove to Carremore. From the road I glimpsed plain fields that held the most megalithic tombs in Ireland. At least 60 graves and stone circles fill the fields, some dating 5 to 7,000 years ago. Later peoples built their circles over the ancient graves and so this has been a sacred area to many over the centuries.

I stopped at the visitor center and read about the tombs. I wandered in the field, some of the stone structures seemed untouched, huge stones set close together suggesting a precision in the positioning of them. One of the passage graves had been excavated and reconstructed to show the underground passage and chamber, very sophisticated for its time.

A team of people of varied ages, were excavating a small area in one corner of the field. I watched for a while as they methodically sifted the earth from each marked area of the tomb. I saw the pile of broken pottery and tool fragments that had been buried and was now recovered. One man whom I watched for a while told me that they suspected some of the structures here were older than they had originally thought, perhaps older than anywhere else in the country.

I wandered through the field. Some of the big rocks faced a particular way. I tried to see in my mind's eye what a ceremony here might look like. A burial, people coming together, maybe within the circle of rocks, maybe outside of them, honoring the elements, looking to the sun, turning up the earth, working closely with fire.

What did death mean to them? Was the funeral a sad occasion or a blessed relief from a harsh life? Did they hope for a better life after this one or did they only fear the powers outside of themselves and had the service to appease them? I longed to know if they were comfortable with death. I wondered just how deeply this transition affected them.

Perhaps death was just another time to come together, pray, dance, and drum. I began to feel that these people were closely tied to the rhythms of the earth, and the rituals for leaving this life were simply another part of it.

I walked up and down the little hills, losing myself in musings of the centuries. To the west stood a mountain, Knocknarea. One could see a burial mound at its summit. Supposedly it was the grave of Queen Maeve (Mebdh) from Irish folktale: "Tain bo Cualnge" (The Cattle Raid of Cooley). According to legend, she is buried standing up to face her enemies in Ulster.

The cairn is probably much older than the famed queen, but locally they like to honor Maeve and prefer this explanation to any others put forth. I decided I would like to climb the mountain sometime if it were possible. But for now I was starving and would go back to Sligo.

That evening I saw the play, "At the Hawk's Well," done on a very simple set, with few characters and elaborate masks. I watched the slow, graceful movements of their bodies that were meant to impart information about the feelings and temperaments of the actors.

The story is of an old man who sits beside a dried-up well. The water which springs forth periodically gives the drinker the gift of eternal life. It is guarded by a hawk. Every time, just before the water comes forth, the old man falls asleep. Cu Chulainn comes along and offers to wake the man when the water comes and they'll both drink.

The hawk becomes a woman and seduces Cu Chulainn, who misses the water's coming and once more the old man misses his chance at immortality. Far off is a battle cry and Cu Chulainn rushes off, for that is his life and that attracts him more so than the promise of the well. Anyway, it is through his heroic life that he lives on and on. That was how I understood it and I sat for a moment when the play was ended, thinking about the simple thought of living in the moment. There is an eternity in every minute.

I watched people stand, put on jackets, and shuffle out to the lobby. In the open area of the lobby, I saw Mary Ann and her family standing in a circle, talking. I came up to her and said, "Hello."

Mary Ann introduced me to her family and then asked, "Well, what did you think? The play?"

"It was very well done. And I found it rather touching. What about you?"

Mary Ann hesitated, tightening the corners of her mouth, almost as if trying not to speak but the words were working their way out anyway, "Well, it's not *Chorus Line* is it? But you gotta love Yeats, don't you? No one like him, is there?'

We all agreed there was no one like him, and together the five of us walked down Temple Street to John's Street and on to Rose's Lane..

At midnight, I put down my book, rinsed out my teacup, and fairly crawled up the stairs and into my little bed in my now familiar room. I could not keep my eyes open any longer than it took to shed clothes and shut the light. I fell soon into a deep sleep. And later, near the middle of the night I awoke from a very vivid dream.

I was back at Aillwee Cave. It was night. Just inside the entrance, on the walls, were unlit torches. I took one and dipped it into a large bowl of oil. I lit it from a black flame so that my torch became a carrier of darkness. I entered the tunnel blindly. A bird in a cage told me to use my other senses.

I smelled the wind, the dirt floor, and the walls. I heard where the air rushed from large openings and where it was silent. With each step forward, I felt myself re-created. I gracefully negotiated the tunnel. At a central chamber were rings of fire. My eyes burned and teared. An old woman stepped forward and asked, "Are you here for the sacrifice?"

"No! No!"

The woman still close to me smiled and said gently, "Why do you struggle so? Perhaps it is something you wish to surrender to."

I listened to the old woman. I relaxed. I could sense my internal organs struggling with one another as if I had a window into my body. The distance to the outside seemed great. As the tension within the organs let go, they seemed to soften, expand, and float easily into one another. Then the space separating my insides from my outsides lessened. The space between the woman and me diminished. Then the difference between me and all people seemed to disappear completely.

I awoke feeling very peaceful and whole - the feeling one gets at the end of a mystery novel when the case is solved and for the moment, there are no questions. The slate is wiped clean. One exhales. At last it all makes sense.

I lay very still, enjoying the contented, completed sensation, feeling my entire self all at once. I began to play the dream backwards in my mind - the oneness, the surrender, the struggle. Now as I recalled being trapped, I saw bears and men in the shadows. There were fires all around as I walked into darkest darkness and my heart began to beat rapidly. I was frightened. What had I let myself into?

I turned on the bedside light, looking at the little table, the lace doily on it, and my book on that. All familiar, all ready to come back and become my world should I need it. I needed it now, needed the light and the table and the lace and my book. I moved the book and there was my watch; 3 am. The hour for doing yoga.

CHAPTER TWELVE

I had fallen asleep with the light on and didn't wake until 8:30 a.m. Opening my eyes to such brightness, it took me a moment to orient myself and turn out the light. How grateful I was for the morning.

After breakfast I drove out to the waterfall at Glencar. Eight miles out of Sligo, on the main road I spotted a little sign, "waterfall." I turned and drove down a narrow lane and into a small car park. Across the driveway, I followed a narrow, steep path that became steep steps winding through trees and scrubby green growth.

A roar like a giant fan or the rush heard standing over a freeway drowned out any other sounds. When I came to the top of the steps, to a platform that was level and led to a downward set of stairs, I saw the full rush of the waterfall. For 65 feet the water fell. It flowed and broke, leaving wide gaps and tumbled down heavily into Glencar Lough. Above me towered the Partry Mountains - silent, unmoving, and constant.

A slit in its imposing face had formed to allow the stream from above to become the twisting, tumbling, noisy water in its rush to reach the bottom. Yeats had written, "There is a waterfall...that all my childhood counted dear."

The car park was along the lake. I looked across the lake at the mountains that took up the whole view on that side. Flat lake, snug against fuzzy green and brown mountains. Looking up I saw the strangest thing. Another waterfall, very high up, was flowing upwards. How can that be? Was this an illusion? No, the water was actually flowing upward, it clearly sprayed from a narrow lower point to a broader higher point. It tumbled against gravity. Or did it?

Back on R286, I traveled to Parkes Castle that is perched above peaceful, large Lough Gill. Swans sailed by on the lake as I walked to the entrance of the Castle which was really a fortress enclosing a restored manor house. Long ago a round tower had stood here for protection and later in 1609, the Parkes family had built the house, two turrets, and a gate house.

As I wandered through the great house with its huge fireplaces and tower windows strategically placed for fighting and its subterranean escape routes, I felt the draftiness of the rooms. They could probably become very cold at times despite the fires or the usual decor and implements of day-to-day life. These large stone rooms, constructed with the intention of fortification, even when filled with friendly people, a family and servants, food and sewing, and conversation, even busy with the activity of living, these rooms stood for protection.

They were big and solid and unyielding. The idea of danger, of an enemy somewhere out there, of fear of attack loomed large. And as strong as any of the fortresses in the area were, someone always broke through. Are we ever truly safe?

I continued to drive along the lake. I was looking for a little park now where wooden sculptures of animals and legendary figures were placed in a natural habitat outdoors to show the harmony of man's work with Nature. I saw a sign for Hazelwood and turned down a narrow lane. It split and I went one way and then another and suddenly the lane became a gravel drive and it looked as if it would deteriorate further.

I had no idea of the way I had come and I saw no sign, no clue which way to go. If the road got any worse, my tires might puncture. I stopped the car and sat. It was quiet here in the warmth of the early fall afternoon. Wiry bushes sprawled out on both sides of the road, suggesting they'd one day take over the area completely. To my left was a small stone bridge over a stream.

Then I saw a little old man bent over with a huge hay bale balanced on his back. A little black dog ran at his feet. He walked right up to the driver's window and set down his load. He put his hands on his low back and with effort stood straight up. Despite the warmth, he wore a long sleeve black coat over a white cotton shirt. He had a rumpled cap atilt on his head and an unlit pipe in the corner of his mouth. "Can I help ye?"

I was startled and then wondered what exactly to ask for in the way of help. He seemed so removed from today's world that I wondered if he had any idea what roads went where. I couldn't picture him going far from here let alone driving. "I'm looking for Hazelwood. Do you know where this road leads to?"

He studied me a moment. He looked down at his beaten up shoes. He looked up as if trying to catch sight of the wind. Then he looked at the direction my car was pointed and cleared his throat.

"If ye continue on this road, you will be nowhere and very quickly at that." He laughed and shook his head. "Ye know yer pretty far afield right now. Ye want to back up and mind it's tight, and go back to the first left, go about a quarter mile and take the right fork. Ye'll be lined up with the lake then and Hazelwood's another mile down the road. Do ye think y've got that?"

I nodded. "I guess I did get pretty lost here."

"Ah, don't think of it as lost. Ye'r never lost, ye know. Ye'r here and nowhere else. Ye know that." His thin, wrinkled lips turned up at the corners and his heavily-lined eyes twinkled. "That's not to say ye know the name of the place or how on God's green earth ye got there. Everyone else may be lost to ye. But ye'r here plain as the nose on a cow. Ye'll like Hazelwood. But after ye see it, walk on up the hill. About ten minutes. Now there's a cairn for ye. Don't miss that one."

He bent down and picked up his bundle. His little dog ran around him in circles, barking. I said "good-bye" and watched him walk on down the rough road "going nowhere" before I backed up and turned around.

I had Hazelwood to myself as I wandered among the wood-carved sculptures of animals placed well-apart in this natural setting. I saw a path running up the hillside and decided to follow it. Was this what the old man was talking about?

As I climbed higher, the trees were closer together and gradually the path grew narrower and darker. Was the sun clouding over or was I just in the shadows of the tall pines? At the top of the hill was an open field. I walked out into the light and found an old walled-in fort - a stone cashel. Within it was a large, ancient circle of stones. Adjoining it was a smaller circle of stones.

One would be a burial chamber, the larger, perhaps, was where the rituals took place. The air felt quite still here. Did the pines break up the wind and smother the sound? Or was this quietness the mark of a sacred space? I felt as if I were in a chapel and looked about trying to sense what had happened here. Who had been here? What had they done? Did anyone mind that I was here now?

I stood in the larger circle and faced the smaller one. Was this area only for burials or was it routinely used for services? I thought of Carremore and the tombs there. I had just assumed that their structures were to protect themselves from the spirits or to honor them. Perhaps, though, they were communicating with them. Perhaps they embodied the notion that we are never alone, that we share this world.

I stepped outside the great stones. How did they ever get these huge stones up to this high place? I began to walk around the circle clockwise, no longer pondering, no longer aware of any thoughts. I circled the stones three times then stood before the entrance stone. I pulled the stone, shaped roughly like a bear, out of my left breast pocket, held it in the palm of my hand in the rays of the sun and set it on the entrance rock.

I walked into the large circle, feeling clearer and freer now. I walked around the circle counterclockwise three times, then clockwise three times. I raised my arms and faced the east, then south, then west, then north. I placed my hands over my heart, then over my eyes. After a minute I opened my eyes and began to dance, just dance, just energy taking me up and down, round and around. I danced faster and fiercer until I could hardly breathe. Then I faced the north again and lifted my arms.

My voice started out low, a low note, a wail, coming from deep in my belly. It was a lament, a cry, a roar. It grew and filled the air, a bellow, a storm. And then it had spent itself and high notes took over, singing themselves in graceful tones of a flute, singing of beauty and giving in and letting go. Song floating now, lifting itself above the circle. Then dreamcloud gave way to laugher and I shook to my belly, to my feet, into the ground, with raw joy.

Then stillness reigned and explained everything to all, to those who need not listen. Quiet and grateful for a long while, I stood. A cloud blotted out the sun and the gray rocks looked black and rough, the earth gave off a dull cast. Stillness. The cloud evaporated and once again, or as never before, the sun flooded the circle. I bowed to the north, then to the west, then south and east. I backed out through the space at the entrance stone and reclaimed my little stone.

I left the cashel and looking back over my shoulder at the circles, saw a rugged arrangement of rocks bathed in light. Rocks and memories. Memories and mysteries. Mysteries and patterns. Patterns and rocks.

I walked down the hill, down the narrow path and back through Hazelwood and to my car. I met no one along the way.

CHAPTER THIRTEEN

I continued to drive, with the lake in sight, in the direction of Carremore. I turned on the radio and caught the end of a talk show. "And our next caller?"

"Hi, I'm Annie. I'm twenty-three. My mother committed suicide and I was adopted. How can I find out who my mother was and if I have any brothers or sisters?"

I thought of one of my patients, Elizabeth, in her twenties, whose mother though still alive was oppressive and manipulative and often threatened suicide. Elizabeth was so pretty, so soft-spoken, so gentle and likable but her eyes held such darkness in their depths if you truly looked.

She was manic-depressive and I liked her, would go out of my way for her more than for anyone to find time in my schedule when she'd have to change appointments. It was funny, I wanted Elizabeth to like me, almost felt I needed her to trust me, needed her to know I could negotiate those dark alleys with her, needed her to know I wouldn't just abandon her in the light and call it healing.

"Well," a male voice boomed over the airwaves, "I guess you'll have to ask your adoptive parents then."

"They died in a car crash last year. That's why I'm looking to see if there's any family left."

My eyes focused, just noticing the road ahead. Suddenly I realized a truck was coming towards me, not just close to me, but in my lane, passing a car but unable to get back over in time. There was no shoulder on this small, two-lane road, only thick, gnarly bushes at the edges of the pavement. It was bearing down fast.

In a flash, I saw the accident, saw my car smashed and sent spinning - metal and glass and plastic in pieces across the road. Heard the screeching of brakes and wheels wrenching, metal bashing, windshields shattering. Heard the sirens of police cars and an ambulance, the shouts at first, the hushed voices later.

They would erect a sign with a black circle marking a fatal accident. I saw all this together in an instant as if I was watching a movie. I froze, my hands gripping the steering wheel.

And then, all of a sudden, the bushes on my left receded, the shoulder opened up, and with no thought I turned the wheel and my little car veered onto the dirt lane and the truck whizzed past, half in my lane. Then it was gone. I turned the wheel and once again I was on the paved road going straight ahead. It was as if I was driving in a tunnel. There was no air, just pure sensation. The tunnel opened before me as I drove.

My past spiraled out behind me. In that one instant, it could have all been over - my plans, my strivings, my interactions with people. The signs along the road, where I was heading, how long it took to get there, all seemed quickly insignificant. And as everything in my life came before me in this minute, I never felt more alive. So alive, so crystal-clear and vibrant as the glimpse into Life reflected the rider at my side to be Death. And though it was the constant passenger, the lifelong companion at the edge, it was never so evident as now.

I came to the turnoff for Knocknarea and gratefully parked the car and got out. How safe to feel the ground, the ground that was always there, once more beneath my feet. There was one other car in the carpark. I looked up the narrow path that led up through fields and grassy hillsides then rocky footholds high up to a large pile of stones, a huge pile in a dome shape, the grave of Queen Maeve.

I started up the path, past bushes and wild flowers with much energy. Here I passed a middle-aged couple on their way down. "Is it a rough climb?" I asked.

They smiled, a bit out of breath, both of their cheeks ruddy. "Not at all. It's an easy trek."

I was on the grassy slopes now, looking for clumps of grass for a foot hold. I came to a gate and a stone wall perched sideways at this height. I unfastened the gate, stepped through, and closed it again. As I continued, I saw many sheep standing and lying and generally rather unaffected by my presence. I was struggling a bit now as the way grew steeper and was not so worn in any one place as to denote a particular path.

Several ways branched out. One had to make a personal choice for negotiating the last steps to the mountain's top. It had taken me about an hour, and I stood at the foot of the grave that loomed maybe twenty feet above me. The clouds seemed close above that. Lines of small stones were arranged at my feet in no discernible pattern.

I turned now and looked down over the path I had just come, the rocks, the sheep, the winding path through brush, the tiny carpark with a little red speck in it. And everywhere green, green, green. Twenty different shades of green, small patches of browns and blacks and whites, but everywhere else ran rampant with green.

I scrambled up the stones. These were small stones piled together. At first I could stand and maintain my balance by continuing my momentum forward, but the last few feet I was forced to crawl, pulling myself up and over the loose top stones. On my hands and knees, I had reached the summit amidst clouds and sunshine. Looking over the edge, I felt as if I were much higher than I'd imagined I'd be when I'd stood at the cairn's foot.

The lines of stones on the ground next to the tomb, I now saw, spelled out, names and places and things like: "Kate loves Tom." I laughed at the realization and the minor diversions one may engage in while standing at the top of stunning beauty. I had my bearings, the narrow top seemed calm and secure. I stood up, looking all across the valley. A cloud moved across the sun and darkened the view.

A fierce wind came up all at once from nowhere and roared across the mountain nearly knocking me off. I almost crouched back down but felt differently. Instead I dug my heels in, connected through the stones to the earth, felt my thighs grow strong, my back tall, my head high. The wind rushing over me was exhilarating. "Go ahead," I called to the wind. "Do what you will." I stood my ground, towering over the fields and footpaths.

The wind roared even louder. Beside me seemed to stand another figure - a stocky woman whose golden hair danced madly in the wind. "Intoxicating!" a voice on the wind seemed to shout.

I almost lost my footing with the spiraling rush of air. Unable to turn away from the wind, I tried to sense who or what was in my peripheral field. I got the impression of bare arms rising to meet the wind. Was this the spirit of Maeve who stood beside me on this mountain, challenging the forces of Nature? Or was it the wind now clapping me on the shoulders? There was too much warmth in the presence breathing beside me to be merely a vertical whim of the wind.

Was this the brave and generous queen who chose nine kings and before they could be crowned at Tara, had to take her to bed? The villain of the Cattle Raid who was told by husband Ailill how much better off she was since she'd married him, discounting the inheritance from her father and the property she'd acquired on her own?

Was this the woman who made this a challenge and inventoried coins, jewels, clothing, linen, vessels, sheep, horses, and swine and found all equal between her and Aillil but for a prize bull? And was she the one who, unable to obtain an equally impressive brown bull peacefully, decided to fight for him? And so began the war between Ulster and Connacht?

Was I here with the spirit of she who ignored the prophecies of Fedelma and the druids warning that Cu Chulainn would destroy her troops? "Red, red, I see Crimson," had been revealed to her. Was this the magnificent leader who rode her chariot into battle, encouraging, threatening, bribing the soldiers, doing what she had to do to win? Was this the queen loved by some, hated by others who nonetheless picked her battles and when she did, threw herself into them with all of her heart?

I felt great strength as the wind rushed at us. Side by side, we held the mountain. Together we stood, dug in, facing whatever came at us. The dark swirl raced overhead, thickening the air I struggled to breathe. Then like a wave, it was gone. The air was still, the sun warm and constant. I stood alone. I was a bit shaken, but for one moment, I had tasted my power.

CHAPTER FOURTEEN

By the time I arrived back at the B&B, it was getting dark. I parked the car and walked back down to the pub at the bottom of the street. I took the guidebook with me and browsed through it as I had a Guinness and a shepherd's pie. Tomorrow I'd head north, curving around Donegal Bay and then due west, out on the peninsula to a little country town called Glencolumbkille in the heart of a Gaeltacht area, where 75% of the people still speak Gaelic.

The route looked like I'd be close to the sea all day, and I looked forward to meandering along the coastlines on the little roads. Someone was setting up a microphone, two guitar cases soon appeared, and I decided to stay and listen to the music tonight. It was funny when you had no tight schedule how quickly and magically a Saturday night could appear.

The next morning, I was up early and went to 7:30 mass at the Cathedral. The altar was beautiful with gold latticework and fresh flowers. The stained-glass windows brought rays of blue and red and yellow and green from the holy scenes and distributed them across the carved wooden pews.

I was almost surprised to find myself each Sunday in church. I truly didn't believe anything bad would happen to me if I didn't. So why did I come? It was the ceremony. I loved the mystical quality of the mass. I loved coming together with people anywhere who moved from a flat, everyday world, for this little bit of time, to a higher, symbolic world of the spirit. I loved these rituals enduring through time in a form I knew by heart.

Afterwards I had breakfast at the B&B and said "good-bye" to Mary Ann who was deeply interested in all my plans and then wrapped the leftover breakfast muffins in a paper napkin for me to take along in case I got a "bit fidgety" on the trip.

In about a half an hour, I was driving through the neat but busy little town of Ballyshannon where many come for the traditional music festival each August. I continued up to the town of Donegal in the county of Donegal. This was a delightful town that had been founded by the Vikings and means, "Fort of the Foreigners."

Here the Eske River meets the sea. At the center of town, called the Diamond, I stopped to see and take pictures of a tall obelisk to honor four Franciscans who wrote the earliest history of the Irish people. When I went back to my car, I was unable to move it. The street was suddenly full of people walking. Some were barefoot as they walked. There were many people all close together.

A woman in a long black dress, her head covered by a black scarf, walked alone. Behind her six big men shouldered a casket. The solemn group passed on quietly and was gone. I stood still for awhile afterwards in reverence for the moment, the person, the passing that moved like a slow train, of time.

As I continued out along the peninsula, the scenery was dramatic. The coarse beauty of great rocks by gray-blue waters, open expanses of rugged, wind-swept plains, were all here with no fanfare. No billboards announced their grandness, no cosmetic touches. Here was an undressed-up estate, maintained mostly by Nature and relatively unchanged for years and years.

When I pulled into Glencolumbkille, I felt as if I'd traveled back in time. This was a quiet little village that lay in a valley. I came over a hill and to an intersection. Beyond it lay the blue and white town hall and a post office. To the left lay the main street with a bar, a church, two convenience stores, and a dry goods store. I rolled on down the hill past another bar and later a small red firehouse, then came to a knitting mill, a small restaurant and a boarding school for studying the Irish language and culture.

Across from this main street, in the distance, perched another old church and churchyard and a soccer field. And that was it. Little roads branched off of the main road, with colorful little houses tucked away in the hillsides. Towards the end of town, lay the beach and the sea, curving in and around all but a narrow strip of road leading several miles further to the actual end of the peninsula. Across the beach, rose mountains, covered in green grass. Sheep dotted the mountain sides as did mounds of rocks.

I pulled into the parking lot of the restaurant called "An Cristin." Inside, wonderful smells of stews and soups and sauces and breads surrounded the several booths and many small tables. As it was late afternoon, few people were there. I went up to the counter and asked one of the servers if there was a hotel or B&B in the area.

A hotel lay at the end of the peninsula, but adjoining the restaurant was the school that held weekly classes in Irish. Since classes weren't starting up again until tomorrow, there might be a dorm room available.

I went into the next building and in his little office, I met the man who ran the school. A highly energetic man of about 50, he was only too glad to offer me a room, though during the height of summer classes, there would never be a spare bed. He walked me up the hill to a communal house with a kitchen that was neat and fairly new. He gave me linen and showed me my bed in a little room with one other bed.

The bathroom had a sign that asked that you shower between 7 and 9 in the a.m. or p.m. I could buy food items and make breakfast or eat at the restaurant. I walked back to the office and paid him. I mentioned that I'd be going on to Belfast the next day and could he recommend a B&B?

He wasn't sure what he'd suggest, but asked the girl in the bookshop next to his office. She knew of a beautiful place that was run by a very warm young couple. I took the name and number and decided I'd call from the hall pay phone. Before I left the bookshop, I picked up a book to look up St. Columba but my attention was drawn to references to Brigit. There appeared to be two people of that name and I read both of their stories before trying the payphone.

I dialed the number I had been given and a man answered. I asked for a room for the next day and he said he thought they'd be full and he could give me another B&B to call. He asked where I was calling from and I told him of the girl at the school who'd referred me. He asked me to wait a minute and I heard him talk with a woman. In a minute, he came back on the line and said they could work something out. It might be tight, a little room not completely finished; but if that was all right, they'd see me tomorrow in the late afternoon.

When I hung up, I began to tuck the slip of paper with the number and address in an inside pocket of my wallet. There I saw a scrap of cardboard with a number for Mary. Mary? The woman I had met in the pub in Dublin. It seemed so long ago, so far away. I thought I'd lost the number. Now I almost called her. Almost dialed her number just to talk to her. But what would I say? Tell her what I had been doing? Ask her...ask her what? Not now. I tucked the number back into the wallet's pocket.

Squared away, I went back to the restaurant and decided to have a big meal. I sat at a booth and ordered the Fish and Chips dinner. As I waited, I took out the little guide book and looked up Glencolumbcille. Not much was written.

"Are you alone?" I looked up to see a woman of about 70 standing before me.

"Yes."

"May I join you?"

"Please do." The woman wore a tweed jacket over a tweed vest over a jumper with dark stockings and sturdy walking shoes. Her weather-toughened face, with its small eyes and long pointy nose and tight little mouth, softened and she smiled.

"I'm Gwen. I'm from around Bruckless, back over the hills aways." Her hand in a tight fist, rose and her forefinger jutted out and firmly pointed back towards the beginning of town. "Over the hills, a good ways, but not too far. How about you?"

"I'm Michelle Maguire from New York City."

"Hah, I detect an Irish name. Have you family here or are you taking the course here?"

"I don't know if I have family here and I didn't know about the school till I got here. Are you taking the class?"

"Yes, it starts tomorrow. I've come for many years now. I stay in the dorm. I could go back and forth, don't live that far, but that's how I do it. Left my husband at home and took off. We have a fair-sized business next to our home with a hand loom. We make very fine tweeds."

She opened her jacket and pulled the lower corner of her vest out and showed the inside and the stitching at the edges. "See the workmanship here? You won't find this everywhere. This is artwork. We worked very hard to establish a name, can relax now a bit, but I still get my hands in the work now and then. Good quality and it lasts. See here these tight little stitches and the quality of the wool. It's almost a mystery how we start with that and it's transformed into this."

Her hand flew out in a gesture of drama, a magician dispelling any logic for the trick. Her eyebrows rose and she tilted her head and laughed.

The waitress came over and she ordered Chicken Masala, an Indian dish that I hadn't noticed was on the menu. "And no garlic in that," she said firmly. "I can't tolerate garlic. And a pot of tea."

She studied me closely for a minute, pulling her upper lip into her mouth and gnawing on it a bit while she thought.

I sat quietly a moment and then asked. "Do you enjoy studying Gaelic?"

"It's wonderful! Just a wonderful language." She came to life, sat up, crossed her legs and leaned forward. "We spoke it at home when I was a wee child, but I lost a lot of it by the time I was grown. So I come back here from time to time, have to stay sharp with it. I'm always learning, usually I'm relearning what I learned last time." She laughed hard, a low raspy laugh that someone from another table might have taken for a cough.

"It's a grand language - a Celtic language - in the family of Scottish Gaelic and Manx - but you won't hear Manx anymore. All gone. But Irish, well you know, it is an official language of the Republic of Ireland."

She nodded her head firmly, jerkily, with a very serious face. "Most people don't know that. There's at least 30,000 people here who speak it every day. And if people learn it again, maybe there'll be more."

"That's great. I'd like to learn more about Irish, maybe someday I will look into it."

"What you should do is take a course. Come back some summer and stay the week and start learning."

I smiled at the strong enthusiasm. If Gwen hadn't been so charming, I'd have felt like I'd just been given an order. "So how do you say, 'hello'?"

"Dia dhuit." It sounded like 'djia ditch.'

"Dia dhuit." I repeated.

"You say, 'Dia dhuit' and I say back, 'Dia is Muire dhuit." This sounded like 'djia's mare ah ditch.'

"So to say 'hello,' I say, 'Dia dhuit.' and you say 'Dia is Muire dhuit.' It was a difficult task for me saying a 'd' and 'j' together and then adding an extra sound from the bottom of the mouth at the end of the last word. I knew that what I said sounded nothing like what Gwen had said.

"Exactly, you're a natural. Sounds just like it. What you're literally saying first is 'God is with you.' The response is 'God and Mary are with you."

"That's a riot."

"A riot it may be. But as nice a touch as warm honey." Our dinners came - great plates of food and a basket of breads and two pots of tea and jelly and butter and milk. We both dug in heartily and said little for a while.

"So what have you seen here?" She looked up and queried taking a break from her exotic meal.

"You mean in Donegal? Well, nothing yet. I just got here and got a room before I met you."

"Oh, this is a wonderful area. Even when I'm not taking a course, I come out here. Often by myself, just to walk down by the beach or up to St. Columba's well - have you heard of that?" I shook my head. "Oh, it's famous. People make pilgrimages there. It's up the top of yonder mountain."

She pointed out the window and across the street at one of the high hills in the distance. "To be sure, you'll have to go there. And cairns - such amazing ones around - if you're into that sort of thing. These hills here are made for walking. I'll tell you what. When we're done here, I'll run you out to some of the sights so you can see for yourself what I'm talking about."

"Oh, no, really. That's all right. I don't want you to go to that trouble. I'm sure you've got to settle in?"

"Settle in? Hah! I never settle in till I'm done for the day. There's plenty of time for that later. And it's no trouble. No, this is something you should do while you're all the way here." A tall man with white hair came over to their table.

"Well, Gwen, I see you're back." He bent down and she pecked him on the cheek.

"Ah, Paedar, it's you who've come back for more! Michelle, this is Peter. Paedar's his Irish name. Paedar, this is Michelle."

I smiled. "Dia dhuit." I looked at Gwen for confirmation and got it.

His eyes lit up. "Dia is Maire dhuit. I bet Gwen here has been teaching you. If you're not careful, she'll do more than teach you a few words - she'll plan your whole life for you."

"Paedar is from California. A doctor - doctuir - heart doctor," she thumped the left side of her chest very hard. "He's been coming for four years to study Irish. He's in my class."

"That's great. How did you get interested in Irish?" I asked him.

"Well, my father was Irish. Came to the states as a boy. He talked of this place often. The pipes were calling, but he never came back. I thought a lot about visiting Ireland, but with medical school and starting a practice, I was too busy. The year after he died, I just had to come see it. And it felt like home. I come back all the time. Maybe I'll retire here."

Gwen pounded her fist on the table. "And who says a heart doctor has no heart! By the way, Paedar, speaking of plans, I'm going to run Michelle here out to Malin Beg and Silver Strand and all later. Will you join us?"

"I'd love to, but after I have some soup, I think I'll walk into town. Maybe stroll into Biddy's. I'm a bit stiff from traveling. But thanks. Michelle, I hope I see you again. Are you in class?" I shook my head. "Well good luck to you, hope you find your stay in Ireland as pleasant as I have." He shook my hand good-bye. "Slainte."

"She hasn't learned that yet, Paedar. But will I see you at the hall tonight. You know they're dancing?"

"Definitely." He bent down, touched his cheek to hers and walked up to the counter.

We finished and paid and Gwen insisted she drive. We climbed into her beat up sedan and she turned left out of the parking lot, heading west toward the water, at a pretty good clip. She spoke rapidly as she drove, giving me bits of information about flora and fauna and little pieces of history and local gossip all together.

We passed a pottery shop that was the front of someone's home and she told me I must stop by the shop sometime for the woman created "pure artwork". Gwen complained that many of the homes here were not lived in all year. "Rich people can buy these cottages, for high prices at that, and just come for holiday if it suits their fancy. Isn't that disgraceful?"

We traveled to Glen Head, a great rock jutting out to the sea, and Malinbeg. We passed the hotel that was large and grand and famous for oysters. When we were near the end of the peninsula, Gwen zipped the car into a grassy lot and parked. We got out and Gwen moved very quickly to an overlook with a railing. She leaned over and thrust her open hand downwards. "There!"

I looked over the railing and far, far below lay a little cove - a pure white-sanded beach surrounded on three sides by cliff walls. The water in the cove was emerald green, the color of mermaid's territory. Large black rocks could be seen at various places in the peaceful water before it left the protected area and joined the sea. "This is beautiful."

"Beautiful, yes. But no one comes here anymore."

"What do you mean?"

"People would come here all the time, bring their children to picnic and swim. Mind you the water can be a bit treacherous. See those rocks? Not safe for ships. The current's a bit strong and if you're not careful, it'll pull you out. But if you take precautions, you're fine. Today, now, people will come, look at the water, dig in the sand, and never go in. Wouldn't think of it."

"Why not?"

"Well for one thing, in the past, if an accident happened to a child, they didn't haul the parents into court. It's a different world, it is. And also, people aren't as hearty. They say the water's cold and it's not sterile and who knows what else is wrong with it. When I was young, I'd come here and it was paradise. Nothing grander in the world. The lovely water, the rocks, it was a magical place, still is, but the world's a bit crazy now. And people are too busy." She started hiking along the railing to where an incredibly steep set of steps led down to the beach.

"Are you going down?" I asked incredulous.

"Of course. Are you all right to go?"

"Sure. Fine, I guess." If she could, I could.

"These steps weren't always here. Used to have to climb down, holding on to the grasses, what with your picnic basket and towel and all. And usually you'd just slide down the last half on your bottom!"

On the beach, we walked on the fine sand. Pebbles lined the lip of the bay, easy, low waves lapped the edges and immediately receded. It was calm and protected and hidden here. The view into the darker waters of the North Atlantic Ocean hinted at cold, dangerous disasters awaiting anyone who left this miniature, safe harbor.

We drove back and took some side roads where we saw many a dolmen - a big rock balanced on two smaller rocks that marked a burial site. Gwen pointed out the Folk Museum and told me that much more information than she was prepared to give would be there, about the local area and of course the famous St. Columba (Colmcille) who was here ages ago.

We were almost back at the restaurant. "You still have the light, you should walk up the mountain to St. Colmcille's well. I'd go but I've got to check in and all. But you go, if you've a mind. I think you'll be glad you did. What do you say?"

"I'm game."

"Fabulous. Now I'll let you off here." She pulled the car to the side of the road. She pointed with her index finger across the road. "You see that break there, by the big stone? Take that and wind uphill past that white cottage, then go past it aways - see the low wall there – then head directly up. And mind, take something you find or have as an offering to leave at the shrine."

I thanked her and got out. "Have a lovely time. And come to the town hall tonight at 9 if you can. They'll be doing some set dancing and maybe you can have a go at it." She winked at me and smiled and nodded and peeled out of the ditch and back onto the little country road.

I crossed the road and covered the flats that ran parallel with the little beach. I climbed past the house and as I got higher, I began to realize that the top was actually very far up. Much further than it had seemed from the road. The climb became steep and I was sweating and was somewhat out of breath. I opened my shirt and rolled up my sleeves. I passed some sheep who moved back and forth at this near vertical slope with ease.

I looked down to the road - it was a pencil line in the distance. At my feet lay a seashell, a lovely pink and white, perfectly round shell. I picked it up and rubbed my thumb across the smooth surface. I placed it in my left breast pocket with the stone bear.

It was becoming impossible to go higher. I searched the terrain frantically for something that resembled a well. Was I in the wrong place? Suddenly I saw below what I had missed on the way up.

An enormous pile of bleached white rocks had been gathered as a monument. Working my way back down carefully, I came to the long arms of a rock pile. In its center, a roof of rocks arched over a little shrine. Clear water flowed within it.

Along the ledges of the shrine were small gifts, coins, a large statue of a woman, animal figurines, pretty stones. I knelt down and touched the water. It was cool, startling to my warm hands. I took out the little shell and placed it among the offerings. There were handwritten letters and a child's ball. Who was St. Columba? And was this always his well? Before he came to this area, teaching and practicing Christianity, was this once a well named after someone else? This place far above the valley floor, with its miraculous outpouring of cool, clear water, must have always been a sacred spot.

The statue of the female seemed almost to glow. I bent down and studied the delicately carved face. It was radiant. I was certain that this was a statue of Brigit. Had this at one time been her well? Was it in honor of Brigit the goddess or the saint? I stood there thinking of how there were two influential women with the name Brigit. I thought about the similarities in their stories and then it dawned on me. They may very well be the same person.

She could first have been the goddess concerned for the welfare of this land as a mother would be. Later, because of all the religious confusion through the land, she could have been born and then become a saint. It would reflect what people needed at a particular time. And individuals, themselves, had to grow and change with the times also.

There are many stories about her. Her father was Dagha of the Tuatha De Danann. She had two sisters. She grew up loving poetry and was very good at crafts. She learned to love the land and watched over those in need, especially women in childbirth. She was honored on February 1st, Imbolc, the day celebrating the birth of lambs and the lactation of ewes. She was known as the 'Fire Goddess' and people kept fires going to her. Over the years, many people were able to heal in the name of Brigit, the goddess.

Later, as a mortal, she was said to have been born at sunrise. Her father then was a druid priest who recognized that she could only drink milk from a white cow with red ears and not eat food, because she was so pure. One time, she was asleep in the house with her mother when the house caught on fire. The villagers came, the fire continued, but no harm came to the house. Even before she should have been able to utter a word, she spoke of the land and her love for it.

Wishing to stay a virgin and enter the religious life, she ruined her outer beauty by blinding one of her eyes. She founded the abbey at Kildare and became its first abbess. For centuries the abbey kept a fire burning to her. Crosses made in honor of her are placed in farmhouses to protect livestock and crops. Her feastday is February 1st. Over the years, many people have been able to heal in the name of St. Brigit.

There are many mysteries in our daily lives. And at the same time, there are simple explanations for what we view as a mystery. I looked closely again at her face and then at the little shell I'd found. Her countenance was so sweet, so serene. Her gaze seemed to be directed at the pink shell.

If Brigit were indeed here, I would have asked her for answers. Answers to the questions I struggled with within. The questions formed soundlessly within me. "Where was I heading? What stood in my way?" A sense of peace came over me and I felt as if someone was encouraging me, telling me not to worry, that I was getting answers, perhaps not as fast as I'd like, but true answers and all in good time.

The goddess, who looked on people as a mother looked on her child, had responded in the same language of silence that I had asked. There was the sensation that a mother in one form or another was always with each of us. It was the sensation of a blessing that descended upon me in that moment. And I had nothing further to ask.

I looked around. The sheep continued to lie about on the hillside. Nothing seemed to have altered. It was beginning to get dark. Time to make my way down.

CHAPTER FIFTEEN

I left early the next morning well before anyone in the dorm was up. I made a cup of tea in the kitchen from communal supplies and loaded the car. I laid out some clothes I had hand-washed the previous night on the back seat to dry. In the stillness of the morning air, the dew rising in a mist over the hills of green and rock, I headed north and east on the N15, skirting the Blue Stack Mountains to the west.

The Republic became Northern Ireland around Strabane. As I drove, I recalled the night before. I had met Gwen and Paedar at the town hall. There was no set dancing but a Sean - Nos. A group of men and women sang traditional Gaelic songs a cappella – with no musical accompaniment. Their clear voices singing ballads and love songs had touched me deeply..

I continued north to Londonderry, along the River Foyle where St. Columba had built a monastery. Derry meaning "Doire" or "oak grove" was where Britain had established a major Plantation project. Many of the Irish were driven off of their land and settlers from England and Scotland were set up in packages of rich farmland. This program ensured a loyal, local support for the Crown. So it had become Londonderry, but many people still called it Derry. Here the "Troubles" hit close to home when 13 demonstrators were shot.

With an appetite as big as that day's plans, I pulled into the central market square, changed my money to Sterling pounds and read through the guide book while I ate to my heart's content. I felt very drawn to wind my way around the Antrim Coast along the North Channel near Scotland. It would take a day, though, and I'd probably want that extra time in Dublin and besides, I wasn't sure how open and secure things were in the north. I decided to drive east directly to Belfast.

Approaching from the hills of the north, "Big Smoke" presented itself as a fortress of industry. I drove through the center of the city, past banks, churches, malls, hotels, huge public buildings and a Kentucky Fried Chicken. Many people were bustling along the sidewalks in this neat and well-organized space. Soon I was in the south of the city near Queen's University. Here, the streets were wider and the buildings further apart. I looked for my B&B.

On a quiet, tree-lined street, at the end of the block stood a gray and black house with a gate and flowers in the yard. A wooden plaque read, "Hallowell House." A tall thin woman with chestnut hair and dark circles under her eyes came to the door and invited me in to the hallway. I noticed a large painting of a woman in a red dress whose throat was exposed and sweaty as she worked in a garden.

Vanessa O'Neil gave me two keys and explained how she had originally thought that many of her family would be occupying the rooms, but they had left unexpectedly. She suggested I take the lavender room at the top of the stairs. She was talking a lot. She was talking very fast. Her face said she didn't want to be talking at all.

I looked down the hall at the antique grandfather clock and a mahogany table before a Victorian mirror. All was elegant and spoke of careful purchasing and tasteful placement, but I kept coming back to stare at the painting as Vanessa talked on and on. The colorful figure with her dark hair pulled back by a scarf, her full lips and full hips exuding sensuality and budding life in this voluptuously overflowing garden, was such a contrast to Vanessa with her quick, small tones and her thinness, a figure undefined by a formless black shift.

Later I explored the neighborhood. I walked up and down Botanical Avenue and sat outside at an art-deco style restaurant. The area was crowded with many college students. I watched the golden light of day fade to softer golden tones as the white electric lights of the shops burned progressively whiter.

It was late when I headed back, passing many others also walking. Most people I passed said, "Hello." Although this was a major city, I would not be confused for a moment and think I was in New York. I opened the door of the B&B with my key, anticipating a long bath and an early turning in to bed. As I quietly started up the stairs, Vanessa came out of the dining room.

"I'm so sorry. I didn't mean to startle you. I heard the door open and I thought it might be a nice night for a cup of tea. Will you join me for a cup of chamomile or peppermint tea? Or you could have some port or sherry."

I couldn't resist. "I'd love a cup of peppermint tea. Thank you. I'll drop my things in my room and be right down."

"Marvelous."

When I came into the dining room, the table was set with a linen cloth, a silver tea set, white linen napkins and painted china cups. "Are you sure you don't want some port? I have a very nice one from England."

"No, no thank you."

"So what have you seen so far? Have you liked everything?" Vanessa leaned on her elbows, cupping her chin in her hands as we waited for the tea to brew. She looked tired but said with polite animation, "While you're in Belfast, you must see the Opera House and of course, everyone now wants to see the murals."

Vanessa explained that since the "Troubles" began in 1968, people in both the Catholic and Protestant areas have painted on the gable walls of their houses, full murals of political statements or military slogans and drawings. One could actually take a cab to see them.

"That sounds really interesting. If you're sure it's safe, I think I'd like to see them. So far Belfast has been nothing like I expected. And, speaking of nice surprises, I really have to tell you, everything in your home is so lovely. It's like everything was chosen with precision. It all comes together like a work of art."

"Well, art was part of our business here."

"Really? And are you from Belfast?"

"I'm from outside of Omagh. I'm really a country girl. I met my husband when I was 19 and I came back here with him. That was 24 years ago."

"Do you miss the countryside?"

"Oh, yes, very much. But I like it here. Belfast is really a very good place to live. And two years ago, we found this house and we both loved it. I knew at that point, I would always be here. We fixed it up as a B&B, something for me to do. And I've enjoyed it."

"Your family who visited, are they from Omagh?"

"Yes, it's about an hour and a half away." She began to pour the green tea into both cups.

"It's too bad they had to leave early." I took the cup and added some cream.

"Actually we got into it a bit," she looked over her cup, her large brown eyes soulful. "I asked them to leave."

"Well, that's different then," I said lightly.

"They came to help, I'm sure. But I don't know - I couldn't deal with things. It's been two months, I should be dealing with things by now. But I'm not."

"Dealing with what things?" I took a sip and the warm, fragrant aromas filled my nose and throat and opened my sinuses.

"Two months ago, my husband died."

"I'm so sorry. I thought that was your husband who answered the phone."

"That was my brother. Oh he's trying to help. They all are. But they want me to sell everything and come back home."

"What do you want to do?"

"I don't know. I should know. It's two months. I just don't know." Vanessa took a sip of tea slowly and shrugged her shoulders. "I think I'm sad."

"How does that feel in your body?"

She tapped her sternum. "It feels like a rock." She nodded her head slowly. "I'm very sad. I try not to be, but I am. And also, I'm scared. Every decision, from when I can remember, Seamus and I made together. Now I can't talk to him."

"If you could talk to him, what do you think he'd say to you?"

Vanessa thought a minute, then half laughed. "He'd want me to relax a bit. He'd want me to enjoy my life. He had a heart attack and we didn't see it coming. And he'd say, he always said, 'enjoy what you have.' But also, I think he'd worry that people might influence me badly. Not like bad friends. It's just I'm too trusting. I think he'd worry people might take advantage of me, like in our business."

"It's wonderful to be trusting. Better than being a bitter old hag." We laughed. "How can you be trusting and yet have the space and clarity to know if someone's taking advantage of you?"

"I guess I could think things out, talk to a friend or even my brother for advice."

"So, in that way, you can reassure Seamus, not to worry. You know you'll be all right." I realized I had slipped into my role as therapist. "What do you want to do for now?"

Vanessa nodded. She sat forward. "You know what I'd like to do? Well, something positive and new. That's all I know. And something with the business. Seamus ran it, but I could do it, even though my family thinks I can't. But I think I want to change it a bit. I'm not sure how yet. But make it more of my business."

"Well, with all that I see all around me, you have quite a head start – definitely an eye for art and organization. Maybe you could talk to a lawyer or accountant and see what the angles are." We had a second cup of tea and talked further into the night.

When I got up to leave, Vanessa told me she knew of a person who could take me to see the murals. "If you'd like, I can call him in the morning and see if he's free to come for you after breakfast."

"Fine."

Vanessa stood for a moment facing me. She had started to pick up the teapot and cups and then stopped and set them down. She thought for a moment and smiled. "Fine."

CHAPTER SIXTEEN

We were finishing our second cup of breakfast tea when the doorbell rang. A man stood at the door with very short hair, a short-sleeved white shirt and black pants. "I've come for a Michelle." His accent sounded like Vanessa's, almost musical with its strong, clipped, lilting inflection.

"Oh, you must be Michael. Come in. I'd like to speak with you a moment. I talked to you on the phone, I'm Vanessa O'Neil. Michelle can go out to the cab can't she?"

"Oh, sure. It's parked in the middle of the street. Climb in, front or back. Be right there."

I said, "good-bye" and that I'd probably be out late and went out and sat in the left front seat of the old black, hansom-type cab. In a moment, Michael came out, jumped into the driver's seat and he was off. He was off to a start that never stopped running. Nonstop information ran on and on about every thing and place we passed, various points of history and tidbits of gossip.

Michael had a youngish face with neat small features beneath close-cropped black hair. He was short and small-built, compact, and his energetic body moved animatedly as he gestured and explained the systems that operated in this area of Belfast.

"Now you see my sticker there," he said pointing to the big piece of cardboard with a yellow circle painted on it. "That's yellow. When we go down the Falls Road, that's the Catholic area, all the cabs will have green stickers. When we go down the Shankill Road, the Protestant area, all the cabbies'll have orange ones."

We drove through the center of town. "That's the 'Europa,' - the most bombed hotel in Europe. Bill Clinton stayed there." Then we came to a busy commercial area, many cars, many people with packages and kids on the sidewalk. "This here's the Shankill Road." He pointed out little places. "See the cabs?' Each one he passed, he nodded to.

"See their stickers, all orange. So they can only work the Shankill Road. And probably only want to. Many of 'em are political criminals, have a record. So this is a job they can do. And they keep it clean here. No drugs. If you do drugs here, God help you. You'll be laid out in a minute." He showed me some colorful, well-done murals with men in black guerrilla-type outfits, English flags and soldiers , "UVF, God and Ulster," "Compromise or Conflict."

We left the area passing through a checkpoint gate which was now opened to let cars pass between the high cement walls separating the two conflicting areas. "This here's the Peace Gate. Any trouble, and they slam it shut and nobody moves."

On the Falls Road, also a busy shopping/ living area full of people, he pointed again at the black taxis. "See the stickers? Green. Green for the Falls Road. Now me, I have the yellow sticker, means I can go anywhere. See when I put this yellow one here, it says I'm not green or orange. I'm friends with everybody. Everybody likes me." But he seemed more at ease on the Falls Road, waving to the cabs and people, feigning driving his cab into a guy crossing who feigned being hit and yelled, "Michael! You devil!"

He pointed out the political bars, - "Jerry Adams - you'll see him here from time to time." He identified the police barracks with loud speakers, the housing developments, many of them safe houses and the Sinn Fein Headquarters, which looked like a small, well-fortified storefront. The murals were brightly colored, with a predominance of green. I saw a huge painting of a chained hand holding a lily over a gigantic "1916" and slogans such as "Free Ireland."

He took me through a cemetery and showed me the part where many freedom fighters were buried. As he pointed at the various graves of the slain men, he seemed sad, but full of admiration. "These lads gave all they could. They could not have given more. And thanks to their brave hearts, one day the troubles will truly be over. God rest their souls."

He smiled and was light again, waving his hand toward the tightly packed cemetery. "But there's Protestant and Catholic alike buried on these grounds. They may fight each other in their lives, but God save their tormented souls, they have to lie next to each other for all eternity." He laughed and drove me up to the top of Cave Hill. We alighted from the cab and stood in front of it to get the birds-eye view.

I could see the divided religious areas as miniatures laid out as in a display. And then, there for all the world to see, the whole of Belfast stood behind it. As I looked over the expansive scene below, I caught sight of Michael out of the corner of my eye. He didn't know I was watching him as he dropped his upbeat expression. His lips were tight, set and determined, his shoulders back and wide, his arms crossed over his chest. But in his eyes was a fierce pride, a farmer surveying his fields, a general reviewing his troops, and there below lay his great city of Belfast, Ireland.

He asked me where I'd like to be dropped off and I said the city center. He pulled into the driveway for the "Europa Hotel." "Thank you, Michael. That was very exciting. What do I owe you?"

He held up his hands. "No charge. It was taken care of by Mrs. O'Neil. She said you helped her a lot and I was to show you a nice time and you weren't even allowed to tip." I protested and he wouldn't hear of it. He handed me his business card with just his name and a phone number printed on it. "If you need anything, just ring me, night or day. He touched his fingers to his forehead as one might doff a cap and said, "good day" and pulled out into the traffic on Great Victoria Street.

I looked at the Europa Hotel and the Grand Opera House and then continued to walk up and down the busy Belfast streets. People filled the sidewalks, going to malls and little shops and restaurants and small businesses. I came to the enormous City Hall on Donegal Square with its grand towers and copper dome. People sat on low stone walls and the grassy courtyard, some eating their lunch or feeding pigeons. A sour-faced statue of Queen Victoria dominated one side of the square. Nearby, I found a memorial to the passengers of the Titanic.

I headed towards the harbor. I passed the Neo-Romanesque St. Anne's Cathedral and stepped into the dark interior where workers were doing restoration work. I passed the Albert Memorial's Clock Tower, which is tilted because the ground is shifting. When I looked at it straight on, the rest of Belfast was leaning. Across the way, near the river was the substantial Customs House.

I enjoyed seeing this modern, bustling, friendly city, but I needed a break. Maybe a spot of lunch, maybe a Guinness. I was near the water and to the right I spotted an area with quaint newly-painted little buildings. One looked like a bar and I decided to try it.

Inside, it was quite dark. There were empty tables in the shadows next to a low lit, intimate bar area. A woman stood behind the bar and the only other customer was a burly man with a red beard and mustache and curly red hair and a big smile.

"Hello there. Welcome. Have a seat. I'm Brid." She was a short woman with an impressive girth and a pleasant, tired face. "This here's Eamon. A nice fellow."

I said "hello" and took a set next to Eamon. I ordered a pint of Guinness and asked to look at a lunch menu. "So where are you from?"

"New York City."

"Oh, nice. Nice. Never been there. Have you been there, Eamon?"

"I've a mind to. I've seen it in the films so, I feel like I've been there."

"Eamon works next door. He keeps me company on the slow days, don't ya?" She smiled and asked me what I'd seen on my travels, what I liked, where I'd go next. Her conversation was easy and friendly and I felt as if I had known her quite awhile. I could have been in one of my regular haunts for as comfortable and safe as I felt.

I told them my impressions, and they added some of their own bits about the places I'd been. And I told them of how things were different in New York and also how much things were alike. MAC machines, cell phones, MacDonald's, who would know you're in a foreign country, unless you're driving on the wrong side of the road?

The time was passing quickly and as I was beginning to feel a part of a threesome, the door opened, throwing a surprising splash of light in, and three guys in casual clothes came in. They all greeted Brid and a thin guy of forty with wire-rimmed glasses sat on my left. A dark-haired, dark-eyed guy between 35 and 40 sat to the right of Eamon; and a man of about 70 wearing a blazer over a tee shirt, put his foot on the stool to the right of the dark-eyed guy and leaned into the bar.

Without asking, Brid immediately started to set up pints for them. She introduced them. "This here's James." She indicated the thin man with an artistically fine face and a peaceful look who sat on my left. "James, don't you have a sister or something in New York?'

"Philadelphia. But I've been to New York with her a couple of times. Love it. I'm going back in December."

"And this character goes by the name of Sean." She nodded to the dark-eyed guy. "But the one you'll be wanting to watch out for is our lovable, cantankerous old Padrig." The older man stood back, swung the cap in his hand up and made a great bow.

"Thank you. Thank you very much. And may I say, I am charmed, charmed, absolutely charmed to be here." He spoke very fast in such a garbled, raspy way that it created a delay between his speaking and one's understanding of what he said. His serious demeanor and later the realization of his light chatter, made his whole presentation comical and entertaining.

"Charmed, though others would argue, and reasonably so, that I was charming, but charmed's the word and I shall stick by that and stay here till they bury me six, is it six or seven feet under, that it was charmed I was today to be in the presence of two such fine ladies, if the term lady doesn't offend you and I must say the reality of lady has never offended me. And here you are before my glad old eyes, lovely ladies and in the midst of my best friends, am that I am charmed, tis perfectly true. Perfectly charmed."

I laughed and nodded to him in acknowledgment. "See what I mean?" said Brid. "I hope you boys are done working for the day. James here and Sean do a bit of construction for the owner here. Padrig, well Padrig visits quite often."

"Madame," he stood back once more from his stool. "May I say, and with all due respect and consideration, that my work is never done. God will take me when it is done, of that I am sure, and also I am sure he has no plans for me in the near future. So I must continue my work and valuable work it is, but thankless and skilled, very skilled, specialized labor, I like to think, but thankless."

He walked over, insinuating himself between James and myself and put a hand on each of our shoulders. "My work might be near done if I could get these two young people to see how they were meant for each other." He squeezed our shoulders and brought us close together. "Both wonderful people. Meant for each other, it is written in the stars. Thank God my job is to read those stars and I can still do my job. What do you think?" Brid walked over, "Okay, Padrig, that's enough or I'm cutting you off."

"Set me up, set me up faithful Brid and interfere not the destiny of the gods!" He was putting his face close to mine. Sean stood up, took Padrig's hand from my shoulder. "He's harmless," he explained and began walking the old man back to the end stool. "Now behave yourself," he told him. As Padrig protested, Sean speaking low but firmly calmed him down and bought him another pint.

Meanwhile, James and I laughed together. James told me about Padrig and how he was a widower and came to visit him and Sean from time to time even though they weren't family. He asked about my work and I told him about being a therapist in private practice. He asked to buy me a drink but I said, "no" that I was fine.

And then Padrig was back, his arms now draped across both of our shoulders. "Did you ever see such a perfect couple. In all your days, Romeo and Juliet, met right here and thanks to me, but no one thanks me. And maybe I'm stepping over my bounds, forgive me, forgive me, mea culpa, mea culpa, but how can I stand by and take the chance you'll not see how right you two young people are for each other?"

He pulled us closer together and we smiled good-naturedly. "Now go ahead and kiss. Right here. See what I mean." Sean jumped up, took Padrig by the shoulders and led him to the far stool. "I'll take you somewhere else. You're bothering them, can't you see that. Put your hat on, we'll go."

"I'll be good. I'll be good. See, I'll sit right here and not say a word." He sat down and leaned into the wall, and lifted his glass for a long, slow drink. I looked over at Sean, into his coal dark eyes and mouthed a thank you. I turned back to James.

James leaned forward and said to all, "Michelle is a therapist in the states."

"Michelle is a therapist? What kind of therapist would that be?" Sean asked.

"Psychotherapy. Talk therapy."

"Now isn't that interesting?" Sean commented. He smiled slowly at me and turned to check on Padrig.

Eamon said good-bye, he was off to his home, and he left. Brid set a pint before me and nodded in Sean's direction.

James was telling me about his sister being an operating room nurse when I noticed that Sean had come and sat beside me. "So, you're a therapist?" he said easily changing the subject. I turned to him, his eyes seemed to have infinite depth, like looking into a well with no bottom. It was hard not to keep looking, to see what was there, to see what would emerge as my eyes adjusted.

"Not that many people are as fascinated by it. Do you go to a therapist yourself?"

His mouth broke into an enormous grin. Small even white teeth. Such a contrast with his dark hair and dark eyes. Light skin. Black and white. "Well I just might, you know. I just might want to work all my deep dark secrets out. Perhaps I'd enjoy the process, what do you think?"

I laughed. He told me that although he did some piecework here, his main work when he could get it was as a musician. And what he truly loved was composing. He had a number of works completed with some success.

I told him that I'd had some interesting dreams and such since I'd been here and about trying to find some relatives in Ireland and told him about my dad, how I was close to him and he'd wanted to come to Ireland but never did, how he also had dark hair and dark eyes, and how he'd encouraged me to come. He told me he was from Belfast, had grown up a Catholic in a Protestant area. "That must have been hard for you."

"Well, I don't know. That was the way it was."

"Didn't you feel somewhat different? Like you had to defend who you were?"

"You might say. I sure learned to fight at an early age."

"And when did the fighting end?"

Pausing for a moment and then smiling, he finally said, "You know you ask a lot of interesting questions."

"I'm sorry. That's me lapsing into being a therapist."

"No, don't apologize. These are good questions. They make me think. I'm enjoying this."

I realized we were sitting alone. James and Padrig were in a far corner at a pinball machine that Brid was plugging in. Sean leaned over and touched my hand. "Will you have dinner with me?" I swallowed, surprised. "Nothing serious. Just a bite."

"What about your friends?"

"They're plenty happy here. They're happy doing what they're doing right now and I'm happy talking to you and well, I'd like to continue that. What do you say?"

I was curious about this Irishman who seemed very quiet one moment and full of words the next. I said "yes."

"I know a lovely little place. You'd love it. Near the water. Not far from here."

We bid farewell to Brid and James and Padrig. Padrig bowed and told us to go with God. "That's 'with' and not 'to' now, keep it straight." Brid picked up the empty glasses and said to me, "Now I wouldn't take what Sean here says too seriously." She smiled at Sean. "But he's a good man all the same. I'll see you again."

CHAPTER SEVENTEEN

We walked out of the pub and Sean looked up into the sky, feeling the breeze on his chin. "Let's walk down to the water first. I'd like to show you the harbor."

He pointed out a Visitor Center for the harbor and the ship building company of Harland and Wolff downriver. "It's pretty here, isn't it?" he said with pride as we stood on a little bridge and leaned over the rails.

"Lovely." I stared down into the water watching the movement of the current wiggle through the wavering silhouette of our head and shoulders reflected as a piece. I felt his arm next to mine. My shirt sleeves were rolled up and I felt his skin next to my skin. His arm was warm. The hairs on my arm stood up.

"Very lovely." Noticing my goose-bumped arm, he put his own around my shoulder. "Cold?'

"Not especially. Till now. I think the wind's kicking up." I rolled down my sleeves and buttoned the cuffs and looked up. There were the dark eyes again. Familiar now and deep and drawing my eyes just a bit further in, keeping them there just a bit longer, waiting just long enough until I found what I was looking for.

He touched my throat. He traced a line from my jaw to my collarbone with a rough forefinger, as if he were studying a sculpture on display. The pressure was light and constant. I looked up at him, waiting. My eyes were open to him, waiting.

His arm was around my shoulder again. "Let's go to dinner." He steered me from the bridge, along the water, to a little side street close by.

We stepped from the chilling, darkening, urban street into a warm, cave-like, candlelit restaurant. Sean spoke quietly to a waiter and we were seated at a highly polished wooden table next to a fireplace glowing red and yellow from a wood-burning fire. He turned his eyes to the ceiling, directing them along the walls, to the carved mantelpiece, slowly taking in the individual touches that elicited intimacy and graciousness and suggested traditions stretching back through the ages.

"Look at these old stone walls, the stonework over the mantle, that tapestry, the fire. This is how the ancient Celtic kings must have supped." He did not open his menu, but looked solemnly at me. "I would like to get us a nice bottle of wine. Can you believe it?" He sighed, while never looking up from the cover of the menu. "It's diabolical how they mark these prices up."

"Don't worry. Really. Let me get it." The waiter came to the side of the table.

Sean looked to me fully. "Do you want some fish or perhaps a steak?"

"I'd like fish tonight."

"Fine." Turning fully to his side he spoke. "Do you have a nice Chardonnay?"

I smiled and glanced around. "You're right. Very simple - the decor - but it all comes together magically. I feel like I'm in a castle."

A tall, older man brought the wine, a bucket and two glasses. He let Sean inspect the label then deftly wiped the top and de-corked it. "I am Patrick O'Conner. I am the owner. How are you folks this evening?"

As Sean tasted the wine and nodded for it to be poured, he began, "I love what you've done here. These wrought iron chandeliers, just so perfect here. And the mantle - it looks like original wood."

O'Conner brightened and explained how they had taken the walls and all the wood molding down to the original fish oil paint.

"Have you completed your restoration?"

"We're working upstairs now. Replacing some of the wood of the floor. Someday, we'll have some dining rooms up there."

"I'd be interested to see it some time. I do a little work with that myself. Maybe you could use some help."

"Maybe. If you come by during the day, I'll show you what I'm doing. Maybe tomorrow or so. I'm looking at rebuilding the old window wells."

"Interesting." Feeling warmth and a heady anticipation, I watched the two men. Under their easy conversation, they parried. Back and forth. Up and down with their words. Assessing whether they'll interact further and what each one's role may be. Moving forward and backward, leaning forward and backward. All in the non-threatening context of information exchange. A balanced ending point is reached, a final statement made, a separation.

Sean was back with me fully, his dark eyes expanded enough to take all of me into their charmed depths and dunk me soundly. He raised his glass to me. "Mistress of the castle, we will defend you to our death!"

"More than likely, my lord, I will not require saving. But this is not to say you may not be challenged."

"I am certain to be challenged!" We were smiling. We were light. We were silent. We were serious. Our salads came and a basket of warm bread and a plate of butter.

At a table, on the other side of the fireplace, a couple was seated. A man with a black turtleneck shirt and a black blazer was with a small woman, her red hair pulled back in a French braid.

I leaned forward feeling playful. "Do you think he's a priest?"

"Could be. Could be. His date fits the picture: reserved but attractive. Very attractive."

I considered her closer. "A bit young."

"As it should be." He stared at her, taking in every inch of her, tracing her delicate features, the ripples of her red braid, her full curves, with the slow touch of his eyes. As he lingered with her, I felt like I was spying on an intimate encounter.

"Do you think he knows we know?" I was trying to seem comfortable, unembarrassed.

"I don't know what he knows. And honestly, I don't want to know what a priest is thinking when I'm sitting here with you." The pull of an alluring image had dissolved and he was looking squarely at me.

"I'm sorry. I'm irreverent at times."

"That's not it at all. I want to hear about you. I'm curious what your days are like. Tell me that."

"You mean my work?" He shrugged and I went on, "I work most days during the week. I like to walk each day - mornings. I love to go to the movies. Sometimes I get together with people in my neighborhood and we talk about making some changes, you know, politics. I guess people don't talk a lot about politics here."

"You know, Michelle, we're more relaxed here than you think." He glanced quickly away, dismissing the subject as he surveyed the dinner a moment before taking a small bite of the salmon. "Marvelous, don't you think?"

I tasted the fresh broccoli, the warm potatoes. "It's perfect. Just perfect. So, are people more hopeful now with the peace talks and the agreement?"

"It's hard to be too optimistic."

"I took a taxi this morning through the Catholic and Protestant areas." I was hoping to brighten his outlook with my general enthusiasm.

"Oh, you did, did you?" He poured some wine into my glass. "You know it's not really a Catholic/Protestant thing so much. There's a lot of Protestants here working right with Catholics. The division lies in the legal considerations. Republic versus traditional ties. All changes are complicated but not necessarily antagonistic."

"But there's still a lot of tension here. I can feel it," I said quickly.

"Very few people condone the violence. All the work is being done at the table. Trust is a personal struggle."

"But there's still the threat of violence. How can people begin to let their guard down and trust the process of peace when there's still a threat?"

"What do you know about threats? What do you know about living side by side with someone raised to distrust you? This oppression goes through the genes - son to father to grandfather. Who can sort out what may be the final solutions for some? Who do you think you are to come here and analyze us? Put us into a category, make us out to be small and screwed up? You think you know me because I'm like your father. Look into my eyes. I'm not your father."

"I know you're not my father. I know that! I'm not trying to tell you what you should do. I'm just trying to understand what you feel." My face was hot; my chest was tight. Where had his words come from?

"Nice words, doctor. Is that your standard response? Placate the madman?"

I felt shaky. The ground was not there under my bench next to the fireplace. It had been there a moment ago, hadn't it? When all was possible. When all was new. When we were unwrapping each other's comments like presents. Delighted and floating I had been. Was that when the ground had slipped away?

"Is this how you talked with your father?" he continued, his voice droning on evenly with restrained hostility beneath it.

"No." I had never felt on equal footing with my father. The air was a stone wall between us. A break in the fortifications allowed a stream to cut through.

"Yet it's because of him that you're taking up our sword here, isn't it?"

"My father loved Ireland. He spoke highly of it." My voice was rising, hitting higher and higher ranges, as I forced the sweetness I had held into coarse expression, here in this heartless arena.

"But he never came here, did he? What else did he value? What else did he deeply love?"

I half stood up. "I'm leaving."

He grabbed my arm and pulled me back to sitting. "I'm sorry. That's not what I meant. It's the drink. Please." His eyes were pleading his case.

"I'm not your enemy."

"I know. I know." His eyes soften and he seemed genuinely understanding.

"I don't want to tread on your territory, but I don't deserve this."

"Of course not. You're an incredible woman. I see such an incredible woman before me and I don't know how to handle her. Such an incredible blend. Such a child. Such a woman. Please forgive me." I sat back slowly.

I began to relax. I studied my hands on my lap and turned my ring around and around. "I should be grateful for your input. On our own, we hardly have sorted out this muddle. And we've been at it for 700 years or so. Maybe we could use a little help now and then." We laughed. And slowly, we picked up silverware and quietly finished our dinner.

As we finished, a fiddle player and a flutist pulled up chairs before the fire and began to play. The heavy cloud of harsh words broke up with the lilting notes of the flute and playful song of the fiddle. Sean spoke, "I guess I had my Irish up. You were pretty mad at me yourself."

"I was, wasn't I? And rightfully so."

"Your blood was boiling, it was. But you have to admit, it felt a bit good to blow. A little fight makes it interesting. You know you're of this world then."

"I'd never admit enjoying such a thing."

"Ah, still defensive. What shall we make of that?" We listened to the music. A ballad. A reel or jig. A soulful lament. "I wonder if they know *Mo Ghile Mear*." He stood up and went over to them, bent down with a question and very soon they were all talking in earnest.

I watched how easily he got along with people, as if he'd known them all his life, and liked them to boot. His posture was open, his movements fluid, but I noticed he kept his gestures very close to himself. Broad shoulders lifted muscular arms as he explained something. One foot in front of the other, he punctuated his sentences by shifting his weight. Back and forth, stocky legs moved slight hips and stomach back and forth.

The fiddle player, a young man with a mustache and long hair stood up and handed his instrument to Sean. As natural as a seasoned jockey straddles his mount, he positioned the fiddle on his shoulder and raised the bow. He sat and leaned forward and conferred with the flutist. Sitting back, he began a tune.

He was so alive, his fingers so exact, the music he made was not music, it was a bridge and it went from him to you, through you to all people of all times. He was a shaman, a healer, an immortal; but his cry carried the pain of the human and it made all humans who heard him immortal. I watched his serious face, his hands, his feet. Who was this man?

When he finished the piece, the small group of people in the restaurant enthusiastically applauded. He stood and seemed to hesitate when they called for more. Then he handed the fiddle back to its rightful owner and came back to the table. As he passed the waiter, he spoke a moment.

When he sat across from me, he smiled broadly. His dark eyes fairly glimmered blue/black. "That was wonderful," I told him.

"You liked that, did you? Well thank you."

"You are an artist."

"No more now or I'll become mad and they'll toss me out of here. It was a nice little fiddle, it was. I also play the melodeon and the flute and I've even been known to finger the bagpipes. The Irish bagpipes. I have quite a collection at home. If my two cohorts weren't sitting up at this very moment in our apartment waiting, I'd take you round to my place and show you." The waiter brought two glasses of whiskey.

"I'd have liked that."

"You would, would you?" He thought a moment. " Not be terrified of the prospect of coming to my den in the dead of night?"

"No." We sat looking into each other. Each coming back to ourselves and finding that space empty, flowed into one another again.

"So, you might not be opposed to spending a bit of this night with me?"

"I might not."

"This woman must have the Irish blood in her for in no way can I get a definite answer from her."

I thought for a moment. "This is about as definite as it gets."

He smiled. He understood. "We'll go to your B&B."

"No, I couldn't." He tilted his head sideways and waited. "The woman there is so nice." He waited further. "I don't know what she'd think."

"What do you care what she thinks? Aren't you comfortable just being yourself?"

"No," and slowly, "I'm not comfortable flaunting myself. And I don't want to make others uncomfortable."

"That's not true, Michelle. You want people to see you as good."

I felt myself withdraw. I stopped. I wasn't going away this time. I punched my knuckles into his hand. He caught my hand and kissed it. "You're not comfortable, that's fine. We'll get a room."

"If you're worried about money..."

"I'm not. I'll work something out."

"Okay then, let's go."

He sat back. "What's your rush? We have all night. I'm just getting to know you. I want to explore you. Take our time." He looked around and the waiter came over. "Let's have coffee. All right?"

I paced myself. "Coffee it is."

"And how about dessert? You don't care do you? I think it's important." And to the waiter, "Two coffees and bring something with chocolate for us to share."

Over coffee and chocolate cake, I told him about my brother Patrick. How we had been buddies when we were young and how we had drifted apart when we were older. How Patrick was the first guy near my own age that I had a crush on. He listened closely, watching me, asking questions, accompanying me further and further into myself and into my family and into my relationships.

The owner brought a small glass of whiskey over and set it before Sean. "Fancy notes there. Very nice."

"Thank you, can I buy you a drink?"

"Oh, no. I'll be good for awhile. But again, nice fiddle playing."

"You know you really should have more professional type of musicians in here." I heard Sean say the words and for a moment I braced for the sensation of someone about to be hit with a sledgehammer. Fear dissolved to embarrassment as the owner took a deep breath and leaned away from our table.

"I don't think that's really necessary. These lads are fine. One's a nephew of mine."

"But this is a nice place. The music should reflect that."

"What I'm doing here..."

I stopped listening to their words and heard the tones. Rising, rising, rising. When the tones crashed into each other, I reached over and took Sean's hand. "Let's get the check and go."

He pulled his hand back and said tightly, "I'm talking here." He turned back to O'Connor.

I brought my hand back as if he had slapped it. I cradled this hand in the other. I needed to go to the bathroom. I stood up. "Excuse me a minute." He nodded, but continued talking to O'Connor. The volume was more even. The argument had become more intellectual and complex. Back and forth, back and forth, they parried.

I began to look for a bathroom, getting further away from the dining room. This was to have been a special night, wasn't it? I passed the waiter and then walked back and handed him a twenty pound note. That would more than cover the wine. I pushed through the door. I stepped from the candlelit cave out into the cold, dark, clean and clear urban air.

Taking long strides, I moved quickly away from the restaurant, away from the docks with their lingering ships and tangled netting. I headed towards the belly of the city. I fairly marched, my face hot, my throat burning with steam rising from a crude visceral boiler somewhere below.

I didn't have a voice, yet electric sparks snapped back and forth, gathered into frantic balls and threatened to erupt from my vocal chords. I wanted to rage against the dark, cloud-filled sky above me. I wanted to scatter the gray blankets of confusion far and wide with my thundering. I wanted to clear the firmament with a resounding rush of air. For once I did not rush to calm myself. In Macha's words, I had balanced the score and was now moving on. But moving on at my own pace.

As I pushed onward across the dark, deserted sidewalk, I was not alone. Although I was independent and sure in my purpose, intact and bristling within my separate skin, others walked beside me. A column of women warriors, transported across many towns and eras, proud and tall, flanked me.

As we marched together across the battlefield, with our home-made weapons, we pulled our separate strengths into one unassailable force. We kept our gait constant. Having overcome a current foe, we did not languish in victory, but continued to advance. What next would rise from the bowels of the earth and take its form in the congealing mist? Let it challenge us. We were ready. I made each step signify a renewal of purpose.

CHAPTER EIGHTEEN

I walked for a quite a while before I realized I didn't know where specifically I was heading. I did not recognize this part of the city, but I knew I was a long way from my B & B. I came to another pub.

Yellow lights from its many windows spilled out and swam into each other, creating a hazy cushion of warmth that softened the pub's squat, square exterior. It invited me in. Just inside, many people standing in little groups around the bar, seemed all to be talking at once. The many conversations rolled into each other creating a chaotic drone. This cushion of noise seemed insular and did not invite me in.

I went to the bathroom. In the old mirror with its peeling silver paint, I saw my reflection as I ran cold water over my hands. The green eyes were open wide, flashing - some spark from an uncurbed genetic fire now lighted my eyes. I did not recognize the unrestrained expression on the face that looked back at me.

Outside of the washroom, I spotted a telephone on the wall. I pulled a business card from my wallet and coins from my pocket and dialed the number.

"Hallo."

"Hello, Michael. It's Michelle Maguire. You took me in your cab today - from Vanessa O'Neil's - Hallowell House."

"Oh, right. Hello, Michelle." His voice was soft and easy. His tone rose slightly at the end of each line.

"I'm surprised you're there."

"I'm a bit surprised myself. What can I do for you this evening?"

I had no idea what I wanted to say, so I barreled on. "Well, I'm out this evening. I'm in town."

"Ah, having a bit of a night out, are you?"

"Yes, and it's getting late and I'm on my own and I think I'm pretty far from my place."

"Well, a young lady like yourself shouldn't be out and about by herself on such a night as this. Shall I come for you?"

"If you don't mind. I just need to get back to my B & B."

"Where are you, Michelle?"

"I don't really know for sure. I think I'm on Victoria Street, maybe a quarter mile from the docks."

"What's the name of the place you're at?"

"Wait." I put the receiver down and walked to the bar. I saw no written sign and so I asked an older woman, her hair in a long braid down her back. She stood with her foot on the bottom rung of a stool speaking in short sentences to a young man. I came back to the phone. "Michael? It's Flannagan's."

"Of course. I know the place well. Sit down, have a drink and I'll be there in no time. Give me fifteen."

I glanced over my shoulder at the noisy, conversing throng; even with its cheerful demeanor, I did not feel like being taken up and into this group. I was unwilling to let my energy disperse only to soften and cool the ramrod poker that radiated vertically from my core.

Michael pulled up before the pub in his rounded black cab and I opened the passenger door and slid in next to him before he could get out.

"I'd have been glad to come in for you," he offered as he waited for me to adjust to the car's interior.

"I hope you weren't in the middle of something when I called."

He raised his eyebrows together comically. "Oh, I'm a very busy man. Very busy and with very important things," he scoffed. "Actually, I was just tying up some loose ends at home. Mundane loose ends. So your call was welcome. After all, this is what I do."

I sat quietly for a moment watching his hands on the steering wheel. Strong hands, wide with short nails. They opened and closed on the steering wheel as if they were kneading dough. His easy words told of someone with confidence in communication. His hands told the story of one who was unsure. His face was young, with fine small boyish features. His grin was the simple curve of a youth. But his eyes - his eyes were dark and deep and ancient.

Was he forty? Or had he had a hard life and he was in his early thirties? Something about him seemed weathered and experienced and hardened despite his playful demeanor. "Myself, I was thinking about heading out again anyway. The evening, as they say, is still young. And I'm sure you haven't seen the whole Kingdom Come yet, now have you?"

"No, there's a lot I haven't seen here. Are you suggesting a guided tour?"

The corners of his mouth rolled up like the ends of a waxed mustache. The corners of his eyes wrinkled mischievously. "Not such a formal proposal as all that. To tell the truth I was thinking strictly off the meter. If you wouldn't feel put upon, I'd be honored to show you some quaint little places in our fair city."

"Are you free?"

"I told you strictly off the meter."

"I mean do you have any previous commitments for tonight."

"I have no outstanding commitments and so offer to be your escort this evening."

"My escort? Does that mean you're unattached?"

"Unattached?" He struggled for my meaning. "Ah, you mean am I married or betrothed, right? Not for a moment. I'm free as a bird on the wing. So will you take flight with me then?"

I nodded. He was being uncomplicated and relaxed. I was becoming stiff and formal again, losing the lifeline to the strong feeling I had within. "But I can't bear to walk into another pub tonight."

"Well that narrows it down a bit. Where would you like to go? I could take you to my house and show you my etchings." He looked over and tilted his head, one step away from a wink.

"You have etchings? Are you an artist of some kind?" I asked lightly.

"You mean like a con artist, Michelle?" I laughed and nodded. "For sure. But I do have etchings. They were done by my sister and given to me. She does lovely work and that's how she repays me for letting her stay there."

"Do you live with a lot of people?" I wondered how crowded his place might be at the moment.

"No, it's my little, attached house in the middle of the block, bought and paid for with my own sweat and tears. My sister stays with me when she has a contract job in the city. She's away now. It's a lovely little place, simple, quiet, and artwork all over creation."

"It does sound nice," I said and the thought of a quiet home with a friendly person seemed to beckon to us as a rest stop might on a long trip. I started to say more and stopped. I looked into Michael's large dark eyes. They held my own intensely, as a hawk might latch his gaze onto a motion in the grass and steadfastly stay with it. He leaned forward and tucked his thumb into the cleft of my chin and cupped my jaw with his large, rough hand.

"You know you're lovely, Michelle. As lovely as the dew on a spring rose."

My chest quivered. The words went in at heart level and shook me deeply. I touched his hand. His hand dropped to my shoulder. I touched his collarbone. It was vibrating, moving quickly with the expanded motion of his ribcage below. A pulse in his neck signaled a body moving into higher gear, each part talking to the other, each part ready to move. My own heart entrained with his rhythm and the drumming within my breast mounted.

I felt a curious disappearance of the boundary of my body. My edges felt soft, unformed, blending with his edges, reforming as one. I was losing my sense of separateness, and I welcomed it. My belly felt as if it were glowing orange with hot coals. The sensation was too much to contain and I leaned backwards, pressing against the door. He continued to hold my gaze and in that moment I saw him hold himself separate, pulling himself together, formulating a decision rather that reacting to the tugs and tremors of his body.

In the moment before he spoke, I sat with my own chemistry racing, feeling my legs, my pelvis, my stomach, my heart. Such a rush was all this feeling at once. Were all of the stories of the passionate, spontaneous goddesses changing me on a deep level? And how could I feel so much for someone I hardly knew?

I looked closer at Michael, trying to see him as he was here in the present. His chest was small, his ribs were prominent through his tee shirt. His arms were very muscular. His hips and waist were narrow, but he had a rounded abdomen. The short, stocky legs seemed well-defined where the material of his jeans pulled taut against his thighs and calves. Although his frame appeared wiry and slight, I could imagine a powerful, compact body beneath his clothes. His body was like his manner: deceptive – graceful ease shrouding intense pressure. He gave the impression of being underfed and overworked. A man pressed into a boy's body.

"What would you like to do, Michelle?" His voice was husky and slow. Beneath his calm surface ran a strong current and a clear consciousness.

This talking was disturbing me. I didn't want to talk or think at all. I furrowed my brow, but I knew full well what he was asking. "I want to do the right thing," I said finally.

"The *right* thing?" he asked. He leaned forward. It seemed as if he was studying my nose. "What exactly do you mean?"

"You know – what you feel. What is honest. That's what is right." I made no sense and knew it. I just didn't want to unravel this. Underneath I was feeling something strong. It felt like something from long ago that had surfaced here, and all I wanted to do was embrace it. If it were something primal from the most basic wiring of my being, so be it. Something from my past was pulling at me in the present, and finally I had the means to act on it. There were no words for it.

This wasn't good enough for Michael. What was it with this man? "So, you want to do the right thing? I hear you saying one thing and your breathing's saying another. And I want to do the right thing too, but I think we're seeing this from two different directions. If we could get together on this, Michelle, I'd be delighted. I'd move forward and not look back and not ask you one more question. So, are you sure you're not doing something you feel is wrong?"

"You mean like pre-marital sex?"

Michael began to laugh. "You know, it *is* a sin, Michelle?"

"Everything is," I said, turning my head and looking out of the windshield. I crossed my arms in front of me. I didn't want to be discussing anything let alone sin. "It's not a big one, though. Not technically. It's not fundamental Catholic doctrine."

"Fundamental, is it?"

"Well, like the infallible proclamations like Christ being the son of God, the resurrection, the bread and wine being his body and blood."

"And what about all the blasted rules?"

"They were made up by Irish monks – many years after Christ – in the Dark Ages. They wanted to keep everyone in line. Thus the rules – going to mass, confession..." He tilted his head and rolled his eyes up toward me. Trying not to laugh, I continued, "Christ had two commandments: love God and love one another."

"And so we should." He looked longingly at me and I met his gaze. My heart swelled with hope. He threaded his fingers in my hair and lifted it away from my face, back from my neck. His fingers came back and smoothed my cheek, spreading the warmth from my cheekbone to my ear. Then in a somber voice, he recited what to me sounded like a mantra, a prayer, a love sonnet. "You are the dew on the morning rose."

This was too good to be true. My heart was satiated. My prayers were answered. Only they were the prayers of an eight-year-old. For a moment, Michael's dark eyes were his own. Then they were the dark, soulful eyes from my childhood. The eyes that had only ever seen me as a child and nothing more. I let the eyes of he who had only wanted to sing to me and tell me stories and see me on my way, slip away.

The fantasy that had drawn me towards it with its poetry receded. It was the product of a child fashioning a story to heal her misgivings. This same child had dreamed of sleeping princesses being rescued by brave kings. The hero had worn the face of my father, my father who rocked me and would touch the tip of my nose with his finger and call me his "wild Irish rose."

I closed my eyes and laughed. I looked up and saw Michael's quizzical look and I laughed harder. Then, I must have seemed funny, tears in my eyes, coughing and laughing at the same time for he began to laugh too. "I'm sorry," I managed to get out between coughs and cackles. "I'm losing it, Michael, I'm sorry."

"Did you have some rude awakening, then?" he asked seriously.

"It's just what you said reminded me of something – someone –

from the past. And I guess I got carried away on a memory."

"Well, I'm not surprised You were looking right past me, and me here all along and alone." He stuck out his lower lip and looked way too forlorn.

I looked into his eyes now. His eyes were dark like my father's, but they now reminded me of someone else with whom I had unfinished business. Were they like Sean's? I shook my head and took in Michael's sad, comical expression. "You're not alone and if you hadn't played twenty questions with me, you would have had to peel me off your walls at home."

"I don't think so, Michelle."

"Are you kidding? I haven't felt so on fire – I don't know when I ever felt so much."

"Oh, I'll grant you, you're a little tiger, Michelle. But when you were looking into my eyes, you were looking for someone else to look back. I felt like a pane of glass. If you were going to get to whoever it was, I was going to have to be shattered in the process."

I closed my eyes and tried to see us moment ago. I tried to picture what I saw when I looked into Michael's eyes. I couldn't capture the expression there. "What color are your eyes, Michael?" I asked in sober contemplation.

He put his wide hand over my face and turned it side to side playfully. "Forget it, Michelle. No good." Then he turned and started the car. "Let's drive around a bit. Get some air." He rolled down his side window and the cool damp air flooded the moist interior of the steamy cab. His hands moved in graceful patterns as he guided the car into the traveling lane of the quiet road.

Traffic was light, and I took scant notice of where we headed or how long we drove. I watched through the windshield for pins of light from passing cars grow larger and mix with the gold mist of the street lamps to throw some relief onto the shapes outside of the close-set buildings of Belfast. In the brightening and dimming light, I tried again to find the eyes I may have searched for when I was close to Michael.

Michael must have noticed me staring into the lights, staring into space for all he could tell. "So, Michelle. When you're not dreaming, it seems you like to be arguing the finer points of the law." I thought of our discussion on Catholic doctrine.

"What about you?" I wasn't going to defend anything at the moment.

"I'm a bit versed in the fine points of some laws." We were bantering with words now and I knew we had come out on the other side of the close encounter as friends.

"Some laws? You're into the country's politics, aren't you?"

"Politics is people. I'm into people. I hope they stick around on this planet a while longer, yet." His tone was light, but his manner was heavy. He was waving me away from this topic.

So I switched topics. "Were you ever married?" I asked.

"No, mind you, I never even considered it."

"Why not?" I was surprised.

"Well, I would make a lousy dad."

"Being a husband doesn't necessarily mean being a father." The therapist in me was resurfacing.

"Sure it does, Michelle. It's always there in the background once you take the step. Don't kid yourself."

"I think you'd make a good father." I truly meant it. He seemed steady and kind, honorable, likable.

"You don't know what you're talking about. But good or bad, kids need a dad to just be there. I know that well and it's something I can't promise. Life's too risky."

What an odd thing to say. "It's risky for anyone."

"True enough. But for some, it's more," he said vaguely.

"Why is it more risky for you? What are you into Michael?"

"Let's just leave it lay there, all right?" He patted my leg with his hand and then it placed it firmly back on the wheel.

"What do you think I am? An informer for the UVA?"

"Oh, God, is that what you think? That in Ireland, all we do is concoct plots and blow each other up?" He laughed half-heartedly. "You better tell your imagination to take a holiday, okay?"

I didn't want to be put off like a child with his dismissive remark. "But you do care about politics."

"I'll tell you what I care deeply about, if you're interested." His tone was soft but his words were pointed and bore through rhetoric and casual conversation and right through me.

"I care about my countrymen and I care about their rights. I care about history and the memory of our ancestors who fought and lost their lives for those rights. You have your autonomy in the States. Perhaps you take it for granted, but for some of us, it's still a burning issue. I have no patience for those who are willing to compromise at the drop of a hat and forget about the years of hardship and loss."

His hands were closing into fists and he stared straight ahead. "You'll go home and forget about all this. One day you'll open your paper or turn on your CNN and find that we did at long last become one republic. And you'll nod your head and assume it was a simple deal, easily negotiated, just a matter of time."

The muscles of his neck pulled hard on his jaw. His voice continued as from a deep, dark, solitary place. The softness in the sound belied the grimness there. "But that won't be the case."

I still didn't know that what he was into – if anything. But I did know for certain that this was a powerful man, possibly a dangerous man. His eyes had been intense, but they had barred the way for me to enter inward into the dark underground he guarded carefully. There was music in his voice when he had spoken, and dancing as his eyes had moved softly over me, but I suspected that what I glimpsed briefly there was unrest and determination. They lined his cramped personal lair.

A pure ideal had been draped in a heavy wrap, and I wondered if it was the thinly veiled darkness that was part of his attraction. Was there a kinship in his quiet strife that I had recognized from my own childhood? Was that why I had so easily called him to come out tonight?

"Michael?" I spoke softly to him. "We're not so many worlds apart."

He smiled and turned the car onto a side street and then down another. He pulled the car off to the side of the road. "Where are we?" I asked.

"This is the dock area. There's the river Lagan."

"You know, it's funny. I never thought of Belfast as being on the water"

"Are you kidding?" He pointed his finger out of the front window and across the water toward a group of buildings in the distance. That's where the Titanic was built. How'd they get it out without the water, I ask you? If they hadn't launched it, of course, it'd be a fine restaurant now, or a grand hotel or a floating casino. They just didn't plan it out properly. Now, you don't see any stray icebergs wandering into this harbor, do you?"

I laughed and thought about people leaving here long ago and heading for America. Some like those aboard the Titanic had a tragic end, others like my ancestors did fine. And here I was some generations later, on this distant land. All was new to me here. I was just another displaced person who didn't know what they would find in the new environment. "Michael, don't you think I have some understanding and concern for your ideas? After all, we have some common history, don't we?"

"What exactly do you mean?" He seemed truly confused.

"I mean my having an Irish background."

"Michelle, you're American. A Yank." I must have looked crestfallen. He laid his hand over mine gently. "I'm sorry, Michelle, but it's not the same thing."

"But I came here, I mean these are my roots. I came here to find something, something I'd recognize, something of me here."

"Your roots? Your roots are in the States. You grew up there didn't you? What did you expect to find here?"

"I heard of this place all my life, heard songs, heard stories. I expected to find something like family, connection, belonging."

"But you have that. You're a member of the tribe of the human race. We're all connected in that way. Isn't that enough for you?"

My eyes were full of tears. "I don't think so." I waited, but he said nothing. I went on, "I thought a sense of belonging was a birthright. I thought it was here."

"And now you feel like you're out of the loop?" he asked.

"Now I feel like I've been kicked out of the only club I ever tried to join." My cheeks were wet and hot. I felt embarrassed.

"Michelle, that's just the way it is. Let me tell you," he said slipping his arm over my shoulder. "My mom's sister and husband left Ireland when they were newly wed. They went over to Glasgow because they couldn't get any work here. So, their daughter was born, my cousin Julie. She's a teacher and she even speaks the Irish. However," his hands kneaded my shoulder, "she's a Scot. She was born there – she's a Scot and that's that. She's not out of anything, and I think she'd laugh if I proposed anything different."

"So, your cousin's not Irish then? She's a Scot." I pushed my eyes into my palms. My shoe had slid off and I searched for it with my foot.

"Absolutely. Anyway, it's just a term."

"I know it means more to you than that." My shoe was sliding further and further under the seat as I tried to coax it out with my toes.

"It does. But anyway, she's got this strong Scottish accent. "Oh, koosin Mihil, wear air yer minners?"

I reached down under the seat to retrieve my shoe and my hand closed on something scratchy and thin that was caught against the heel. I pulled it out. It was half a roll of white crepe paper. I reached again and found another roll beneath the cushion. "What's this for?" I asked in amazement.

"Oh, I had the cab in a wedding party two weeks ago. We taped some of streamers on to the whole line of cars. Pretty fancy, yes?"

"Do you have tape now?" A picture was forming in my mind.

"No tape. I was the one that brought the paper."

"Never mind," I said unrolling some of the paper and slipping my shoe on. "Do you have a flashlight? You know, a torch?"

"Oh, sure, in the glove box." As he leaned over to open it, I slid out of the car and began to rip off strips of paper.

"Michelle, what are you doing?" I heard him say from inside the car.

But I was tying streamers to the door handles, the bumper, the grill, the windshield wipers and the antenna. "Michelle, are you sure you don't want a drink or something now?"

"Not a drop," I said taking the flashlight from his hands.

"No, you don't seem to need one. If I may ask –"

I jumped in and slammed the door. "You may not. Now please drive on. You want a Yank, I'll give you the Yankee Doodle dandiest." With much reservation, he edged the car into the street and began what I imagined was a procession. I tied a strip of white around my forehead and turned on the torch. Leaning out of the window, I proclaimed that I was Lady Liberty to anyone who might be interested. And Liberty's escort for the night was none other than the Irish Ambassador, Michael.

We drove and I waved and he seemed to get into it after a while and even tooted the horn as we passed other cars. The white decorations streamed out behind us and made our passing that night a grand occasion – white tails and black tux.

We had made our way and my arm was tired. "Michael, pull over, will you?" When he did, I pulled the paper from my hair. "You know, the thing about roots is, well, you can't help what you're given. You start with those roots. You put them down where you're born, yes. But, unlike a tree who can't move on its own or can't choose to, I can go to where I decide. And my roots are still growing, still looking for purchase in the ground below my feet. So, I chose to connect to this wonderful place whether you or anyone likes it or not. So there!"

Michael smiled at me and tussled my hair. "I like it just fine, Michelle. And that's just what we need here – some mighty spirit!"

We headed to Hallowell Hall. It was the wee hours of the morning and I was exhausted. Michael looked like he was only in midstream. As my eyes half closed in the misting lights of the city as we crossed its streets, I was haunted again by the thought of the eyes that I had searched for earlier in the face of a new friend.

I thought of the different people in my life for the answer, and it was like trying to fit a series of keys into one lock. I thought of my relatives. I thought of my boyfriend in college. I thought of my friend in college. I felt a sense of settling. The key fit the chambers of the lock perfectly. All came to rest in open conclusion. I could almost picture him.

When Michael dropped me outside of Vanessa's house, he kissed me softly good-bye. He told me not to lose the card with his number on it. Both of us knew that the card was tucked away for the present, maybe for good. I watched the dark car with its papery white trailers slip off into the peaceful predawn.

CHAPTER NINETEEN

Later, lying in my bed, in the dark, I stared out of the window. The sky was a black quilt sequined with yellow stars. I fell into a deep sleep. I awoke later that morning not only wrapped in the soft white duvet but also enfolded in the warm feeling of a dream. Slowly, like a Monet painting coming into focus, the separate parts of my dream appeared before my eyes and retold their story:

I had married a very old man, noticing nothing about him except a golden string like an electric cord that connected my abdomen to his. There were many happy people at our wedding, even his ex-wife who felt like a friend to me. At our marriage bed - a blanket on the grass under the stars - he had lifted my breasts in his hands and now a ribbon flowed from my chest to his. We slept curled into each other.

When I awoke and looked over at him, I realized how old and wrinkled he was. I was horrified and started to slip away. He sat up and talked to me. He seemed to know so much, his words were so wise. A new line from my forehead jumped to his and with that hook-up, a circle formed around us - a round thread connecting the area just outside of us. I could not tell which of us was the old one, which was the young one. I felt wonderful, deep, complete love.

I stood beside the bed, feet straight ahead, knees slightly bent. With no effort, a warm stream, thick like a mineral spring, flowed up from the ground and filled me with energy. With an empty mind, a beginner's mind, I did my Tai Chi as if for the first time. As if I was discovering each move in turn, developing this form myself, from a silent conversation I was having with Nature, I turned gracefully in balance.

When I came down to breakfast, Vanessa had made eggs and also French toast. She was very excited to tell me that she'd been writing ideas down on scraps of paper since yesterday.

She had talked on the telephone to a business advisor who was going to see her tomorrow and who told her in the meantime to write down any ideas she had for the business. She was to note such things as the strengths she had in her business and her weaknesses, what she liked about it, and what were the directions she was drawn to explore. She was going to put a new kind of business together even if it took her a fair amount of time.

I was very happy for her. Since I would be leaving Belfast later that morning, I asked Vanessa what I should definitely see before leaving. "You have to go to the garden," I was told.

I packed up my car and walked over to the Botanical Gardens. I went through the tall wrought iron gate and along the many paved paths that wound through gorgeously planned Victorian gardens. Benches had been placed outside of a glass fernery and a glass and wrought iron house. Exotic plants and bushes in stunning colors were arranged neatly throughout the grounds.

Also there was the Ulster Museum. Inside was such a diverse collection of historical pieces, scientific information and archeological specimens. I saw a special exhibit commemorating 200 years since the 1798 uprising when Wolfe Tone's United Irishmen's Rebellion was put down. I walked back through the garden, a lovely oasis in a big industrial city and headed to the B&B.

"Thank you for your encouragement," said Vanessa.

"You could drop me a line, if you get a chance, and let me know how things are coming. It sounds like a bright beginning of something wonderful. Oh, that reminds me." I reached into my left breast pocket and took out the little stone. "This goes with you now. It's traveled with me only a short while but I think it's speeded my journey. See if it doesn't encourage you now as you begin something new."

"It's lovely." Vanessa took the carved stone and turned it over in her hand. "It sort of has the face of an animal on it, doesn't it?"

"You don't see a bear there, do you?" I said quickly.

She studied the gray and black stone closely and then shook her head. "No, it's more like a fox."

I started to drive in the direction of Dublin and then quite suddenly turned around and headed north. I had wanted to see the Antrim Coast and so I would. Schedules be damned! I had a lovely day, singing to the tunes on the radio and following little roads here and there but for the most part, hugging the coast.

The coastal scenery was spectacular. I felt daring and new as I wove through the rugged landscape, passing through the little fishing villages. Graceful beauty came in blues and greens, sky grays and blues, rocky silver and browns, sandy browns and white. Birds were everywhere.

I stopped at Carrick-a-rede Rope Bridge, a contraption of ropes and wooden planks and wires stretching 65 feet across a chasm 80 feet down. I made my way across by blocking out the dangerous view and staring straight ahead. I made it, but it was rather unfulfilling.

On the way back, I stopped in the middle and looked straight down. The planks began to twist in the wind. My stomach felt as if it were falling, falling, falling and crashing into the rocks and water below. Then I began to move with the planks, feeling their support, at one with the bridge. The view had been stunning - deep blue water and black rocks lay in the shadows of the cliffside drop.

I had read about the Giant's Causeway, and longed to see it, but no description prepared me for the actual site. It was like landing on another planet. I parked the car and walked towards a huge conglomeration of rocks. Everywhere were basalt columns, extremely tall and rather small columns, in even polygon shapes. Almost 40,000 columns rose from the cliffs above the sea.

Moving through the small crowd, I climbed on to the tops of a large section of the four and five foot columns. I teetered on one foot as I reached my other leg cautiously toward the next step. Losing my balance, I pitched forward. A hand caught my arm and steadied me.

"I got you now." I turned to face a black woman with long curly black hair standing beside me.

"Thanks."

"Girl, you're taking you life in you hands, tiptoeing on those stumps. You got to jump!"

"Jump?"

"You know, like this." The woman in a blue sweatshirt and jeans stood on one foot and then hopped to another column, landing on her other foot. "And you got to keep jumping."

We crossed the wide belt of stones together, jumping form one to another, continually moving until we reached the end of the row and climbed down. We were both laughing and breathing hard.

"I guess that's one way to get across," I said.

"Yeah, if you've got a death wish. I'm Didi. I live pretty close so I know these rocks like the back of my hand."

"I'm Michelle. I've never seen anything like this." We began to walk along the seaside away from the basalt structures. "I read that this was all made by a giant."

"Finn MacCool."

"Right. And he made this as a highway to get to his girlfriend in Scotland."

"And you believe this? You're not buying the theory that lava burned up all the plants and chilled quick, making all these nice geometrical shapes? Then when the Ice Age ended, the sea split the whole thing wide open?"

"You have to admit the first one makes more sense," I said, and we both laughed.

"Well, I don't know about old MacCool, but he's not the only game in town. This place is full of stories, some true."

"What I'm learning is that everyone has a story and it may look different today than it did yesterday."

"You got that right. What's your story? Or better yet, what was the story yesterday?"

"Yesterday? You don't want to know. But seriously, it's a story that is hard to tell."

"Was it really all that bad?"

I could feel my eyes water. "Yesterday was terrible, but then it was great. It was very confusing. It had to do with one guy and then another and my father and whether I had a choice or not."

"And did you?"

"I did." I nodded and smiled and told her what happened - the pub, the dinner, my walking out; making a call, the closeness of the night. Saying good-bye to a new friend; remembering an old one. I couldn't believe I was telling her such personal things. But she seemed to be right with me, understanding my feelings as I talked. Who was she? How did she seem to know me so well?

"You know, when you start talking guys, it always gets confusing." She twisted her hair into a knot on the top of her head. "And you did just fine. The only thing I take issue with is you paying more than your share – you know, at the restaurant."

"That's what I was comfortable with. I don't like to owe anyone."

"Really? Well, that's a neat trick if you can do it. It's a touching story, Michelle, but I suspect it's not over. I do know what you're talking about, though. You could say I've had my share of trials."

I turned and looked into her large dark eyes, deep pools of experience. "What happened to you?"

"I just recently moved back to this area. I was born around here. When I was pretty young, my mom died and my stepdad decided to raise me. I don't know what he had in mind for the future, but he did take care of me then.

"We moved to the States and he raised me as his own. But he'd say things like, 'Your mama always said you'd be trouble, but I took you anyway.' And things were fine until in high school when I met this guy and fell for him and brought him around to the house. Well, my stepdad threw him right out, and scared him terribly. I told the guy we should run off and he said 'no' being afraid and all. But I convinced him and we took off, traveled all around."

"Then what happened?"

"He didn't turn out to be too steady. He ran into my stepdad at some auction and took off for good that time. I decided to go back to my stepdad's - he lives in Chicago. I went back, but he made my life miserable, saying no one would ever be good enough for me. So, he was pissed and mean about the whole thing, but I burned all my bridges with the man. I came back here on my own, absolutely broke, but on my own."

"It seems like you've been through a lot," I suggested. "Do you like living around here?"

She smiled broadly. "There's no place like home."

CHAPTER TWENTY

Later, I drove on to the town of Ballygally and found a room for the night. In the morning, I was heading down the A1 en route to Dublin. By early afternoon, I had crossed the border, finding myself soon after, "just beyond the Pale."

The countryside on the Midlands was green fields with many small lakes tucked among them. In a secluded spot, I came to the ruined monastic settlement of Monasterboice. I walked among the high Celtic crosses and sat on a wide carved stone. I took in the peace and quiet, the elaborate unchanging stone structures in the midst of the simple ever-changing landscape. I got the slightest sense of my father. As he came alive in my memory, I felt his presence even stronger.

"Hi, dad," I told him softly. "I wish you were here with me now. Of course this would've been quite a different trip. Actually we'd probably be touring the Old Bushmills distillery right now." I laughed lightly.

"But I wish we could have made this trip together once. We could have walked around this beautiful country and together have met some of these beautiful people...And in our walking, maybe all the things that have lain unsaid and misunderstood between us, well, maybe they wouldn't need to be said after all.

"And if mom were here, I think she'd enjoy it. She'd be amazed at the all the plants and tiny animal life. She'd keep us walking while she investigated little things on the trail, sending us on ahead. By the way, I met a guy who, in some ways, reminded me of you. Yes, he was quite a character. He led me down the garden path..." I began to cry.

After a while, I sniffled and lifted my shoulders. "I walked away from him, but whom I walked to was not exactly my knight in shining armor either. It's kind of a relief to not be depending on a knight just now. I'm not sure where I'm heading, but I do know it'll all turn out all right. So don't worry, dad, because I turned out to be all right. In fact," I smiled widely through tears, "that's really what I wanted to tell you. I turned out just fine."

As I came into Dublin from the north, the sight of the tall buildings and bridges was at once familiar and welcoming. It was like returning to an old haunt from one's past. With little trouble, I located the guesthouse I had stayed at before, checked in and got settled.

Getting very hungry, I walked outside and toward the city center. I'd see what restaurant tickled my fancy. I stopped to buy an Irish Times to read at dinner and taking out my wallet, noticed the hidden compartment. Opening it, once again I was surprised to see Mary's number on the piece of cardboard. It had popped out one time too many. I found a phone booth on the street and dialed her number.

"Yes?"

"Hello, Mary?"

"Yes."

"This is Michelle."

"Do I know a Michelle?" Children's voices were loud in the background.

"Remember me? I'm the woman from New York? When you were with Adele? I'm the one who wanted to get you on CNN for the Irish Pyramids."

"Ah.....yes! The lady who solved peoples' problems."

"Right. Anyway, I'm back in Dublin and I just thought I'd call you and see if you could get away. Maybe we'd get together, have something to eat?"

"You mean tonight?"

"Sure."

"Oh, Jeez, I got kids bouncing off the walls here and I haven't the foggiest where Dan is."

"Well, that's okay..."

"Now hold on, Michelle. Are you about tomorrow?"

"That's Friday. Yes. I don't leave until Saturday morning."

"There you go. I'll meet you tomorrow afternoon. Would you believe I haven't been out since I saw you? I'll grab Adele too, if she's around. Where will we meet you?"

"How about Bewleys?"

"Bewleys? You mean for a cuppa?"

"Sure."

"What do you say to this? I'll meet you around happy hour at the bar I saw you in and we'll have a pint?"

"Practically the same thing I was suggesting."

I pored over the Irish Times, looking to see what was going on in Dublin that evening. Taking a chance, I walked over the O'Connell Street Bridge and down to Parnell Square to the Gate Theater. On the right side of chance, I was able to purchase a single ticket for the play that night, The Weir by Conor McPherson.

I went into the theater and sat in a seat near the front. The chair next to me was empty. Not until after the lights had been turned down and the play began, did someone make their way to the seat. I watched the Irish play that took place in a bar. It was a virtual conversation of fairies and ghosts and spirits. It was both funny and touching.

At the end, a female voice beside me whispered, "What do you think? Was it all you hoped for?'

"I don't know what I hoped for."

"Then you aren't disappointed?"

"Not at all."

"And you don't feel manipulated?"

"Not for a moment."

"Wonderful." During the last of the applause, the woman beside me made her way out. The house lights came up and I turned around towards the exit in time to see the back of a tall woman with yellow hair wearing a green cape.

CHAPTER TWENTY-ONE

The next morning, after breakfast, I took the bus out to the harbor. I walked the many paths around Dun Laoghaire, a grand port center for ferries and yachts. Lovely with its bright houses and lighthouse, and busy with many people coming and going, it had a lively, energetic feel to it. I was able to see Howth Head, a great rocky outcrop at the northern limit of Dublin Bay.

In the early afternoon, I enjoyed just walking through the streets of Dublin, basking in the familiarity of this friendly town. I stopped and had a "cuppa" tea at Bewleys. There I bought my souvenirs: tins of tea and boxes of shortbread and toffee.

As I passed the storefronts along the streets, I began to watch for my reflection in the glass – the profile of my neck and chest, my abdomen, my pelvis. My stomach became a bit queasy and I began to walk in the direction of my guesthouse. Watching my shape in the shop windows, I felt like I was one step behind myself.

The night before last, I had been more daring than I could remember. Having dinner with a stranger, calling Michael and sharing with him some of my innermost thoughts and the stirrings of passion. I was comfortable being a person who was more open and honest with her feelings, but I was different. And integrating such a shift was a bit unsettling. I could see myself beginning to trust my gut when making a decision.

I knew that that method sometimes was a bit dangerous. For hadn't I been one step away from a physical encounter? What if that had gone too far, too fast? Not only would there be the awkwardness of having been intimate with someone I knew for too short a time, but the truth was I could even be pregnant right now. Instead of window shopping, I could be purchasing a pregnancy test.

I was nauseous with all of the feelings now flooding my abdomen. Was this how morning sickness felt? Earlier, I had had a bad moment in the bathroom of my guesthouse and had sat on the floor next to the tub unsure if I would throw up. How close to the edge we skated on the blade of a moment of unguarded passion. With precautions, I knew that the chance of conception would be rather slight. It would also hardly be fair. The memory of the "world's not fair," came back to me and I briefly smiled.

I wondered how my mom felt waiting, maybe even weeks, to see if she were pregnant. And was I what she had hoped for? Did she even want a child? Did she want me? At times she seemed so burdened with me. She seemed to have struggled through the years - my lovely, suffering, patient mother. That is how I always saw her, but maybe that was not the whole picture. And where did I fit into this process? What did I want myself?

I couldn't even think. I couldn't imagine having a child, even if it came as a surprise. I'd consider having a procedure back in New York. It was only fair to the child. The child? When I began to picture an actual child in all this, I wasn't so sure about what was right.

I have always believed that a woman has the right to make an individual choice here and that she had to make that choice considering what was best for all. She had to look at all sides of the situation, her own health, the child's health, the ability to care for the child, the child's environment. The child, the child – what exactly would have been right? But then, I wondered, what could be wrong about having a child?

Of course, I wasn't pregnant. I knew this. I knew I was getting carried away with anxiety. But the thought of a pregnancy now shook me to my very core. I let myself imagine what that experience would be like. Suddenly it was hard to breathe.

My chest and throat felt even tighter than they had earlier. I had a sense of me as a mother and immediately I knew what I would do. I was thrilled and scared. I would have carried the child. I would have gone home and gone back to my practice, but now there would be a new dimension to my life. I would spend more time with Patrick and my nephew, Evan. I would share the joy of this child with everyone in my life. Perhaps I would call Mark, perhaps he would be a part of this plan. Whatever would be, would be. Also, I would have to learn to breathe again.

I let out a sigh and came back to reality. There would be no baby. No new little one to cradle, to bring into this world to love. At least not yet.

Once more I thought of my mother, but it felt different this time. Now I wasn't feeling so distant from her, so critical. There was an aura of softness around her as I recalled a walk we had taken together when I was in junior high. As I got older, we took fewer walks together, but they were something I usually didn't pass up. Sometimes she'd be describing all the little plants and bugs that we were passing and sometimes she'd be very quiet.

I realize now we had a heart connection and many times we didn't have to talk. In those times I felt her underlying acceptance of me. We were walking through the woods near the house and the dog was running ahead of us on the path. I told my mom I was trying to decide what to be when I grew up.

"You can be whatever you want," she said. "What do you want to be?"

"I'm not sure. It's such a big decision," I answered.

"Didn't you tell me you wanted to be a teacher? I think you'd be a great teacher." She stopped to pick up a leaf. It must have been autumn for she was always saving the colorful leaves in one scrapbook or another.

"You don't understand. I have to be sure. I don't want to make the wrong choice."

She was folding another leaf into her pocket. "Whatever you choose will be fine, Michelle dear, you'll see. The choices we make create our lives. You can't see it all yet because you haven't made your way yet. But it'll be what it is. And you know, we all make mistakes. I probably shouldn't have rushed into marriage with your father. We only knew each other a couple of months, but I lost my head. And we're very different people. But I did marry then and because I did, by some miracle, you came along and you are my sunshine."

I could see her eyes brighten as she looked at me with love. She had always been there somewhere for me. Sometimes she withdrew her energy to somewhere within, but she hadn't withdrawn her love for me. She had died three years ago and for the first time since then, I let myself feel my loss. I cried, as I hadn't before. This was the lump in my throat, the stone in my gut. This was what was working its way up and out since I had been at the statue of Brigid.

I cried as I thought how, after she died, I continued to look for her. In church or a store or at a play, I would start when I'd see the back of an older woman whose hair may be tucked into a bun. My heart would leap and for a moment, I'd strain to see if it could be her. They would turn or I'd go past them and see a sweet, unfamiliar face, and feel silly. I'd been looking for her for a long time.

After a while, my stomach felt easier, not sick anymore, maybe a little lonely. I had to call someone. I went to the lobby and found a phone. I took out my phone card and automatically dialed a familiar number, not sure why this had to be my first call.

"Hello."

"Hello, Patrick, it's your sister."

"Mickey! You little leprechaun. Are you home?"

"Not just yet, Patrick. Not even close."

"So, still on Emerald Point? Having fun, are you?"

"It's beautiful here. The people are so nice. They don't spend a lot of money going out. They seem to entertain each other, make their own fun, have fun with one another..."

"Maybe it's the connection, Mickey, but you sound downright sad."

"Do I? Oh, by the way, I have some Irish coins for Evan."

"Great. He collects everything now. And what do you have for me? Those family jewels that you tracked down?"

"As a matter of fact, I did find the family's wealth. But it's a buried treasure."

"Buried treasure, huh? I see you're still lucid and verging on sanity."

"Our genetic legacy."

"Hey, sis, don't make fun of my family."

"Oh, only you can criticize mom and dad?"

"Mom - never."

"You better not." I smiled into the receiver.

" Dad - well it may surprise you to know that not all of my memories of the old man are bad."

"I'm waiting."

"Let's see. Hold on, I'll think of something. Well, he did take me fishing a few times. It was pretty cool hanging out by the stream, nothing to distract us. Except then you'd show up and start asking all your questions. I'd love it when he'd say you were scaring all the fish and he'd send you up stream to scare the fish our way. It was peaceful then. He'd say, "This is what men do," and I'd feel like a regular guy.

"And I remember laying under the stars on a summer night. He'd tell us stories of the constellations."

"He knew mythology?"

"Some. Like Venus and Cassiopeia and especially Orion and what was the dog star? Canus. In fact, that reminds me. You remember that pup you had that ran away?"

"Yes."

"And remember a couple of weeks later, a lost pup turned up in the yard and you found him and adopted him? And dad said that lost pups were always found by good owners. He said that Cannes, the Dexter star balanced things out and sent you that one."

"I remember Laddie. I remember mom wasn't too fond of him. What's the story?"

"Well, dad took me to a pet store and had me pick him out. Then we had to orchestrate putting him in the yard right when you'd come out so it could all happen by 'chance."

I laughed. "I never suspected."

"Yeah, dad was a bastard at times, chewed up my behind from time to time and deserted us on a regular basis, but sometimes when he was there and trying to be a father, sometimes it was good. In some ways he helped me to be a good man. Not a perfect one, but basically good. I hope I can pass some of that onto my son."

I felt tearful at his words. "Then why did you always joke about him?"

"I had to. You were so defensive of him."

"And now?"

"Well the miles have a way of smoothing out the hard lines, don't they? But hey, this is costing you. Can I pick you up at the airport or something? When do you come in?"

"Thanks, but Shelly's supposed to. I'm going to call her now. And if not, I can easily call a cab. Pat, when I do get back, I'd like to have dinner with you and talk. I miss you and I have a lot to tell you."

"You got it. I'll have you over and we'll have ham and cabbage - yum. Oh, and bring that buried treasure with you. I've got some leads for investing."

I sat and collected myself. I hadn't given Patrick much space to talk, but there was more talking between us than in a long time. I had one more call to make and dialed Shelly's number. To my surprise, I learned that Shelly had delivered her baby and all was well. I was happy to make other arrangements for my airport arrival tomorrow.

Tomorrow and tomorrow. But for tonight, I still had to meet Mary and I was looking forward to it. I put a jacket on over my long sleeve shirt. The breast pocket felt a bit empty now. I brushed my hair and walked back outside. I headed to the bar and to find Mary.

"Well, if you aren't a sight for sore eyes?"

I turned in my chair to see Mary coming across the barroom floor towards me. "Good to see you. I'm glad you came."

"Wouldn't have missed it for the world. Adele says 'hey.' She's cooking dinner tonight for the mother-in-law and couldn't break out." A waitress came over and we each ordered a pint of Guinness.

"I'll get this," said Mary.

"Absolutely not! No argument. It's on me!"

Mary sat back in her chair and smiled wryly at my forceful declaration.

"Dan says 'hi'," she volunteered.

"Dan says 'hi'?"

"Yeah, he says he was sorry he couldn't tuck you in that night."

"Oh, my God, he told you?"

She was laughing heartily now. Almost falling out of her chair. "Sure that little fart tells me everything. He's harmless. Loves to joke with the women, get 'em going. Thought you were precious. But he's just playing. When you get to know him, you know. He's a good man. Good to me."

168

I bent my head in a posture of caving in. I had been so serious, but no one else had. With their accepting way of looking at life's shortcomings and their easy way of talking to each other, they had paved the way for a simple, trusting relationship.

"So tell me about your travels. What's happened for you?"

We drank our stout and talked about the places I had seen. Mary made comments on the places she'd been to and asked questions of the ones she'd like to get to. At one point, Mary leaned over and said, "You know, you seem somehow...lighter. Yes definitely lighter than when I first met you. The air here must do you good."

We had some dinner and talked further about the different types of women that we were at times. Finally we decided we weren't locked into one specific type. We were vibrant, sensitive, ever-changing women so the world better just look out.

A guy with a bodhran, one with a fiddle and a woman with a tin whistle, began to play some lively tunes. "Well, I guess it's time," said Mary. She stood and took my hands and pulled me up on my feet and into the middle of the floor by the music. "It's time you learned to set dance."

She showed me the joyous steps of set dancing and before long, people were joining in. We stayed until very late, celebrating the energy of music moving through people enjoying life.

Tired and sweaty and satisfied, we said a simple 'good-bye' with a simple hug and went our separate ways in the late Dublin night.

The next morning, I woke early. I was excited to be going home and sharing my experiences, but at the moment, there was an ache in the pit of my stomach. I felt a sadness to leave this little island for yet another one. Though I hadn't actually left, I felt a longing to return. Evidently the connection I had made here ran much further back that a mere two weeks.

I took the M1 to the airport and dropped off the little red rental car. In the terminal, I changed back my Irish pounds and British sterling into US dollars. I filled out customs forms and checked in. I had a couple of hours to kill before my flight. I bought a cup of coffee and sat down near the gate and took out *Ulysses*.

Stephen is on the beach. He's trying to determine if what he sees or hears is real. He remembers his past, trying to figure out who he is now. He is changing. Stephen ponders many things such as two women passing by, monks whose sashes join them to each other and God, navels, and if his true father is his dad or God.

He has never done anything heroic such as saving a drowning man, as Mulligan once did. Unlike his friend, though, he lives his life sensitively and tries to be genuine. Once he dreamt and wrote poetry. Now he must learn to balance his conflicts or he will be drowned or crucified by life. There is some promise of renewal and rebirth as he tears off part of a page and begins to write again.

After sitting for awhile, I walked around the airport. In a little alcove was a cozy bookshop. I glanced through the titles and picked up *The Celtic Goddesses and Their Stories*. I came across the tale of Deirdre. It had a haunting familiarity about it.

Long ago, King Conchobar had a bard who had a daughter. The king's druid priest foretold that Deirdre who would be very beautiful, would cause sorrow for Ulster and should be put to death immediately. The king kept her alive, and had her raised in private.

One day she sees red and white and black together, and she knows this has something to do with the man she will marry. There is a young man, Naoise, pale with black hair and red lips in the kingdom. She manages to meet him and falls immediately in love with him. She tries to convince him to run away but he is fearful of angering the king. She finally convinces him and they travel all through Ireland avoiding the king's men. They even go to Scotland and are safe until the king there has designs on Deirdre.

About that time, an envoy says the king of Ulster has pardoned them and they can return. He has sent three famous warriors to escort them back. Naoise is eager to return but Deirdre knows it is a trap. The protectors are lured away by an invitation to a party that they are not allowed to refuse, and Eogham kills Naoise and his two brothers traveling with them.

Deirdre returns and is locked up for a year. At the end of that time, King Conchobar asks her whom she hates most. She says, "Eogham." He says, "Then that is who you shall marry."

He and Eogham took her in a chariot to the wedding. She jumped out of the chariot and smashed her head against a rock. Deirdre chose to chart her own fate. Except for the woman smashing her head on a rock, that story was strikingly similar to one I had heard just a short while ago.

I bought the book and returned to the boarding area. On the plane, once again I sat next to the window. Beside me sat a woman in a skirt and sweater. In the aisle seat was a teenage boy. I asked the woman if she was on vacation.

"No, I'm a chiropractor in Dublin. I'm on my way to New York City to take a course in Zero Balancing."

"Zero Balancing?"

"It's an alternative healing modality. I'd like to add it to my rather conventional practice. I hear it's lovely work. Do you know New York City very well?"

"I live there." I was settling in. I slipped my new book in the seat pouch in front of me and set my jacket on the floor.

"Grand! Then perhaps you wouldn't mind telling me what I should see when I'm there."

"How long do you have?"

"The course runs all of four days and I'm there a week. So that gives me three days, and of course evenings."

"Where exactly is your course?"

"It's in a place called the Queens."

"Wherever you go, I'm sure will turn out to be interesting. I'll give you some places to visit like the Metropolitan Museum of Art and the Empire State Building and Broadway, but if you have time, walk through Manhattan and just feel the pulse of the city. Oh, and see all – all that you can." I smiled inwardly and then wrote a little list for her.

For the first time, I actually watched the plane take off. I even enjoyed the sensation of leaving the ground. I picked up the new book again going through the stories of the individual goddesses, one by one. I began to realize I had been encountering goddesses on some level since my journey began. And what an incredible trip it had turned out to be.

I looked up Eriu and learned that she was the one who gave Ireland her name. Eriu was a nurturing goddesses, who had brought forth flowering plants and who selected and consecrated the early kings by bringing them a sacred goblet of wine. But when the Milesians, also known as the Celts, attacked their shores long ago, Eriu rose to the occasion. She encouraged her fighting force, but the Milesians were fierce.

One by one, she watched her brave soldiers fall and die. In fury she picked up handfuls of the blood-soaked earth and threw the mudballs at the enemy. The balls dried in the air and when they hit the ground, warriors sprang up, naked but armed and they fought off the Milesians. Although the Milesians eventually conquered Erin, they were impressed with this woman and named the land after her. From then on, she protected all of them.

Over the years, battles had been lost, but not the war. I thought of the image I had seen of her looking out to sea and felt she imparted to me the wisdom to adapt to loss while keeping your goals firmly in mind.

Surely Scathach had come out to socialize as Sonny, the martial arts trainer. What a meeting that had been! While I waited for the ferry, it was she who had encouraged me to relax within myself and to be confident of what I already knew.

Then at the water's edge, in the forest of Killarney, I was sure I'd encountered Clodhia, the Otherworld goddess. The text explained that she stood for the afterlife, bringing some people to her distant land to heal. A part of her still comes to shore with every ninth wave. Her example spoke of giving of one's self in life to help the healing of others.

Niamh was the golden haired goddess whose name means "beauty." At the late party in Dublin, I had heard the story of how Niamh had befriended Oisin and taken him to the Otherworld. Now I read that she assists anyone with the rituals and help needed in passing on.

Macha must have been the old woman who had awoken me at the hotel pool. Her story of racing and childbirth had taught me not to get mad, but to get even. She had encouraged me to do what had to be done. Also she instilled a wonder of childbirth. She had told me the story of Morrigan, who was the triple goddess of war, destruction and death. She flew over the battle often in the form of a raven or crow, taking the spoils of battle during the night. Her fighting and her protection of Cu Chulain demonstrated the life/death cycle that is a part of our world. Accepting those fundamental aspects of the world, women can become powerful and they are able to heal.

The vision of Maeve that came to me as I stood on the mountain, at the top of her grave, was extraordinary. Her presence helped me feel my bravery, feel my own power, and know I could stand up for myself. As I stood at the well in Glencolumbcille, I was certain that I had been comforted by Brigid. In her nurturing way, she had assured me that mysteries would be revealed. I would never be alone or apart from all spirit. I would never be apart even from my mother, when it came down to it.

I was thrilled when I thought of what a wonderful sharing I had had with Didi, how understood and connected she'd made me feel. To think that this could have been the goddess, Deirdre – Deirdre of the sorrows. Their stories were too close to be pure coincidence. Deirdre's life was an inspiration to carve out the life you are to lead. This most beautiful of women was supposed to be the one you called on when you were ready for a prophetic dream. You called on her when you were ready to take the next step in your life.

As I went through the stories of each of the goddesses, I felt blessed to have learned from these powerful models. Whether they were the actual incarnations of these powerful mythic women or not, I still became acquainted with each of the goddesses in some form, and came away with a lesson every time. And I was the richer for it.

I was totally surprised, though, when I read of Fedelma. She was a fairy queen from Connacht. Her gift was prophecy, and she foretold Queen Maeve of her upcoming victory. She was described as having very long yellow hair and wearing a dress of gold and a shawl of green. Her ability to see the future was aided by the triple irises her eyes held.

Haunting images came to me of the woman who sat next to me on the plane, the woman leaving the restaurant when my Greek goddess book went missing, and the woman beside me at the play about fairies and spirits in Ireland.

I laughed out loud as I considered how unawares I had been caught.

After a light meal, I put my head back, just feeling the plane ride as the clouds rolled by. It still didn't feel terribly secure, but I'd handle it. Life was an ebb and flow of many different feelings. Feelings that may rush right through you and be gone like a summer wind, and feelings that can stay with you and shake your foundations and your faith.

Sometimes in the middle of the night, I had awakened suddenly, feeling a torturing black hole inside of me, afraid that the essence of my life was one flat piece of cardboard moving hour by hour, closer to some unrelenting incinerator. And then, in the light of day, I would be whole again, would know that someone watched over me. I learned to wait for the light. And I was thankful for the light.

Faith carried me through the dark nights with its promise of a sun. And yet I had turned away from someone whom I'd stood in the light with. Had turned away without a word. So much of life was timing. Perhaps I could not have turned back to the light, as I did now, until I had turned away from it completely. I thought of the phone conversation I'd had yesterday when I'd called Shelly's number. A man answered, not her husband, Bob.

"This is Michelle Maguire. Who is this, please?"

"Michelle!" a voice with much pleasure bounced back to me. "This is Mark – your old best friend."

"Oh, my god, Mark. What are you doing at Shelly's?" I was worried something was wrong.

"Well, Shelly had her baby, very late last night. Bob's at the hospital with her now and she's just fine."

"The baby?"

"A beautiful baby girl – 8 lbs., 1 oz. Big."

"Heavens, I didn't know she had it in her."

"She did, and now she's relieved she doesn't. She did a great job, was so pushing for this event that she brought her in two weeks early. I was just about to make some calls to announce it. Anyway, she'll be staying in the hospital until tomorrow."

I couldn't picture her swinging by the airport on the way home, but then you never knew with Shelly. I was just about to sign off with Mark when I knew that now was the time to break an old pattern. "How are you, Mark? I've missed talking with you."

"Have you? I've gone into withdrawal without our long conversations. That's why I spend all my time writing. Seriously, I am writing a lot, but I'm doing well. I'm back in the area now. Writing a book."

"A book?" I was excited. "That's wonderful. What's it about?"

"Well it's a documentary tracing Jewish roots into modern times, focusing especially on the Kabballah – particularly Kabbalistic healing."

"That sounds impressive but outside of my range of knowledge."

"It sounds heavy, but don't let it close you out with its specialized focus of study. As a matter of fact, I'd have no problem dedicating it to someone who inspired me to explore my beliefs and my roots – even if it was a Catholic girl. I have a lot of material and I'd love to share it with you."

"Really? I guess I'll never stop learning at this rate."

He laughed softly, "I don't suppose any of us do. So how's your trip? I'm guessing from your comment that it's been a learning trip of sorts."

"It started out as a vacation, I think," I said wryly, "but I could use some time off to integrate all that I've learned. And that may be something I could share with you. But look out, buddy, it'll knock your socks off. It's about some pretty powerful women." Where would I begin?

"Great! You know, you sound different, Michelle. I know it's been a long time since we have talked but there's something's new about you."

"Oh, yeah?" I was about to ask if that was a problem.

"Hey, don't get me wrong, I like it. Do you remember when we worked on that Oscar Wilde play together at the college?"

"*The Importance of Being Earnest*?"

Yes, and there was a character, a Miss Fairfax, who tells Jack she hopes she's not quite the perfect person he's picturing her?"

"'It would leave no room for development and I intend to develop in many directions.' That was fun."

After a moment, he said in a quiet tone, "I've changed too, Mickey."

"How?"

"You'll have to see for yourself. Change is the stuff of life, isn't it? I wonder if things will be different now between us."

Maybe that would be good, I thought. "You're piquing my curiosity."

"I can't tell you what you're doing to mine."

"Mark? Will you pick me up at the airport tomorrow?"

"I'd love to. What time?"

"One o'clock in the afternoon. Aer Lingus."

"I'll be there. And I'll bring you to see Shelly's baby – Emily. You'll fall in love with her."

"I have a feeling I just might."

"Tomorrow?"

"Tomorrow."

I sank back into my headrest as the memory of the conversation faded and "tomorrow" slid into today. I was grateful for this journey. I was grateful for what I had learned. I thought of the Vision Quest of the American Indians. To have a quest, you had to remove yourself from your daily life and face the elements alone. Besides learning about yourself, you were to receive a gift. You were to bring that gift back to your people to share it with them. What was my gift? Perhaps it was the appreciation of the profound resources a woman could find within herself.

The stories of the goddesses told of their complexities, mysteries, sensitivities and powers. In truth, these were aspects that lay within all of us. Understanding our feminine depths, understanding the masculine richness we attract and then cultivating the balance, enriched all of our lives. But this was only part of the gift. There was much more. Could I really take the changes I had made within myself home as a gift to share? I closed my eyes and slipped into a light dream:

A black dog runs along the beach and jumps into the sea, joyfully paddling further and further out. The dog turns into a baby. Rising and falling with the swells, the baby kicks little feet into the air. Long strings appear from a mobile above the baby. The baby stretches both hands up and finally catches the ends. It is a parachute, but instead of landing, it rises, lifting the baby high. Free, floating, flying easily above the ocean. A crow flies by with a sunflower seed in its mouth.

At a little after noon, I saw the familiar shape of New York rise majestically from the translucent surface of the sea. I felt a welling up of anticipation in my belly, curious to know what was next, but fascinated with not knowing. And my path? The ground waited for me. Would always wait for me. The path would unfold as I walked it. I would make my map while listening to the music of my own inner rhythms.